Murder in an English Village

Murder in an English Village

Jessica Ellicott

KENSINGTON BOOKS
http://www.kensingtonbooks.com

KENSINGTON BOOKS are published by

Kensington Publishing Corp.
119 West 40th Street
New York, NY 10018

All Kensington titles, imprints, and distributed lines are available at special quantity discounts for bulk purchases for sales promotion, premiums, fund-raising, educational, or institutional use. Special book excerpts or customized printings can also be created to fit specific needs. For details, write or phone the office of the Kensington Special Sales Manager: Attn. Special Sales Department. Kensington Publishing Corp., 119 West 40th Street, New York, NY 10018. Phone: 1-800-221-2647.

Library of Congress Card Catalogue Number: 2017944856

Kensington and the K logo Reg. U.S. Pat. & TM Off.

ISBN-13: 978-1-4967-1050-5
ISBN-10: 1-4967-1050-9
First Kensington Hardcover Edition: November 2017

eISBN-13: 978-1-4967-1051-2
eISBN-10: 1-4967-1051-7
Kensington Electronic Edition: November 2017

10 9 8 7 6 5 4 3 2

Printed in the United States of America

Acknowledgments

Every new book is an exercise in faith. It helps to have someone standing nearby, whispering encouraging words in your ear, and allowing you to firmly grip their hand. This book was no exception.

I'd like to thank my agent, John Talbot, for placing this series in front of the right editor. Thanks goes out to John Scognamiglio for being just such an editor. I'd also like to thank all of the marketing, sales, and art department staff at Kensington for all they do to shepherd a book from the manuscript stage to bookstore shelf.

Also, I'd like to thank my extraordinary blog mates, The Wicked Cozy Authors: Sherry Harris, Julie Hennrikus, Edith Maxwell, Liz Mugavero, and Barbara Ross. It would hardly seem worth doing without all of you to share the journey!

I'm exceedingly lucky to be surrounded by a supportive family. I'd like to thank my sisters, Barb Shaffer and Larissa Crockett, and my mother, Sandy Crockett, for their support and patience when I never seem to answer the phone. My children, Will, Max, Theo, and Ari have all unflaggingly cheered me on during this project. Thanks, guys!

My last thank you goes out to my husband, Elias Estevao, who believed in my writing long before I ever did.

Chapter 1

Beryl Helliwell read the advertisement for a third time, not quite believing her good fortune.

> *Well-bred lady with spacious home seeks genteel*
> *lodger. Reasonable rates. Breakfast and tea in-*
> *cluded. Kindly direct enquiries in care of Miss*
> *Edwina Davenport, The Beeches, Walmsley Parva.*

The sign she'd been seeking stared up at her from the evening edition of the newspaper. Beryl circled the advertisement with her fountain pen and sat back to consider. Winter was fast approaching and she had no desire whatsoever to return to America just in time for the cold and the damp.

To the casual acquaintance Beryl appeared a good ten years younger than her age, an admirable state of affairs she attributed to a love of quality gin and an adamant refusal to bear children to any of her ex-husbands. Despite her appearance, the cold had started to fiddle with her joints. Add to the weather the fact that the recently enacted Prohibition was putting a crimp on the supply of quality gin. No, remaining in England was by far the best choice. And now she knew just where she would like to stay.

Beryl hadn't felt so alive in weeks. With little fuss and even less time she settled her bill and determined to set out at first light. Her new automobile, won during a feverish night of card playing the week before, sat tucked up in a garage behind the hotel and would likely be itching for a run out to the country. A vehicle like that deserved to be taken out on the open road and run at full tilt.

The next morning the sun was still deciding if it wanted to get out of bed when Beryl tugged her kid driving gloves up over her broad hands and double-checked that the porter did indeed know how to strap a suitcase to the trunk. Miles of road stretched in front of her and Beryl was determined to be amongst the first to respond to the notice in the paper. As the early morning chill seeped into her joints she was even more determined not to return home to the States for the winter.

Edwina Davenport awoke with a vague sense of disquiet. She lay motionless under her chenille bedspread and ran quickly through the list of worries that plagued her of late, the most pressing of which were financial. She mentally checked off the coal bill, the greengrocer's account, and the disturbing smell of damp issuing from the back hall. All of these worries were faithful and familiar companions. The source of her unease was not amongst them. She opened her eyes and spotted the peeling chunk of wallpaper along the north wall. Which is how she remembered. Honestly, her memory had become shocking of late.

The paper. There had been nothing else for it but to swallow her pride and to place the notice in the newspaper. While America's economy galloped along at a steady clip, that of England was sharply in decline. The post-war boom had busted and Edwina had found herself amongst the many who had felt the pinch.

Advertising for a lodger was a distressing enough proposition, but the parade of unsuitable people who appeared in front of her and demanded consideration was quite shocking. Why was it so very difficult to attract a tenant with even minimal standards of personal hygiene and a firm grasp of the English language?

Edwina may have been short on funds but her imagination was a rich one. It had taken very little to convince her the majority of the respondents were up to no good. Those applicants who didn't shed great clods of earth on her carpets looked like they were sizing up the place for a possible break-in at a later date. Each time she answered the door to another unsuitable applicant she envisioned a web of criminal activity wrapping its sticky string round the village, her own beloved home the centre of the operations. It was times like these Edwina longed for a sister with whom to share her concerns.

Still, there was no use grieving over what was never to be. That was hardly the way to get things done. Edwina slid from beneath the bedspread and tucked her bony feet into her threadbare carpet slippers. Crumpet darted from his basket and appeared at her side ready for a morning outing and a hearty breakfast. Chiding herself for her late start to the day, she almost tripped over her little dog in her hurry to dress. The evening post had brought a whole new slate of candidates requesting appointments to view her spare room today and she couldn't very well meet them in her dressing gown.

She made due with a dish of gherkins and a slightly stale roll left over from tea the day before. Crumpet seemed to look at her askance as he rose up on his hind legs to beg for a bit of her breakfast. But preparing meals never seemed worth the bother. If Edwina were to be utterly truthful she would have to admit she was not only in dire financial straits but also desperately lonely as well. In the secret little room of small dreams tucked deep in her heart she held out hope that the right person would see her advertisement and be the answer to both her most pressing troubles.

But she didn't admit such a thing even to herself because that would be greedy. With so many troubles in the world a bit of solitude was nothing to complain about. And while it was bothersome, like the twinge of rheumatism in her left elbow, it was endurable. One simply ignored such things and soldiered on.

Crumpet pranced eagerly next to the door as she plucked her thick wool jumper from the hall tree and slipped it over her head. She grabbed her gardening gloves and the sturdy old basket she used for weeding, then stuffed a brimmed hat on her head to ward off the chill. She could at least get a few minutes in the garden while the dog had a good romp round the grounds. She wrested the door open, thinking as she always did that its difficulty in opening was another source of concern. Crumpet shot through the door and dashed ahead of her down the drive, a black and white flash through the dense greenery.

As she made her way down the drive she paused to view the yews flanking either side. Long gone were the days when a head gardener and two boys for the rough work kept the shrubbery in trim. Now Edwina made due with the halfhearted ministrations of an antiquated jobbing gardener named Simpkins as well as her own passionate but insufficient efforts. Shaggy green growth stuck up above the shrubs and gave the hedge a neglected air. If the shrubs could have clucked their collective tongues at her she was certain they would have done so. And she couldn't very well blame them.

She pulled her shears from the basket, determined to make amends when she heard the squeal of tires and then a tremendous crash that vibrated up through her feet. She dropped the basket and ran down the drive towards the lane. There, at the end of her driveway sat a dazzling red beauty of a motorcar, its magnificent bonnet crumpled against one of the stone pillars flanking the drive. Her heart lurched as she forced herself to look down at the wheels for signs of black and white fur. Her heart thumped to life again when Crumpet raced towards her from the other side of the road.

Turning her attention to the motorcar once more she felt her fear returning. Hissing clouds of steam issued forth from beneath the motor's damaged bonnet. A tall figure slumped in the driver's seat, its forehead pressed against the steering wheel. Edwina stared at the back of the driver's head of platinum blond hair peeking from beneath a cloche as red as the motorcar. She knew better than to move a patient without being sure it wouldn't do more damage than good. She just wasn't sure how one figured that part out without medical training. Should she run back to the house to use the telephone? What if the woman came to her senses all on her own and wandered off into the hedgerows to die of exposure?

Before she could decide how to proceed, the driver stirred and groaned ever so slightly. One hand, clad in an elegant glove, reached up and patted the fashionable hat back into place then straightened back against the seat. The woman turned to Edwina and smiled.

"Hello, Ed. Remember me?"

Chapter 2

"Do stop fussing, Ed. I've told you I'm fine." Beryl Helliwell pressed back into the depths of the threadbare wingback and assessed the situation. It was even worse than she had suspected. Shelves in the bric-a-brac cabinets were more empty than full. The velvet draperies were faded and frayed along the edges. Worst of all, the fire in the grate sputtered and fizzed the best it could with only a single log to fuel it. Beryl had feared finances were at the heart of Edwina's advertisement and now she was sure of it.

"I'd still feel better if you'd let me send for the doctor." Edwina leaned forward and her spectacles slid down the bridge of her nose just as they had when she'd been a schoolgirl. Beryl's heart gave a squeeze at the thought of all the years since then and felt the ennui of the past months slipping away.

"I've no confidence in modern medicine. I'll only allow you to bring in the village witch with a basket of vile-smelling tinctures and poultices. You must have one of those tucked up round here somewhere."

"Honestly, you haven't changed a bit." Edwina shook her

head. "What are you doing here? According to the papers you were last seen in a hot air balloon over the Kalahari."

"You've read about me then?"

"It would be impossible not to with the way news of your exploits have been splashed across every paper in the English-speaking world. But what are you doing here in Walmsley Parva?"

"The truth is I'm feeling a bit at loose ends."

"Loose ends?"

"Yes. Loose ends." Beryl wished she had thought of some other reason for her visit than the truth. But now that it was out in the open she might as well continue. "I'm desperate for a change."

"From all accounts, you do nothing but change. You're always dashing from one thing to the next trying your hand at one lark or another."

"But that's just it, you see. I'm all dashed out. I feel a great need of a bit of peace and quiet. A spot of serenity, if you will." At this, Edwina released a most unladylike snort as she poured a cup of tea for her guest.

"I would hardly describe your arrival as serene. What does bring you to my little village?"

"I shouldn't like it become common knowledge but I feel in desperate need of a rest, Ed." Beryl took the offered cup of tea, declining a dusty cube of sugar with a firm shake of her head. Beryl paused for dramatic effect and returned her teacup to the table beside her, hoping to give the impression that holding it had become a bit too much for her.

"I shouldn't wonder, after what was reported concerning the hot air balloon incident."

"That did take it out of me a bit." Beryl had been sorry to discover the crash landing in the middle of the desert had not delighted her, as it once would undoubtedly have done. Even the handsome Bedouin wielding a curved sword who appeared from nowhere and had cut away the layers of silk collapsed atop her had not set her blood fomenting as usual.

"At our age I should think it would have." Edwina whisked a lace-edged handkerchief from inside her cardigan sleeve and gently blew her nose.

"Age is a state of mind, Ed. Nothing more or less."

"I've tried telling that to my joints but it doesn't seem to make the slightest difference." Edwina sipped at her tea. "Are you telling me you are in Walmsley Parva for a rest cure? There are no sanatoriums here, Beryl. It's hardly the sort of place that would attract a woman like you."

"You've put your finger on it exactly, Ed. I am looking for a place with absolutely no excitement whatsoever. I find myself in the odd predicament of being bored by excitement. If you live at a fever pitch for too long even that feels dull."

"I'm certain you are pulling my leg."

"I'm not. Gallivanting from one end of the globe to the other can be just as monotonous as living one's whole life in one quiet, out of the way village. After too long, one camel caravan is very much like another. And the tips of daggers are all more alike than you'd think, even when they're pressed against your neck."

"Tips of daggers, indeed." Edwina put down her cup. "Surely you haven't had a knife held to your throat even once, let alone enough times for the experience to leave you unimpressed."

"Not all places share the same rules of conduct. You'd be surprised at all the ways a body can get itself into trouble. There seems to be quite a mania about women's hair and having it covered in many parts of the world. I remember a tall man with remarkably white teeth in Damascus kicking up quite a lot of dust about it."

"Not many ladies run round hatless in Walmsley Parva either."

"Nevertheless, I shall soon adapt."

"You don't mean you intend to stay?"

"Of course, I do. I'm here about your ad in the paper. "

"I expect it was too much to hope no one I knew would see it," Edwina said.

"That seems at odds with the point of an advertisement."

"I was rather hoping that no one of my acquaintance would be in need of a place to stay and so would not be reading the rooms to let section."

"Well, I need a place to stay until I feel quite like myself again and I am delighted to have discovered your ad. Shall we consider the matter settled?"

"I can't think of anyone I'd rather have in my home." Edwina's cheeks flushed. "All the previous applicants have been entirely unsuitable. Would you believe the vast majority of them have been men?"

"Any good-looking ones?" Beryl couldn't resist teasing her old school friend just a bit.

"That isn't the point and you know it. I hardly knew where to look when the first one came to the door. And now I can't show my face in the village. That's why the larder is so bereft. It's not just that my budget's tighter than an old-fashioned corset. It's that I can't bring myself to face the flood of rumors. Every time I pop down to the post office or to the greengrocer I'm beset by twittering giggles and cackling whispers. " Edwina lifted her rumpled handkerchief to her nose and gently honked. Beryl noted the sheen of tears threatening to spill down her cheeks. If there was one thing she couldn't stand it was mean-spirited gossip.

"There's only one way to deal with a mess like this, my friend."

"What do you plan to do?" Edwina gulped down the dregs of her tea and rattled the cup back onto the rickety table beside her.

"A rumor can never truly be quashed. It can only be displaced by an even more interesting one," Beryl said. "So tell me, who's the most vicious gossip in the village?"

Prudence Rathbone would have sworn if she ever permitted herself to indulge in such a vulgar vice. She was just finishing up an inventory of the penny stamps when a squeal distracted her from her duties. Inventory was always on her list of weekly tasks and now she would have to start over.

But since the damage was already done there was nothing to keep her from sliding out from behind the counter to look for the source of the commotion. She peered through the sparkling windows of her post office-cum stationer-cum sweet shop. A scarlet motorcar with a disreputable dent in the bonnet had screeched to a halt directly in front of her store.

A great bulk of a woman poured out of the vehicle and slammed—yes, slammed—the door. Prudence scarcely had time to return to her place of authority behind the counter before the woman was in the shop making a beeline for her. There was something familiar about her that Prudence was just about to identify when the woman stopped in front of the till and removed her driving goggles.

"I wonder if you could direct me to the nearest garage? My car is in dire need of service."

"You're Beryl Helliwell." Prudence's mind boggled. The closest celebrity encounter she had ever had was when as a small girl she had been the second runner-up in an egg in spoon race where the prizes were handed out by the owner of the local cricket bat factory. And now the face she had so often seen beaming at her from the pages of the newspapers was there in her shop.

"Yes, I am."

"What are you doing in Walmsley Parva?" Prudence realized her mouth was hanging open and snapped it shut with such ferocity she heard her jaw pop.

"Are you the owner of this establishment?" Beryl Helliwell gestured round the shop with a gloved hand. She tipped her head this way and that as if she was really taking in the scene around her and not simply making conversation. Prudence felt a surge of pride and a desire to impress.

"I am. It belonged to my parents before me and my mother's parents before them."

"Then you must enjoy a certain standing in the community as a respected business owner." Beryl raised her eyebrows and nodded. Prudence realized they understood each other perfectly.

"How kind of you to say so. I like to think I hold myself, and my shop, to a certain standard." Prudence flicked an imaginary speck of dust from the gleaming counter.

"I feel quite certain you are a person known for her discretion. Is that not the case?" Prudence felt warmth rise to her sallow cheeks as she basked in the compliment.

"I shouldn't like to presume to know what my customers have to say about me. But I do take pride in keeping myself above common gossip."

"I always trust my instincts and even though I probably shouldn't, they're telling me to let you in on a little secret." Beryl leaned over the counter and lowered her voice. "I'm here answering a coded distress call from my dear friend Edwina Davenport. Perhaps you know her?"

"Edwina Davenport? A distress call?" Prudence's mind reeled. How could a mousy thing like Edwina Davenport be friends with the likes of legendary adventuress Beryl Helliwell? Let alone involved with something as thrilling as a coded distress call. "You mean like something out of a spy novel?"

"I knew you'd understand. Ed is such a rare talent. We would have clobbered the Kaiser in half the time it ended up taking if the agency only had a few more like Ed."

"Do you mean to say Edwina Davenport is a secret agent?"

"Shhh!" Beryl pressed a gloved finger firmly against Prudence's lips. "The war may be over but there are still enemy eyes and ears everywhere."

"My apologies. It just spilled out. After all, I've known Edwina all my life and never would have guessed she was more than the daughter of a country solicitor who had run out of money." Prudence could not believe her ears. It was simply unfathomable. "After all, there was that advertisement in the papers seeking a lodger."

"Quite sporting of her, that bit was." Beryl leaned even closer and winked. "Even though she knew it would cause unpleasant conjecture in the village, Ed went ahead and placed the ad. It was our coded distress call, you see."

"You mean she doesn't actually need a lodger?" Prudence chewed furiously on this bit of information. For weeks the subject of Edwina Davenport's finances had been on everyone's mind thanks to her determined efforts to keep it there. The story would have died down if Prudence had not shown her customary vigilance in reading the advertisement section of the newspaper.

"Certainly not. Ed is up to her eyeballs in liquid assets. She could buy up the entire village at a whack if she were of a mind to."

"But she owes money at the greengrocer, the chemist, and although I don't like to mention it, even here."

"All part of the cover story. Very convincing, wasn't it?"

"So she besmirched her reputation in aid of a secret governmental agency?"

"There's nothing Ed isn't willing to sacrifice for His Majesty." Beryl cleared her throat. "He told me so himself." Prudence gasped. It was all too thrilling. In her wildest dreams Prudence would never have dreamed up such a startling turn of events. It was just like something out of the pictures.

"But if she sent you a message, she must be on a mission." A delicious shiver crept between Prudence's prominent shoulder blades.

"As I'm sure you can appreciate, I cannot possibly confirm such a report. Suffice it to say Ed has never needed to call me in to assist before now. I trust I can depend on you to keep this to yourself?"

"My lips are sealed," Prudence said as her glance wandered over Beryl's shoulder and out onto the street landing on her friend Minnie Mumford who had stopped on the street to ogle the red motorcar.

Chapter 3

"You did what?" Edwina paced the rug in the hallway with such determination that little puffs of dust billowed round her ankles.

"I quite cleverly implied you are a secret agent."

"Implied it or said it flat out?" Edwina stopped and faced her old friend.

"Somewhere betwixt the two I suspect." Beryl finished polishing an apple she had bought after settling Edwina's bill at the greengrocer and held it out. "Eat this. You need to keep up your strength if you are to effectively remain in the service of His Majesty." Edwina shook her head and waved away the fruit.

"Tell me you did not lead people to believe I work for the King." Edwina sagged against the wall, her knees threatening to give way beneath her.

"Quite a stroke of genius that was. Besides, I'm not the one telling people. I only told Miss Rathbone who assured me she would keep it to herself."

"But Prudence is the most brazen gossip in the village. She

won't be able to eat, sleep, or remember to breathe until she's passed what she knows to every resident of Walmsley Parva over the age of nine."

"Exactly. No need to thank me, Ed. It was a pleasure to watch the old bat's eyes bulge from her face."

"She's younger than you are, Beryl."

"As I always say, age is a state of mind. I meet very few people who seem younger than me. Besides, your new reputation as a superior sort of secret agent has shaved years off you, at least in the eyes of your neighbors." Beryl took a loud bite of the rejected apple and smiled.

Edwina pressed away from the wall and gathered herself to her full height.

"You must return to town and tell Prudence the truth. I cannot abide lies."

"Then you must have changed a great deal over the years." Beryl squinted and took a step closer to Edwina. "Do you remember the chocolate box incident?"

"That was an exceptional circumstance. The games mistress would never have let Bertha James live down the shame of helping herself to those sweets. You know how cruel she was."

"What about the stories for Frances Beddoes? If it weren't for the little white lies you told her about the older girls who were bullying her, she wouldn't have had the courage to stand up to them."

"She needed a bit of a boost. It was all for a good cause. Besides, I was a child at the time. You can't hold that against me."

"What about telling your mother that my parents were nudists and that they were planning to induct me into the group over the school break so that she would invite me to spend the holiday here with you instead?"

"I seem to remember you crying yourself to sleep every night thinking about how much you didn't want to go home."

"You saved me from a great deal of heartache, Ed. Your lies are always motivated by concern for others. It was only fair that I did the same for you. Frankly it is a relief to be able to pay you back at long last."

"Even now I can't believe I used the word *nudist* with my mother. Or that she survived hearing me say it." A dimple appeared in Edwina's cheek. "Still, I feel quite wretched about deceiving everyone."

Beryl handed Edwina a smooth pear from the folds of her fashionable duster coat and noted with pleasure that her friend accepted it. As a schoolgirl Ed's moods could be gauged by her appetite. Beryl knew if Ed would just take a bite it would signal that she had accepted a way out of her embarrassing predicament. Edwina bit.

"Then the only thing for it is to make the lie the truth. We shall set out to uncover some dark doings here in Walmsley Parva."

"There are no nefarious goings-on in the village. There never have been," she said after swallowing a large chunk of pear.

"If there's one thing I've learned rattling all over the globe it's that everywhere you go someone is up to no good." Beryl dropped her apple core into the nearest plant pot. "Even in Walmsley Parva. Haven't there been any unsolved crimes in the area over the last ten years?"

"Not that come to mind."

"Surely there's something. Pennies missing from the alms box? An errant husband who died suddenly of an unidentified stomach ailment? A hunting accident?" Beryl watched a flicker of an idea cross her friend's mind before she shook her head.

"I shall have to think about it a bit more before I should like to say anything. Accusations are hard to withdraw." Edwina crossed her arms over her chest and Beryl knew there was no hope of persuading her to speak before she was ready.

* * *

Edwina rinsed out her cocoa cup and Beryl's brandy snifter and placed them on the drain board. The clock on the wall ticked quietly and the night sounds of the house gathered in around her ears. Edwina had insisted on clearing up the dishes on her own while Beryl went off to bed with a book on local history. As much as she was glad of the company, having someone around all the time would take some getting used to.

Wind whipped round the house and wriggled between the glass and sash of the windows. Edwina told herself the creaking she heard was just the normal sounds of the house as it settled for the night. Any creaking above her head was just the unfamiliar sound of Beryl moving between the guest room and the lavatory. She felt a murmur of unease when Crumpet scratched at the scullery door to remind her of her duties as his mistress.

"Are you sure you must?" she asked. His urgent prancing between the door and her feet announced that indeed he must. Edwina was loath to head out into the dark. She had spent the evening considering whether or not to mention the Wallingford Estate to Beryl. All that dwelling on the possibility of criminal behavior had spooked her. Still, she was even more reluctant to allow Crumpet to head out into the darkness alone. Especially not after the scare she had when she thought she had lost him beneath the squeal of Beryl's tires.

She plucked her wool coat from the peg and wound her extralong muffler round her neck for good measure. Edwina impatiently flipped the scarf ends out of the way as she bent to clip Crumpet's lead to his leather collar. She wasn't prepared to go chasing him about in the dark. She lifted a torch from the shelf next to the door and commanded herself to be sensible. Unbolting the door she allowed Crumpet to tug her into the garden before she could change her mind.

The wind ruffled her hair and played with the end of her scarf. Edwina trained the torch on the ground in front of her. Crumpet hurried as fast as the length of lead would allow and made straight for his favourite part of the garden, an overgrown wedge of shrubs used to screen the brush pile.

Edwina turned back to the house and felt comforted by the glow of light coming from the guest room. It was nicer than Edwina wanted to admit to have someone in the house with her. She hadn't realized quite how lonely she really was until she wasn't.

Crumpet tugged at her again and she took a step deeper into the unfinished part of the garden. She believed in preserving wild areas in the garden for birds and insects to create shelters. More times than she liked to consider she had argued the point about the brush pile with her gardener Simpkins. In fact, more than once Simpkins had threatened to quit over her insistence on keeping what he considered an invitation for bothersome rabbits and hedgehogs.

But it was her garden and so the pile was heaped up with clippings of yew and trimmings from a pollarded row of beeches that led to the summerhouse. Simpkins always tut-tutted as he tipped each wheelbarrow full onto the pile but he had followed her instructions. Crumpet caught the scent of something beneath the pile and began to dig beneath it with a will. Deeper and deeper he dove beneath the crisscrossing branches. Edwina gave a sharp tug on the lead and found it had become entangled. With a sigh of frustration she leaned forward to pull it free.

Just as she did so she felt something yank on the ends of her scarf. "Not me, too," she thought as the scarf began to tighten around her neck. "What can I have gotten caught on?" Below her, Crumpet began to bark and to growl. Panic rose in her chest. Edwina's heart thrashed and thumped like the sparrow she had once discovered caught in her gooseberry netting. The scarf drew tighter and tighter from behind. She realized the scarf was not caught but rather that someone was deliberately pulling on it. She tried to twist round to view her attacker but felt a knee raise up and press into the small of her back, pinning her in place.

Energized by the thought she would not give Simpkins the satisfaction of finding her dead on the brush pile, she tilted her head out of the way then sharply raised the hand holding the torch over her shoulder with all her strength. She felt it make contact with something firm and heard a sharp intake of breath from her assailant. The scarf went slack and Edwina twisted, hoping to get a look at her attacker. Whoever it was streaked off into the velvety dark of the wood. Edwina knew she would never identify the attacker if she didn't give chase but she simply hadn't the strength. It was all she could manage to free Crumpet from the brush pile and to stagger back into the house.

Beryl had returned to the kitchen to look for her brandy snifter when Edwina burst through the door and sank into the nearest chair, dropping a bedraggled scarf on the floor in a heap. She looked as though she had gone ten rounds with a tornado. Bits of evergreen needles and twigs nestled in her hair as though a bird thought to settle down to raise a family on her head. Crumpet stood pressed against her leg, his ears pricked and nose twitching. He didn't look any cleaner than Edwina but he did look ready to spring into action.

"Is it really that difficult to walk the dog around here? You look positively done in." Beryl reached over and plucked a tiny leaf from Edwina's shoulder.

"It is when someone tries to strangle you in your own garden." Edwina reached up and spread apart the lapels of her coat. Beryl couldn't quite believe her eyes.

"What happened?"

"I was walking Crumpet at the back of the property when someone grabbed the ends of my scarf. Before I knew what was happening I couldn't breathe. I've never felt so frightened in my life." Edwina did look grey. Beryl spotted the clean brandy snifter on the drain board and then hurried to the drinks tray in the parlor for a large tot of spine stiffener. Beryl had a great deal of experience with people in the throes of shock. It tended to happen to others at an alarming rate when she was in the vicinity.

She pressed the glass into Edwina's trembling hands and waited for her to swallow more than half of its contents before she allowed herself to ask questions. "How did you get away?"

"Bashed him on the head with my torch." Edwina sat up a little straighter at the memory.

"Very resourceful. How do you know it was a man?"

"I suppose I don't really. I assumed it was because one is always concerned about being attacked by violent men. And whoever it was seemed very strong."

"I don't think we can assume anything. Barehanded strangling would surely indicate a male attacker. However, anyone becomes much stronger when they employ any sort of a garrote to assist them."

"How do you know so much about such a nasty subject?"

"One of my ex-husbands authored a thick volume entitled *The Mechanics of Violence.* He would read his favorite bits aloud in bed to me before turning out the lights."

"He sounds like a dreadful sort of man."

"He wasn't my worst ex-husband but I did use his choice of bedtime story against him when I wanted a divorce. The judge saw things my way quite quickly when my lawyer read some of Tristram's favorite passages aloud in court." Beryl leaned in to peer closely at the darkening bruise around Ed's throat. "You realize what this means, don't you?"

"It means I'm going to have a lie-in in the morning." Edwina raised her glass to her lips and finished the brandy in one fluid gulp. Beryl saw her wince as she swallowed.

"It means there really is something going on in Walmsley Parva. We've scared someone so terribly they've made an attempt on your life."

"You think this is because of the stories you told in Prudence's shop this afternoon?"

"What else could it be?"

"It could be a coincidence."

"I don't believe that and neither do you."

"What are we going to do?"

"I should think it would be obvious. We are going to investigate."

Chapter 4

"I've been thinking about last night," Edwina said, spreading a heaping dollop of jam onto a slice of thin toast.

"I thought as much." Beryl leaned forward on her elbows, a slice of crisp bacon poised in midair. "Come on then. Out with it."

Edwina settled back in her chair with a creak and folded her slim hands in her lap. Once a thing was said, it couldn't be unsaid. And unless Beryl had changed more than Edwina suspected since their shared girlhood, it would be very difficult to distract her from a course of action. Edwina cleared her throat, noting the pain in doing so. That decided it.

"Are you familiar with the Women's Land Army?"

"The organization that sent women into the fields as agricultural workers during the war?" Beryl asked.

"The very one. The government needed all the help they could get in keeping the soldiers on the front and the people at home fed and the Land Army helped to do just that. It was important work and many farms in the area took advantage of the program," Edwina said. "The Board of Agriculture even set up a large farming operation which served as a training centre here on the Wallingford Estate."

"Am I right to remember that the Land Army had some trouble being accepted by the general population?" Beryl said. "Thought to be unladylike or some such a thing."

"They did have a bit of difficulty at first. The shocking look of their masculine uniforms and the way so many of the girls bobbed their hair struck many of the farmers and other local people as scandalous. Still, they needed the help and it wasn't worth the country starving because one objected to women using trousers," Edwina said. "Besides, the cause was greatly helped in this area by Lady Wallingford who gave over the estate into the care of the government for the greater good."

"How generous of her," Beryl said. "Or do I detect there is more to the story than a self-sacrificing act of patriotism?"

"It was a good way to save face in the district. Her husband died and left her with far too little capital to keep the place up." Edwina sighed and looked around the kitchen. The cooker could well do with a fresh coat of blacking and the floor hadn't had a truly decent scrubbing since Edwina had been forced to economize. Keeping things up with a single live-in housekeeper had been difficult before the war. A daily girl working part-time had been even less helpful. By the time Edwina's mother died she couldn't justify even that expense and had been forced to curtail those inadequate services. Edwina couldn't imagine how much more difficult things had been on an estate as large as Lady Wallingford's. "Lamentably it is an altogether too common state of affairs of late."

"I'll pitch in and we'll get things straightened round. You'll see." Beryl nodded vigorously and Edwina felt a faint flicker of hope for the first time in ages that things might just be looking up. She couldn't truly imagine Beryl being much help with the housekeeping but one never knew what one was capable of. The war had taught that lesson for certain. "You still haven't said what any of this has to do with someone trying to throttle the life out of you last night."

"I'm coming to that bit. Once Lady Wallingford made such a public show of her support for the Land Army scheme folks around here grudgingly accepted the idea. The scheme was also bolstered by respectable local women championing it by participating themselves."

"Which brings the tale round to you?" Beryl remembered her bacon and took a large bite.

"I volunteered to serve as the village registrar," Edwina said.

"That doesn't sound like you were out digging potatoes or mucking about in the cow barns."

"I wasn't. My duties involved keeping a register of all the Land Army workers in our area including the details of their availability and their skills. Local farmers came to me to help find workers for their farms." Crumpet crossed the room and lay down at Edwina's feet and placed his chin on the toe of her worn, brown shoe. Edwina bent over and scratched his ears.

"You acted as a sort of job placement agent?"

"Yes, I suppose that was the job in a nutshell."

"You believe that position has something to do with the attempt on your life last night?"

"I do." Edwina reached for her teacup and took a sip. "I got to know many of the girls quite well, you see. Which ones were hard workers, which were conscientious, and which of them regretted ever signing up in the first place. Which is why I never quite believed that Agnes Rollins would abandon her duties without a word to anyone. I would never have put her down as that sort of girl."

"What happened?"

"Agnes simply vanished in the night. She was the leader of her gang and one morning she was simply gone when the other girls awoke. As far as I know no one ever heard from her again."

"Did she leave a note? Had anyone seen her go?" Beryl leaned back in her chair and gazed up at the ceiling. Edwina followed her gaze and added painting the kitchen ceiling to her list of necessary repairs.

"No note, no word of any kind." Edwina's brow furrowed. "One day she was hard at work on the Wallingford Estate and the next it was if she had never been there."

"Did she not have any family that came asking after her either?"

"I seem to remember her saying she was alone in the world so I was not surprised no one asked after her. I was merely saddened by it."

"Is her disappearance the possible mystery you were thinking of when I asked about nefarious doings here in Walmsley Parva?" Beryl tented her fingers in front of her face and fixed her sparkling blue eyes on a spot on the wall somewhere past Edwina's shoulder. Edwina fought an urge to giggle at her friend's serious look. It suited her far less well than did wide smiles and mischievous winks.

"It was. I never felt satisfied with the response from the matron in charge or the authorities, slack as they were, at the time."

"Who was in charge of the operation?"

"Hortense Merriweather was the matron on the estate. She was herself eager to pitch in for much the same reasons I was. We've been in the same circle of course, her father being in finance and mine a solicitor. Our lives diverged as so often happens when one friend marries and another does not. Her husband volunteered as soon as war was declared and was killed almost as quickly."

"Dreadful. Any children?" Beryl asked.

"No, they were never blessed with them. To make matters worse, her much younger brother volunteered not long after she received the telegram about her husband. His entire unit experienced heavy shelling and a gas attack. The lot of them were wiped out in a single day. Hortense took the deaths very hard indeed." Edwina paused. "While I naturally deplored the circumstances that brought her to the job, I was pleased to be working with someone as capable as Hortense." Beryl nodded her understanding.

"This Hortense ran a tight ship, did she?" Beryl asked.

"Indisputably. Hortense had a real knack for keeping the girls in line. Which was one of the reasons I was so surprised for Agnes to run off on her. She was the sort of young woman who appreciated order herself and expected it from the girls on the gang she led. I couldn't imagine her leaving Hortense in such a difficult position."

"Your friend had no explanation for what had happened to the missing girl?" Beryl asked.

"Not really. I remember she said she was disappointed and that it just went to show how society was becoming completely unraveled. She was quite put out about the whole thing and said you simply couldn't trust anyone to live up to his or her responsibilities. I remember Hortense herself ended up taking over for Agnes for a couple of weeks doing the early milk run."

"What, you mean the matron was out making deliveries?"

"Exactly. The Land Army was still recruiting young women as fast as they could but it was all hands to the wheel. Hortense replaced Agnes until they could find someone else to drive the morning milk float. It wasn't easy but it was certainly less difficult on the body than ploughing or milking or harvesting potatoes."

"You mentioned speaking with the authorities. Who else was there?"

"The police force was depleted here, like everywhere else in the country."

"I suppose a spot with as little criminal activity as Walmsley

Parva would naturally not rate an officer when London and Manchester were understaffed."

"That was just it. When our local officer joined up we acquired the distinction of being one of the first communities in Britain to have a female police constable. Doris Gibbs is a local woman who, despite a lack of experience, somehow managed to be appointed our village constable during the war. She holds the position still."

"What did she think of the whole matter?"

"She told me there was no mystery in it. Constable Gibbs had a very low opinion of the morals of all the women in the Land Army. She felt they were likely to get up to all sorts of trouble." Edwina felt anew the indignation at the conversation she had endured with Constable Gibbs.

"Your constable sounds like she had no interest in what happened to the missing young woman."

"Very little at the time and none as more time passed." Edwina pushed back her chair and carried her dishes to the sink. Beryl, she noticed, did not seem inclined to do the same. In fact, her friend seemed oblivious to all but the notion of Agnes' disappearance. "It was all very unsatisfactory. But with so much grief and so many losses I felt rather foolish pressing the point of one disappearance."

"Who knew Agnes, besides you and Hortense?" Beryl asked.

"The other girls in the Land Army assigned to the Wallingford Estate. But they are all gone except for Polly Watkins. The others came from places all over the country but Polly is a local girl, and when the Land Army was disbanded last year she was the only one to stay. She went back to working as a maid."

"Then we ought to start our investigation by speaking with her," Beryl jumped to her feet, and rubbed her hands together briskly. Edwina cleared her throat and looked into the sink.

"I would rather stay here and do the washing up."

"You can't mean that. No one would rather do the dishes

than to track down a missing person." Beryl stacked her teacup on her plate and plunked them into the sink. "Tell me what is really on your mind."

"It's Polly. She used to work here as a daily but I had to let her go when money got so very tight. I don't think I can face her." Edwina's face reddened. "The fact is it wasn't just the money. She wasn't at all reliable and even when she did show up on the appointed day she wasn't at all good at her job."

"Why does anyone employ her then?"

"Help is so hard to come by that one can't be at all choosy. It is far better to employ a disastrously disappointing cleaner than to admit you haven't one at all. At present, the best you can hope for is that the staff doesn't nick things."

"Did Polly do that?"

"Some of my acquaintances said they thought she found it easier to pocket the silver than to polish it." Edwina sighed. "I never noticed her taking anything here but I'm still not sure I can face her."

"Well, I can. Do you happen to know where I can track down this paragon of domestic help?"

"Would you, Beryl?" Edwina asked. "I believe she'll be at Charles Jarvis' today."

"What are friends for?" Beryl said.

Chapter 5

Beryl paused in front of the hall tree and positioned her fashionable scarlet hat upon her head with a light hand. As much as she'd reassured Edwina that the blow to her forehead during the car crash had been no more than a tap, the fact remained there was a walnut-sized lump just below her hairline. While Beryl did not consider herself to be a vain woman, she was acutely aware of the role appearance played in garnering assistance, especially from men. Bearing that in mind she leaned closer towards the mirror and repaired the damage her breakfast had wrought upon her lipstick.

A steady breeze ruffled the ends of her hair and drove swirls of autumn leaves up the lane ahead of her. The trees were half bare and still the temperatures were mild. If it weren't for the lump Beryl would have been tempted to go bareheaded. She kept her eyes on the crossroad and turned left. Five houses up on the right, Edwina had said. The sign in front of a low-slung stone cottage proclaimed it to be Meadowlark House. Just as Beryl stepped to the door and raised her gloved hand it popped open revealing a bespectacled man with a slight stoop. His eyes widened behind his lenses and he took a step back.

"Miss Rathbone said she had met you but one hardly knows what to believe when it comes to that woman," he said. "You are Beryl Helliwell, are you not?"

"I am. I suspect you are Charles Jarvis as I was assured by my friend Edwina that this is his house."

"I'm so very sorry. I've completely forgotten my manners. I'm not sure which was more of a shock, seeing you there or discovering that Prudence had gossip to share that was actually worth hearing." Mr. Jarvis opened the door fully. "Do come in. Are you in need of legal services? If so, perhaps we should head to my office in town. The daily woman is here and I should like to respect your privacy." A clatter of crockery sounded from a room at the back of the house. Mr. Jarvis winced at the sound of it.

"It was your household help I came to see," Beryl said, enjoying the chance to view surprise playing out across Mr. Jarvis' face once more. In her experience, members of the legal profession generally prided themselves on bland demeanors. Mr. Jarvis was a rare breed. She wondered if he were at all successful. She stepped into the hallway and drew off her kidskin gloves.

"You wish to speak with Polly?" he asked. He lowered his voice. "Does this have something to do with a certain something you might be working on with Edwina?"

"In your capacity as a solicitor I am sure you frequently encounter circumstances require the utmost discretion." She waited for him to nod before continuing. "Why don't we just say my visit here is to ask Polly if she could possibly fit Edwina's house back into her schedule. After all, my arrival signals a change in Edwina's financial situation. There is no longer any need for the pretense of penury."

"Of course. My lips are sealed," Mr. Jarvis said. "Well, right this way then." He led her down the fusty, narrow hallway covered in watercolors all appearing to spring from the same hand. Beryl paused to give them a closer look. They weren't professional by any means but there was something about them that drew the notice and suggested the artist had potential. The English landscape was portrayed in almost simpering sweetness. So bland as to make the one vibrant and successful thing in each painting stand out all the more starkly. In every single one a slim, small woman in modest clothing sat or stood with her back to the painter. Something in the way the figure was depicted reminded Beryl very strongly of Edwina. It made one wonder.

The passageway halted abruptly at a spacious kitchen fitted out with all the modern conveniences. Beryl turned to the unprepossessing man once more.

"May I ask if there is a Mrs. Jarvis?" She nodded to the appointments.

"Alas, there is not. Why do you ask?"

"In my experience most gentlemen living on their own have neglected kitchens, not ones that could be found in a showroom."

"I was once advised by a lady I esteem that a gentleman with a well-appointed kitchen stands a better chance of attracting a wife of quality than one with a hand pump and stone fireplace fitted with a spit. A modern kitchen is even more important now that it is nearly impossible to get any help at all these days. Especially help that does much good." Mr. Jarvis turned to a noise at the back door. Beryl followed his glance. A young woman with glossy, honey colored hair peeking from beneath a kerchief stood in the threshold, a mop bucket dangling from her small hand. "Speaking of help, allow me to present Polly Watkins, the young woman who sees to the cleaning for me," Mr. Jarvis said.

"Ma'am," Polly said. "You're that woman in the newspapers. What is always flying around here, there, and everywhere around the globe. You're as famous a star in the pictures." Polly's eyes widened so much Beryl feared they might not remain tethered to her head.

"That's right. I am Beryl Helliwell. And you're the Polly

Watkins I've heard so much about." Beryl was alarmed to see Polly's eyes grow even larger. The poor girl's mouth dropped open and a small squeak escaped her lips. Polly nodded slowly as if the atmosphere around her had unexpectedly become filled with tomato aspic rather than the usual combination of oxygen, nitrogen, and other gases.

"Splendid. I hoped I might have a word with you." Beryl turned to Mr. Jarvis. "If that's all right with you?"

"I'll leave you to have a word on your own then, shall I?" Mr. Jarvis said. Beryl waited until he left the kitchen then pointed to the enameled table in the center of the room.

"Why don't we have a seat and I'll tell you why I've come," Beryl said. Polly nodded and put down the mop bucket with a trembling hand.

"Am I in some sort of trouble?" Polly asked. She sank into a wooden chair. Her fingernails were short but ragged and she gnawed on a thumbnail, her gaze never leaving Beryl's face.

"Certainly not. I'm the one in difficulties. I'm here on behalf of my dear friend Edwina Davenport. She regrets most sincerely any hardship she caused you when she found it necessary to suspend your services."

"Miss Davenport's a real lady," Polly said. "I was very sorry to hear about her troubles," Polly said.

"Everyone has had them in the last few years, haven't they?" Beryl said. "She sent me to ask if there is any way you could fit her home back into your busy schedule."

"I might be able to do for her again if she thinks herself able to have me back." Polly bit her lower lip. Beryl had the impression that Polly was too well mannered to bring up the subject of money. Being an American, Beryl had no compunction about doing so herself.

"Miss Davenport had good reason to allow her finances to become common gossip. But I assure you, finances are of no consideration at present."

"I heard that the rumors about her being down to her last farthing weren't true." Polly looked at the ceiling as if consulting some sort of appointment diary written in invisible ink. "Will she have my back wages as well? I don't think I could come back without what was owed me."

"Miss Davenport insists upon it," Beryl said. "Along with a small bonus for your trouble."

"In that case I could start again first thing tomorrow if that would suit," Polly said. "I don't mind saying I'd be glad of a bit of extra to lay by for the future."

"We would be extremely grateful. I wished to speak to you not only to procure your capable services once more." Beryl paused to look around the model kitchen once more. Beryl was very much afraid that for all his conveniences Mr. Jarvis would still have a difficult time convincing a lady to be impressed by his home. Beryl wasn't at all sure what Polly was being paid to do exactly. The floor was streaked with mud. Cobwebs festooned the corners of the ceiling and the state of the window-panes left Beryl unsure whether the view was one of a garden or something else entirely. "I also understood that you might have information which would help clear up a distressing event that has taken place in Walmsley Parva."

"I might?" Polly's eyes goggled. "I can't imagine how."

"Do you remember a young woman named Agnes Rollins who worked up at the Wallingford Estate as a Land Army girl?" Beryl spoke softly and kept looking back over at the door. She wanted to give the impression of secrecy. Girls like Polly, in Beryl's experience, liked to have a bit of something that set them apart from the rest of the crowd. What better to do that than to be the source of information in an enquiry?

"That one that went missing?"

"That's just who I mean. Do you remember her?"

"Of course I do. She was the leader for my gang of workers. Her disappearance caused a right ruckus when it happened."

Polly's posture lost some of its uprightness. In her eagerness to help she leaned across the table and drummed her fingers on its white surface. "One day she was there and the next day she wasn't. Not word to anyone. Why do you want to know about her all this time later?"

"May I trust you with a secret?" Beryl asked. "It is very important you keep it to yourself."

"You don't keep a job like mine for long if you spread gossip like Miss Rathbone down to the post office, now do you? People let you into their homes and it's nigh on impossible for the hired help not to know things guests in the drawing room would be shocked to discover. I can keep a secret all right. Especially for Miss Davenport." Beryl leaned a little closer and spoke at barely above a whisper.

"Last night someone tried to strangle Edwina with her own scarf whilst she was out walking her dog," Beryl said. Polly gasped.

"Is she all right?"

"Nothing a couple days of rest and cups of hot tea won't fix. But she thinks there is a connection between the attempt on her life and the disappearance of that girl Agnes Rollins."

"Why ever should she think a thing like that?" Polly looked genuinely confused.

"I made the mistake of confiding to someone that Edwina and I were looking into the possibility of some criminality here in Walmsley Parva. Only a few hours later someone made the attempt on her life. Agnes' disappearance came to mind as something someone might not want investigated," Beryl said. Polly shifted about in her seat and looked at her lap. "Since you are the only Land Army girl who worked on the Wallingford Estate who's still here Edwina suggested I ask you about what might have happened to her."

"I'll give you any help I can but I doubt I'll remember much. We weren't close friends or anything. What do you want to know?"

"Do you remember anything about her daily habits?" Beryl asked. "Or her duties?"

"I remember that she drove the milk float early each morning."

"By herself?"

"I believe so. Everyone had more than enough to do and we didn't double up on jobs that didn't absolutely need it."

"You said she was your gang leader. Did she get on with the girls under her command?"

"As far as I ever heard she did. I think she had a reputation as the matron's pet but she pulled more than her own weight so no one complained too much."

"Did she have any particular friends amongst the other Land Army girls?" Beryl asked.

"I would say that. They didn't complain about her but they resented her a bit I think. She didn't socialize much. None of us did since we were all plumb worn-out by the end of the day. Besides, we all had to make an early start of it every day. Milking happens early."

"Can you remember anything about the day she went missing? Anything at all?" Beryl asked. There was no sound in the kitchen other than the odd clunk issuing forth from the sink pipes. The kitchen was not entirely modern after all. Polly took her time and Beryl let the silence stretch out between them. Finally Polly seemed to make up her mind.

"No one noticed at first that she were missing. All the other girls got up as they always did and got busy with dressing and breakfast. Breakfast and the noon meal were always informal and you never waited for others to join you. You just served yourself and got on with the work."

"Very sensible."

"Agnes was never one for breakfast anyway. She said it made her green about the gills to think of eating at the crack of dawn, and she made up for it at noontime. No one thought it the least strange she hadn't been seen at breakfast."

"Was she there after breakfast?"

"Not that anyone could say later when that poor excuse for a bobby, Constable Gibbs, showed up and started asking questions a few days later." Polly looked at the ceiling again as if in consultation. "Everyone just got on with their milking duties and assumed Agnes was with someone else at the time. It wasn't until she should have taken the milk float out on deliveries that anyone noticed she was missing."

"Was there a thorough search made for her?"

"I'll say there was. We needed every single person available for the work. And all the girls made a yearlong commitment to serve. No one expected anyone to go back on the commitment no matter how much they hated the job. Least of all someone like Agnes."

"Did she hate the job?"

"No, I don't think she did really. I think it took its toll on her like it did so many city girls. They weren't used to that sort of work but they mostly settled down and got used to it before too long."

"Where did you look for her?"

"We checked her room, of course, to be sure she hadn't overslept. When she wasn't there Mrs. Merriweather called Miss Davenport in and asked her to help search the estate while she took care of the milk delivery herself that morning."

"Did you find any trace of her?"

"Not a one. We looked in the main house, which had been turned into a sort of a hospital for recovering soldiers, but no one had seen her there. We searched the fields and the barns. Mrs. Merriweather even went to the train station to ask after her but no one matching Agnes' description had been seen leaving Walmsley Parva that morning or the night before either."

"How long did you keep looking for her?"

"Mrs. Merriweather called off the search after she checked Agnes' room and discovered all her personal items were gone.

She said that we couldn't waste any more time or energy on someone who'd left us in the lurch and that we would be better off forgetting about her and getting back to our duties."

"And that was the end of it?"

"Miss Davenport wasn't as quick to let it go as the rest of us. But she always likes to see the good in people. I don't think she wanted to believe Agnes would abandon her duties like she did."

"And no one ever heard from her again?"

"Not that I heard mention of."

"Can you think of any reason someone might have wanted her out of the way? Any reason someone might have made her disappear? Anything at all?" From the way she squeezed her lips together as she shook her head, Beryl was certain a flicker of an idea passed through Polly's mind. "Nothing at all that gave you pause either at the time or now as you are reflecting upon it?"

"No, nothing," Polly said.

Chapter 6

Edwina waited for Beryl's retreating form to disappear down the drive before she hurried upstairs to dress for the day. While she had given Beryl the impression she would stay in and rest, she had no intention whatsoever of doing so. She slipped into a serviceable day dress and rooted around in a dressing table drawer for a faded silk scarf. She wrapped it loosely around her neck to cover the bruising. She hurried down the stairs and clipped a lead onto Crumpet's collar.

Hortense Merriweather had returned to live in her own home on the other side of the village after the Land Army was disbanded the year before. But it was far more likely that the former Land Army matron would be found continuing her volunteerism efforts. Edwina couldn't blame her. She did her best to stay away as much as possible from her own empty home. The two likeliest places to find Hortense Edwina thought were the village hall or the church. Crumpet would be far more welcome in the hall so she decided to head there first.

Edwina stopped to allow Crumpet to sniff at a rustling pile of leaves before ascending the short flight of steps to the village hall. She pushed open the heavy wooden door with an ear-shattering creak and peered inside. Light filtered in through the door and a beam of dust motes ascended like a sort of holy apparition. At the far end of the room Hortense stood silhouetted against the wavy glass of a long window.

"Hello, Edwina, are you here to lend a hand with the jumble sale?" Hortense's voice boomed across the sparsely filled space. Crumpet cowered behind Edwina's skirt as Hortense approached. Edwina had noted in the past that Hortense was far fonder of dogs than they ever seemed to be of her. "I see you've brought a helper, too."

"He's a fine fellow but if you need things sorted you might want to look elsewhere. He is much better at making things disappear than he is at piling objects into groups." Edwina winced as Hortense stooped at the waist and gave Crumpet's ears what she likely considered a playful tug. Crumpet yelped and wrapped his lead around Edwina's legs in an effort to get away from Hortense's determined attentions. Something had to be done before she was knocked off her feet. Edwina pointed to the tables covered with the castoffs from homes throughout the village. "Are you here on your own with all this to do?"

"I don't know what the world is coming to. You just can't seem to get help with anything these days." Hortense folded her arms across her well-upholstered bosom and tut-tutted at the emptiness of the room. "Why, I remember a time when there were more women to help with such things than there were jobs for them to do. I used to make up little unnecessary tasks just to make some of them feel useful."

"Sometimes it feels as though everything has changed," Edwina said. "I find myself wondering what fresh wave of trouble might be just round the next corner."

"Is the arrival of your celebrated visitor one such of the troublesome changes?" Hortense asked. "I expect you are all at sixes and sevens with her popping up at the Beeches."

"How did you hear about that?"

"The same way as everyone else. I was walking along the high street yesterday afternoon minding my own business when Prudence Rathbone popped out of her shop all agog with the news that she had met the famous Beryl Helliwell."

"Was that all she said?"

"Certainly not. She sputtered on about the very idea that someone like her would be a friend of yours and could I believe it? She even went so far as to suggest you had deceived us all with your appearance of financial difficulties over the past few weeks. She made the ridiculous allegation that you were making it all up as some sort of a ruse to explain Beryl Helliwell's appearance in Walmsley Parva." Hortense let loose an unladylike snort. "I told her she was off her nut. I've never seen anyone so angry in all my life."

Edwina found herself in the unprecedented position of defending Prudence Rathbone. Not only was Prudence known for her eagerness to spread rumors, she was also unparalleled in her ability to take the smallest smidgen of information and turn it into a full-blown tale worthy of the evening papers. One of the grubby pleasures of life in Walmsley Parva was watching with disbelief the stories Prudence invented to condemn her neighbors. It would have been far easier to allow Hortense to remain convinced that Prudence had made up the entire story herself. Still, it would hardly help bolster her claims of solvency if she didn't lend credence to Beryl's rumor. Nor would it help to root out her nocturnal assailant. Edwina gingerly touched her throat and let out a sigh.

"I'm afraid she finally has a tale worth carrying. Beryl Helliwell is indeed here in Walmsley Parva and will be for the foreseeable future."

"Surely you're having me on," Hortense said, planting both hands down on the table in front of her so forcibly that a china elephant, short one leg, toppled over and dashed to bits on the hard surface.

"I assure you, I am not." Edwina stepped forward and with a piece of newspaper began gathering up the white and blue shards. "We were at finishing school together as girls and have kept in touch, however sporadically, all these years."

"You never said," Hortense said. "But then you wouldn't have, would you?"

"It would have sounding like boasting or trying to capitalize on someone else's reflected glory. It was far nicer to read about her adventures in the newspapers. In a village like this one so little stays private. I rather enjoyed having a secret for a change."

"I see just what you mean. In a village privacy is a luxury in short supply," Hortense said. "Does that mean she was also correct in asserting that you sent out a coded plea for assistance in order to get to the bottom of a crime at the behest of the King?"

"How many people in the village do you think Prudence told that to as well?"

"All of them, from what I heard. So, is that true as well? Criminal activity here in Walmsley Parva?"

"Let's just say someone made an attempt on my life last night. I hardly think it was a coincidence." Edwina loosened the knot in her scarf and pulled it aside to expose her bruised throat. Edwina couldn't resist the lure of a little glamour and intrigue. "I doubt very much the King would approve of this," she said pointing to a particularly painful mark darkened to the color of aubergines.

"Are you saying someone attacked you? Whatever for?"

"I think someone is afraid of me asking questions."

"Asking questions? What about?" Hortense asked.

"Helping out with the jumble wasn't the only reason for me stopping by this morning. I wanted to speak to you about Agnes Rollins."

Hortense threw up her hands in the air. "Not that old news again. I told you at the time she was just a foolish, irresponsible girl who had no sense of her duty. Nothing more mysterious than that." Hortense turned her attention to a pile of mismatched mittens and began sorting them into pairs by size regardless of color of pattern.

"We both knew that girl and it wasn't like her to be anything but conscientious. I never felt satisfied with the fact that no one ever could say what had happened to her." Hortense dropped a red mitten to the table surface and gave Edwina her full attention.

"You think that the disappearance of a flighty young woman more than two years ago explains someone trying to choke you last night?"

"Can you think of any other secret someone would be so eager to protect?"

"If you really think there was something unsavory about Agnes' leave-taking, why didn't you insist on following it up more thoroughly at the time?"

"I seem to remember trying to do just that. But I felt as though I was crying into the wind. I understood that things needed to get back to work at the Wallingford Estate for the greater good, and don't blame you for moving on quickly. But even Constable Gibbs didn't seem to be as concerned as I was at the time either."

"She had her hands full with day-to-day troubles. She certainly wasn't likely to borrow any more."

"Still, she did not do what anyone could consider a comprehensive job with the search for Agnes." Edwina thought back to the complete lack of assistance the search for Agnes had received from Constable Doris Gibbs. A female police officer was a new and startling concept for the villagers and Constable Gibbs had shown herself eager to uphold even higher standards of the law than her male predecessors. In fact, her law and order stance had led to her dismissal of the investigation into Agnes' disappearance. She had a list of wayward young women she suspected of khaki fever and the members of the Women's Land Army all were given a place on it simply because of their uniform trousers and the proximity of their housing to the hospital where so many soldiers could be found recovering.

Edwina had been able to say nothing to convince Constable Gibbs to consider the possibility that Agnes was a good girl who might have been a victim of foul play. Unfortunately the crime rate in the village was at an all-time low with Constable Gibbs serving the community and in an unusual turn of events, she was not replaced by a male officer at the end of the war. Edwina hardly expected her to be any more help at this late date than she had been when Agnes first went missing. Edwina certainly wasn't going to report the attack upon her person the night before. Edwina had an uncomfortable suspicion that she might have a place on one of the constable's lists as well. Not for lewd behavior but quite possibly as a waster of police time or even a degenerate debtor. She vastly preferred to have no contact whatsoever with Constable Gibbs.

"I suppose she could have been a bit more enthusiastic about it, but you know what she's like. How is it that you propose I can help you at this late date?" Hortense moved down the table from the mitten pile and began sorting half-empty spools of thread and other sewing notions into neat clusters. Edwina followed and tackled a wooden crate filled with tarnished singleton candlesticks and chipped vases. Under Hortense's watchful eye she lined up the household offerings wondering whom in their right mind might find use for any of them.

"You knew Agnes as well as anyone at the Wallingford Estate. Was she having any trouble with anyone that you can remember? Did she have any particular attachments?"

"All the girls were too tired at the end of the day to do much more than to head off to bed as early as they could manage. There isn't much to get up to in Walmsley Parva, as you well know, even if they were so inclined."

"There was the cinema and the tearoom. The reading room may have had appeal for Agnes. I seem to remember her being an enthusiastic reader."

"Now that you're prodding my recollection, I believe she used to read to patients at the hospital when she had the energy of an evening."

"That's right, she did." Edwina was surprised that she had forgotten such a thing. Her memory really was starting to slip. Sadly, not away from the painful memories though, only the useful or inconsequential ones. "Do you think she might have run into difficulties while she was there?"

"I'm sure I couldn't say. There were all sorts at the hospital at the time and not every one of them was someone it would have paid to be alone with for any length of time."

"Surely she wouldn't have been alone with a recovering soldier if she were reading aloud to the men in the ward."

"The hospital was not my bailiwick. Early on, Dr. Nelson and I agreed to observe strict boundaries between the two halves of the Wallingford Estate. His domain was the hospital and mine was the agricultural endeavors with never the twain should meet," Hortense said. "Even if she did volunteer there I doubt he'd remember her."

Edwina was not sure she would agree. Although her own experience with the male of the species was rather limited and had only included close contact with her own father and her beloved and much mourned brother, she could not quite credit the idea an attractive young woman like Agnes would have failed to make an impression upon the doctor. He might have been a respected member of the community, and a married man, but he was still as likely as the next man to appreciate a pretty face and a fine figure.

Edwina decided once she had spent enough time to consider she had made an effort she would leave Hortense to finish on her own and would use her bruises as an excuse to visit Dr.

Nelson's surgery. Calling ahead for an appointment was always wise but perhaps fortune would be on her side and she would manage to secure the doctor's attention for a few moments.

"Once I've finished up here with you, I think I'll stop by his surgery and ask if he might take a look at my neck. I could do with some sort of liniment for it."

"Suit yourself. If you wish to waste your time I shan't try to stop you."

Chapter 7

Beryl strolled back into the centre of the village lost in thought. Her conversation with Polly had yielded nothing particularly fruitful, which was, of course, discouraging. This detecting business was less exciting than Sherlock Holmes stories suggested it might be. Still, there was no denying Edwina had suffered a very real attack. She might have been wrong about Agnes Rollins being the cause of it, but evidently someone had been thoroughly upset by the possibility that Edwina was on the hunt for criminal activity.

Beryl had to wonder if whatever was going on was more recent than a wartime missing person. It was far less likely that there were no spies in the country than that there were any number of them. What better place to lay low than a sleepy backwater like Walmsley Parva? The ruckus had started because Prudence believed Edwina and Beryl were employed by His Majesty for just such countermeasures. Surely it wasn't too much of a stretch to consider the notion that there was indeed cause for alarm in the village. It might not be spies either. With all the unrest, there was no reason not to suspect labor organizers or even the Irish of working towards goals the King would not be pleased to hear about.

There was still plenty of time before lunch and it occurred to her to check on her automobile. The day before, the garage had been locked and the mechanic nowhere in sight when she had called. She had pulled the automobile to the side of the road in front of the garage, which bore a sign proclaiming it to be BLACKBURN AND BLACKBURN GARAGE AND CAB COMPANY. She had slid a note through the letter slot describing the services she hoped they could render and had promptly put the entire matter out of her mind. But now, with the investigation at a quiet interlude, she decided to stop in to ask after her prized possession. As her vehicle was no longer standing at the side of the road she had high hopes that the requested repairs were under way.

Banging and clanging filled the air as she stepped into the wood framed building whose wide doors stood flung open permitting the daylight to stream in and play upon the shiny scarlet paint of her car. A pair of small feet clad in greasy, leather boots protruded from below her scarlet vehicle. A tall man bent over under the hood and called out suggestions to whomever was stretched beneath. Viewed from behind, he was an attractive young man. After her last divorce, Beryl had vowed to herself she would never marry again. At least not anytime soon. Still, she was never one to shut her eyes when passing a pastry case simply because she wasn't actually hungry. Beryl smoothed the ends of her platinum hair and stepped in out of the breeze.

"Hello, I see you found my note," she called. The man whirled around at the sound of her voice. Beryl noted with a familiar and exhausting sense of pity that one of his sleeves was empty below the elbow and the excess fabric was pinned back out of the way. She wondered at his ability to continue in his trade with such a challenge. The man's eyes widened and a surprised smile spread across his face as he looked her up and down from her hat to her wildly impractical shoes.

"I told you it really was her," he said with a raised voice. The body that accompanied the boots beneath the automobile slid out and revealed itself. An impish-looking young woman with the same dark coloring and bright blue eyes as the young man sprang to her feet and hastily wiped her hands on her coveralls before offering one to Beryl.

"Michael and I laid a bet that the note you left was some sort of elaborate scheme dreamt up by the Prude."

"Prudence Rathbone, the postmistress," Michael interpreted. "Across the way. She said she'd seen you but my sister Norah here has always been a bit of a skeptic."

"Only where that woman is concerned. I can't scratch my nose over here without her reporting to the whole village I've contracted small pox." The young woman shook her head as she peered out through the garage door to the shop across the street.

"I take it I am in the presence of Blackburn and Blackburn?" Beryl asked.

"You are and we hope to have your motorcar back on the road by the day after tomorrow at the very latest." Michael patted the shiny red paint of a side panel with his remaining hand.

"I am relieved to hear it. I miss her already." Beryl felt a tug as she looked down at the crumpled front fender of her beautiful machine. Generally she didn't form attachments to possessions but in the case of the car she found herself utterly smitten.

"I would, too. She's a beauty," Norah said.

"Would you like to take her out for a run once you've finished up with the repairs?" Beryl asked. "Unless that would be a bit of a busman's holiday for you?"

The two siblings turned to each other, identical grins spreading across their faces. "We'd love to," they said in unison.

"That's settled then. Would it be too much to ask you to deliver it to the Beeches once you've tested it out for road worthiness?"

"Miss Davenport's place?" Norah asked.

"That's right. I'm staying there with her for the time being. We were at school together as girls and I plan to be here for some time renewing our acquaintance."

"That wasn't what Prudence had to say. She made up some sort of outrageous story about you and Edwina collaborating on secret missions during the war."

"Did you believe her?" Beryl asked.

"I don't generally, but with what all the papers have had to say about you over the years I thought if it really was you here in Walmsley Parva then the rest of it might be true as well," Michael said.

"What about you, Norah? Did you believe that I was here to assist Edwina with a secret mission on behalf of the King?"

"Truthfully I thought our nosy neighbour had finally gone round the twist. I was quite looking forward to her finally being carted off to the local insane asylum. I quite like the idea of having a postmistress that doesn't read one's post," Norah said. The Blackburn siblings shared a long look and Beryl felt a tingle of excitement. Perhaps there was a bit of a mystery Edwina had not considered. Prudence Rathbone would make a very satisfying villain.

"We've never been that lucky, sis," Michael said. "I don't expect our luck to change now." Beryl caught him glancing at his empty sleeve and she felt a pang for him.

"How can you say that, Michael?" Norah delivered a playful punch to his fully functioning arm. "Did you ever think you'd have the chance to work on a celebrity's motorcar?"

"Perhaps you're right," Michael said. Another vehicle pulled up in front of the garage and a man waved at them. "Another customer. Maybe you really are right." He stepped out into the sunshine and began to speak with the newcomer.

"Have the two of you been in business together long?" Beryl

asked, keeping her eyes on Norah whose own gaze stayed fixed on her brother.

"Only since the war. It was simply Blackburn's Garage before then. When Michael volunteered I took over. I wasn't sure I knew quite what I was doing, but it turned out that I had spent so many years watching him that I had picked up far more knowledge about the job than either of us realized," Norah said. "When he was discharged due to his injury I was determined he'd have a job to come home to so I just kept on. He wouldn't admit it of course but there are some parts of the job you simply need more than one hand for. So I lend him one or two of mine and we keep going."

"It sounds like you are all the luck your brother needs," Beryl said.

"I try to be."

"Do you both drive the cabs too or is there another Blackburn hiding round here somewhere?"

"It's just us. Michael does most of the driving. He says he can think better when he's behind the wheel."

"That is a sentiment he and I share," Beryl said. "I shall be glad to have it back as I have need of a good place to think. You see, Miss Rathbone was not only correct about my presence in the village. She was also reporting the truth about the reason for my visit. Edwina and I are investigating some irregularities here in Walmsley Parva." Beryl studied Norah's face as her words sank in.

"That's about the most shocking thing I've ever heard. Whatever could possibly need investigating around here?" Norah's eyes widened and looked not unlike the headlamps of the car.

"You didn't ever do any work on the Wallingford Estate during the time the Land Army was there, did you?" Beryl asked. "Fixing machinery, that sort of thing?"

"Now and again they would give me a call about something or other. I wasn't there very often though. So much of the equipment was manual that there wasn't too much call for a mechanic. They even had a horse and cart for the milk deliveries. Why do you ask?"

"I just wondered if either of you knew a young woman by the name of Agnes Rollins?" Beryl asked. Norah's posture stiffened and she drew a rag from her pocket and began slowly wiping her hands with careful attention.

"I did know her and would appreciate it if you didn't mention her name in front of my brother."

"He knew her too, I assume?" Beryl watched the men bending over the engine of the vehicle in front of the garage. Michael was pointing at something and the other man nodded as though he had some inkling what all the works under the hood were about. It was easy to imagine Michael as hale and hearty before the horrors of war had dug into him.

"Yes. They were friends of a sort, but she took off without a word. He has never quite gotten over it."

"Were they sweethearts then?" Beryl asked.

"No, I wouldn't say that. It's hard to explain in a hurry. Michael looks quite well now but he was not himself for ever so long. I should be very upset to think anything distressed him unnecessarily and sent him back into one of his dark spells." Both women looked at the young man in the dooryard silently. Beryl nodded.

"I shall be sure not to ask him anything about her. At least for the time being. But I should like to ask you more about her later in private if I may?" Beryl said. "I'll tell you what, why don't you come by for luncheon at the Beeches when you drop the car off and you can tell me all about it then?"

"What will I tell Michael if he wants to join me?"

"Say it's a lady's luncheon and he wouldn't enjoy it."

"You obviously don't know Michael if you think that will dissuade him." Norah looked at her brother again. "I'll tell him you're planning to serve a cold vegetable soup. That should put him off. But don't get your hopes up. I really didn't know Agnes all that well and it has been ages since last I saw her."

"That's the point really. It has been ages since anyone has seen her. Edwina never was satisfied with her disappearance. She truly believes something happened to her."

"Are you suggesting she didn't leave Walmsley Parva of her own free will?"

"I think Edwina was suggesting she didn't leave this village at all." Michael shook hands with the other man and turned to give Norah a smile and a nod. He moved in their direction.

"In that case I especially hope you shan't say anything to Michael. He should find such a suggestion most distressing." Norah's voice took a note of pleading.

"I can promise you I shan't say a thing to him until after our luncheon," Beryl said. She gave her car a loving pat on the hood and nodded good-bye to the younger woman before stepping out onto the sidewalk once more. She raised her hand to Michael and felt Norah's eyes upon her. As she set off for the Beeches she couldn't shake the feeling there was much more running around under the surface in quiet Walmsley Parva than anyone would notice at a glance.

Chapter 8

"I'm sorry, but whingeing at me shan't make a bit of difference," Edwina said to Crumpet as she tied his lead to an iron fence post. "It's one thing to take a dog into the village hall. It's quite another to take one into a doctor's surgery." She patted him on his scruffy head before heading towards the surgery.

Nurse Crenshaw looked up from behind the wide wooden desk when Edwina pushed open the door. "Miss Davenport, I don't remember you making an appointment for today," she said, peering down her large nose at an open appointment diary on the desk in front of her.

"Your memory is as sound as ever. Something has come up unexpectedly and I thought I would take the chance that the doctor might be able to squeeze me in." Edwina drew herself up to her full height. Not that it made her particularly imposing. She was not a tall woman, in fact most would call her short, but she had found that displays of impeccable posture had an effect on others.

"The doctor does not take patients without appointments. It is a strict policy, as I am sure you are well aware."

"Is the doctor marked down with a patient at present?" Edwina asked in a bolder voice than her usual one. In Edwina's considered opinion nurses were sorely inclined to think themselves rather more powerful and important than they ought. Especially Nurse Crenshaw. What the doctor saw in her Edwina would never know. She leaned over the appointment diary and tapped her finger on a blank place. She then gave a pointed look at the wall clock. "I see he is not. I would appreciate it if you added my name."

"Calling ahead is the preferred method for making an appointment. This is not a butcher shop where one simply stops in and begins giving orders. Besides, the doctor will be needing his dinner right now if he is to manage to eat before his afternoon appointments. Isn't that right, Doctor?" Nurse Crenshaw called out past Edwina's shoulder. Edwina turned to see Dr. Nelson framed in the doorway to his examining room.

"I can always find time for my patients. Especially those as infrequently ill as Miss Davenport. Please come through," he said, stepping aside to allow her to enter the room. Edwina felt the hot scowl of Nurse Crenshaw's disapproval attempting to blister her back. Dr. Nelson closed the door firmly and gave her a welcoming smile. "She means well but I don't suppose that makes her attitude any easier on my patients."

"I can come back later if I am keeping you from your dinner. I shouldn't like to inconvenience you or your wife," Edwina said. Dr. Nelson shook his head.

"It's no trouble at all. I find I never have any appetite anymore and Margery never notices if I am coming or going, as I am quite sure you are aware."

"She's much the same then?" Edwina asked.

"Yes. I'm afraid she is one patient completely beyond my ability to cure. I do wish there was some way to convince her to invite a few people over to play bridge again or to serve on the flower committee at the church, but she just won't hear of it."

Dr. Nelson ran a boney hand through his thinning hair. Even after the war began he and his wife had carried on entertaining and had been leaders in social circles in the village. Edwina had been a guest from time to time at their home and had always enjoyed the occasions. All that had changed, however, when the Nelsons' young son Alan had sickened with influenza and died. Margery had taken it very hard and Edwina thought she had blamed her husband for his inability to save their child. She almost never left the house. It was remarked in the village that she had not felt the kiss of the sun on her skin since her son died two years earlier. People, not unkindly, offered advice as to how to cure her time to time but the doctor only changed the subject whenever his wife was mentioned. "But my domestic affairs are not what brings you in to the surgery I am sure. What seems to be the trouble?" He pulled out the visitor's chair in front of his desk. Edwina settled herself and crossed her ankles.

"I had a bit of trouble with my scarf last night whilst out walking Crumpet. I wondered if you might have some sort of soothing liniment?" Edwina unwound the silk scarf from her neck once more and exposed her throat for inspection.

"That looks like a great deal more than a bit of trouble. What have you done to yourself?" The doctor stooped over her and looked closely. "Or should I ask, what was done to you?"

"That is the second reason I am here, if you want the truth."

"I always want the truth from my patients. I find things get on the mend far more quickly if one needn't sift through a heap of falsehoods in order to proffer a diagnosis." He seated himself on the edge of his desk. "You haven't been coaxed into feats of derring-do by your adventurous housemate, have you?"

"So, like everyone else in Walmsley Parva you've heard about Beryl Helliwell's arrival, have you?"

"Nurse Crenshaw told me about it before I'd even taken off my coat this morning. I assume the rumors are true then?"

"They are. You heard the rest, too?"

"That you are employed by His Majesty to ferret out nefarious activities in the heart of our green and pleasant land?" The doctor gave her a broad smile. "I had. I can think of no one I'm more amused to imagine bringing wrong-uns to justice than you, Miss Davenport. That is, so long as it doesn't place you in harm's way." He leaned towards her once more and gently touched the side of her neck. Edwina tried not to wince and failed.

"Naturally, that is exactly what Beryl believes happened. In the afternoon she mentioned that she had arrived to help me with an investigation and by nightfall someone had attempted to strangle me in my own back garden."

"Are you quite certain you didn't simply catch your scarf on a low-hanging branch? After all, the entire idea of someone attempting to harm you over such obvious poppycock beggars belief. If such an investigation were to be undertaken it would be unlikely for it to be assigned to a woman and certainly not one of your advancing years," he said.

Edwina wasn't sure she entirely liked his attitude towards her investigation. In fact, if she were to be honest with herself, she would admit he had gotten her dander well and truly up with his lighthearted dismissal of her capabilities. While she had herself protested that it was unlikely Beryl's tale of investigatory prowess would be believed, it had not been on account of her gender or her age but rather her lack of experience in such matters. Still, he was a man and as such should be expected to be saddled with a predictable and unfortunate narrowness of mind.

"I am intimately acquainted with my garden, Doctor, and I assure you that I did not ensnare myself in the branches of a tree. The local flora is not so vicious as to cause a wound such as this." Edwina pointed to her neck once more.

"I shall have to bow to your greater botanical knowledge. Assuming you were attacked, have you any idea what might have caused such a desperate move?"

"Agnes Rollins. You remember the Land Army girl that disappeared."

"Of course. Quite a dither at the time if I recall. Why should you mention it to me though?" Dr. Nelson got to his feet and turned his back on Edwina as he opened a glass-fronted cabinet filled with bottles and tubes. He took his time selecting one before turning to face her once more.

"Hortense reminded me that Agnes made time to read to the soldiers at the hospital whenever she wasn't dead on her feet."

"She was a very dedicated young woman. The soldiers were always very eager to have her there." The doctor vigorously shook the brown glass bottle he held in his hand.

"Did you have any inkling at the time why she might have gone missing? Did anything happen at the hospital that might have explained it?" Dr. Nelson leaned over her and dabbed a bit of liniment on her bruise. His brow furrowed and he looked as though he were debating something.

"Some of the soldiers awaited her visits even more eagerly than the others. One in particular comes to mind."

"Do you remember his name?" Edwina asked.

"Oh yes. Michael Blackburn. He had come to us suffering from shell shock and also had lost a limb. Until Miss Rollins came to read to the men he was almost completely unresponsive. Even his sister could not provoke a response from him when she came in daily to visit."

"I hadn't realized he had been quite so affected. You wouldn't know he had suffered from any disturbance of the mind to speak with him now."

"One never knows what will cause the mind to recover. In Michael's case it seemed to be Miss Rollins who rekindled his interest in the world. He became quite besotted with her by all accounts." The doctor cleared his throat. "She actually came to me for advice about him. She wanted my professional opinion as to whether her visits were doing more harm than good."

"In which way?" Edwina asked. She was surprised. Michael

had always been such a pleasant, even-tempered young man before he was sent back from the front, injured.

"Michael seemed to believe Miss Rollins' attentions were of a more personal sort than she had intended. He became quite persistent about it all."

"That sounds unpleasant."

"It was very awkward for Miss Rollins and for everyone else as well. I finally felt it best to ask her to desist in reading to the men."

"Why was that?"

"Michael began to shout at the other patients if they spoke to her or even if she chatted to them. He threatened them with bodily harm if any of them made the least indication they wished to interact with her. No one needed that sort of outburst and I asked her to refrain from visiting any further."

"How did she react to your request?"

"I believe she was relieved. I think by that point in time she was rather frightened of Michael and was content to be done with the whole experience."

"When did this happen?"

"Not long before she left, I believe, but the whole time period is such a blur I am not clear on the details. There was a great deal of more importance happening in the hospital than jealous rantings and obsessions of delusional young men."

"Did you not think at the time there might be a connection between Michael's behavior and Agnes' disappearance?" Edwina felt stunned. "That he might have either frightened her off? Or worse?"

"Perhaps I should have but you have to recall what the circumstances were like then. The hospital barely managed to attend to the extreme needs of the soldiers we had recuperating there. That doesn't even take into account the myriad patients we attended from the village. I had very little ability to give thought to a missing volunteer girl." Dr. Nelson passed a hand over his face as if to wipe away the memories. "What does it matter now? Michael has made as full a recovery as one could hope and it seems to me there's no reason to go stirring things up at this late date."

"Doctor, someone is worried enough about an investigation into something criminal in Walmsley Parva to do this to me." Edwina touched her neck lightly. "It might be that Michael is not as well as you would like to believe."

"Or it might be that what happened to you has nothing whatsoever to do with that girl's disappearance. Perhaps someone has a more personal reason to attack you and simply used the rumor to cover up their reason. " Dr. Nelson crossed his arms over his chest. "Had you considered that?"

"I had not in any way considered that possibility. After all, who would want to harm me? And why now?" Edwina felt a shiver run along her scalp. Part of her was terrified and a smaller part just the slightest bit thrilled to think she might stir such events into action.

"You advertised for a lodger recently, didn't you?" Despite Beryl's efforts that bit of gossip wasn't fading easily. Edwina felt her cheeks grow hot.

"Yes. I did."

"I assume you provided an address for your house in the advertisement?"

"Yes." Edwina grew uneasy.

"And your name, which identified you as a lady on your own, I expect?" Edwina nodded. The doctor shook his head. "Did it not occur to you that some lunatic took the knowledge about yourself that you provided and took the opportunity to try to satisfy his irrational and homicidal urges on you?"

"You think I was attacked by someone who read my advertisement? You think it was simply an opportunistic and unbalanced stranger who did this?"

"I'd say that is at least as likely as the possibility someone made an attempt on your life over an old and not particularly worrisome missing person's case, don't you agree?" The doctor shoved back his chair and came round the desk to stand beside her. "I suggest you go home and be sure to apply this liniment to your neck a few times each day until the bruising fades. I also advise that you lock all your doors and don't wander around in the dark on your own until you are quite certain all the copies of your advertisement have had time to end up as wastepaper."

Chapter 9

Beryl rounded the back corner of the Beeches determined to find a sunny spot to sit and think about her new situation. An appealing stone bench sat tucked up against some sort of twiggy shrubbery just ahead. Beryl never interested herself in the names of plants. She zigzagged across the browning lawn with the intention of taking a seat. As she approached, a scuffling, dragging noise emanated from just beyond the shrubbery. Considering Edwina's plight the evening before, Beryl felt it foolish to turn her back on the noise without further investigation. She crept around the leafless bush and came upon a man well past his prime dragging sticks off a towering pile and heaping them into a wheelbarrow. She waited while he paused, pulled a tarnished flask from a jacket pocket, and took a long swig from it.

"Hello," Beryl said. Her travels had taught her to always lead with friendly intentions and to expect the best of native populations. Some of her most pleasant and memorable experiences while traveling had been from meeting and forming friendships with locals. Especially over a glass or two of the local variety of potent hooch. Elderly men were one of her particular specialties. But then they should be as she had plenty of experience with them through her numerous marriages to the sort. The man turned to face her and she realized he was even older than she had first imagined. Truly it was a wonder he was still putting one hobnailed boot in front of the other, let alone that he could perform physical labor. Especially if he was as pickled as she suspected him to be. Even in the open air the fumes rolling off his person made Beryl's eyes smart.

"Morning, missus." He swiftly hid the hand holding the flask behind his back then doffed a disreputable excuse for a flat cap with his free hand and bobbed his head.

"I don't suppose you would like to share whatever it is you're sipping back here?" Beryl's tone was playful and friendly.

"That depends."

"On what?"

"On whether or not you are planning to tell Miss Davenport what I've been up to."

"I shan't be able to promise any such thing until I decide if I approve of the contents of that flask." Beryl tugged off her gloves and held out her hand. The old man flashed a semi-toothless grin in Beryl's direction and she got the impression he would have been a rather difficult man to resist had he been forty or fifty years younger.

"I won't tell Edwina about the spirits if you don't." Beryl took a healthy gulp of the old man's refreshment. He wasn't much of a dresser but he did know his liquor. "I can forget about the flask but I cannot promise anything without knowing what it is that you are up to with the vegetation. Are you stealing her brush pile for some nefarious purpose?"

"That's as Miss Davenport would have folks believe. Right barmy about stick piles is Miss Davenport. But it's only for her own good."

"What is?"

"I told her no good would come of piling up brush. Rabbits and rodents. Hedgehogs even can't resist a grand pile of sticks. It causes no end of troubles with the vegetable plot. But would she listen?" The old man jabbed an angry finger at the offending brush.

"I would hazard a guess that she is not inclined to do so," Beryl said. "Edwina has always listened best to her own counsel as long as I've known her." She handed the flask back to the gardener.

"I'll say she does. I heard at the post office that she almost strangled herself getting all tied up by her scarf in there. Almost lost that poor wee dog of hers too whilst she was at it."

"I think Edwina might not be quite as much to blame as you suggest," Beryl said. The man appeared not to have heard her.

"Here I am on the day I usually oblige at the solicitor's clearing this lot up before she does herself any more mischief. Do you think she will thank me for me troubles? Not likely." The man reached for a long stick and gave it a firm yank. "It's a hard enough thing to keep up with the garden when the mistress doesn't insist on laying out the welcome mat for all manner of pests. I'm all on me own now that young Norman's gotten above himself and has taken against helping out from time to time."

"Who's Norman?" Beryl wondered if Norman was the old man's son. If so, Norman could easily be quite elderly himself. If that was the extent of the help available it was no wonder the grounds at the Beeches were looking as run-down as the house. Even though he hadn't responded to her offer to help Beryl pitched in and carried an armload of sticks of her own to the waiting wheelbarrow.

"Norman Davies, the lad who used to work with me once a week when they could spare him from the estate."

"The Wallingford Estate?"

"That's the one. He was one of those workers of special need what didn't end up in France like the rest of the lads round here." The man shook his head. "Now all he can think about is making a go of that bit of property he's renting. Trying to win back that girl of his. The lad's got no time for the likes of his old friend Simpkins anymore."

"It can be very difficult to find help these days, can't it?" Beryl asked. "I'm sure that Edwina is very pleased to have you even with the disagreement about the brush pile."

"You wouldn't think it with how slowly she loosens the purse strings." Beryl wondered if Simpkins had been talking to the postmistress and the greengrocer. Her payment the day before of Edwina's delinquent accounts at both establishments would likely have been as much a part of the gossip going round as stories of criminal investigations.

"I think you'll find her to be much more prompt at delivering your wages now."

"So you say, missus, but I'll believe it when my pay packet is tucked in me back pocket all snuglike."

"I assure you, fortunes are on the rise here once more. In fact, Edwina asked me to approach the maid, Polly, who used to work here, to return. She starts back at her job tomorrow morning."

"Polly Watkins?" Simpkins gave a mighty tug on a stuck branch and nearly knocked himself off balance with the effort. Although on second thought, Beryl considered it might have been the drink making him so wobbly on his pins.

"I believe Watkins was her surname. Fresh-faced girl with plenty of freckles and honey-colored hair?" Beryl said. Simpkins made a grunting sort of sound then heaved the stick he wrested free from the pile a few yards away. "Do you know her?"

"I thought I did. Until she threw young Norman over without an excuse."

"They were sweethearts, your Norman and Polly Watkins?" Beryl asked.

"They walked out together. Had something of an under-standing, if you know what I mean."

"Were they engaged to be married?" Beryl asked.

"No one had announced the bans, if that's what you're ask-ing." Simpkins grunted again. "Still, young Norman had expec-tations and no one can convince me that Polly didn't lead him a merry chase." Simpkins perched a final stick on the wheelbarrow and grasped the handles. He rolled it unsteadily forward. Beryl followed him as he headed to the edge of the wood at the far reaches of the property. One by one he pulled the sticks out of the wheelbarrow and scattered them on the ground below the trees.

"It sounds as if it may be a good thing that this Norman won't be helping out here at the Beeches anymore if Polly will be coming and going."

"You might be right at that. I shouldn't like to see young Norman forced to see that girl at close quarters. It's hard enough in a village this small for him not to have to see her more often than is good for his temper."

"He has a temper then?" Beryl asked. "Perhaps Edwina is best off without him for even more reasons."

"Nothing that he can't usually control. The boy's a good lad. He never lashes out unless sorely provoked." Simpkins stiff-ened like a foxhound that had caught the scent. "Speaking of women who provoke fellows beyond what any reasonable man can be expected to take, Miss Davenport has returned." Beryl turned to see Edwina rounding the corner of the house. Simp-kins offered Beryl a final swig from his flask before pocketing it, sketching a small salute, and stumbling off through the woods.

Beryl watched him until he disappeared from view. Edwina arrived at her side a moment later.

"Whatever has happened to my stick pile?"

Chapter 10

"I think it most disloyal of you to have assisted Simpkins," said Edwina. "It's taken me weeks to get my pile built back up to a satisfying size again." Edwina had required a great deal of coaxing but Beryl had finally persuaded her to have their tea at the Silver Spoon Tearoom, Minnie Mumford Proprietress. Despite Minnie's encouragement to take a table in the center of the shop where she would be sure to overhear any choice bits of their conversation, they had flatly refused and chose instead a table barely large enough for two near the window overlooking the street.

"How was I to know a brush pile could be such a source of disagreement? If you are so unhappy with your jobbing gardener, why don't you simply stop employing him?" Beryl raised her teacup to her lips and took a sip. As much as she was happy to have escaped the cold and damp of a New England autumn in favor of a milder English one, she would never understand the passion the English had for tea. She vastly preferred Simpkins' notion of what constituted a drink. Give her cocktail hour over teatime anyday. She looked around the shop where china figurines clotted the molding above the windows and faded chintz swathed every flat surface. Beryl wondered if she sat still for too long whether the proprietress would drape a length of polished cotton over her as well.

"I can't do that. Simpkins is the only jobbing gardener to be had for what I can pay. Thanks to your efforts, I've barely managed to convince people I shan't end up in a pauper's grave. If I dismissed Simpkins the rumors would run amok once more."

"If you are so grateful for my help I suggest you forgive me for your brush pile. Tomorrow I'll head out into the woods and gather all your sticks back up if it makes you feel any better. I hate to see you looking so down. Although your attitude does seem a bit extreme. Even for a devoted gardener."

"It's not really Simpkins or the pile. I've just been to see the doctor and it's left me more than a bit on edge." Edwina dropped two cubes of sugar into her cup and gave it a listless stir.

"Bad news at the doctor?" Beryl asked. "It wasn't on account of what happened last night, was it? You didn't suffer any long-term ill effects from the attack, did you?" She leaned across the table and tried to see past the silk scarf swathing Edwina's throat.

"No, nothing like that. But I did leave feeling quite foolish. I went in to ask him about Agnes and the volunteering she did at the hospital housed in the ballroom of the Wallingford Estate."

"Drat. There I was thinking I had a lead to share with you from my visit to the garage." Beryl reached for a scone from the tiered stand Minnie plunked between them on the table. Edwina reached for a thin tomato and cheese sandwich to pass the time while Minnie hovered nearby. Beryl had polished off one scone and had reached for a second before the bell on the door mercifully jingled and announced a new arrival. Minnie scurried off and left them in peace. "Why did you feel foolish?"

"Dr. Nelson pointed out the possibility that the attack on me last night had nothing whatsoever to do with any criminal activity centred in Walmsley Parva. Other than my own making, that is."

"You? Involved in criminality? I'd be as likely to believe your Simpkins was in line to be the next Archbishop of Canterbury," Beryl said.

"He's not my Simpkins." Edwina frowned extravagantly. "The doctor suggested that the attack was prompted by my advertisement for a lodger and that it had nothing whatsoever to do with Agnes or anyone else from Walmsley Parva."

"He suggested the attack on you was your own fault?" Beryl dropped her scone to her plate with a clatter. "The very idea."

"He made a convincing argument."

"Did he now?"

"He did. He said I had provided my address and even my marital status in the advertisement. Truly it had never occurred to me that such a thing could be dangerous." Edwina let out a deep breath. "But considering the potential tenants I refused I have to concede the doctor made a strong case for a random act by a total lunatic."

"You think there is nothing to investigate? Regardless of why it happened, someone tried to choke you to death."

"I haven't forgotten that, thank you very much. It's just that I fear we should consider that perhaps we've been making a bit of a fanciful fuss where really the truth is just sordid and ordinary."

"I have often been accused of my life being sordid, Ed, but I refuse to have anyone call it ordinary. If you don't wish to continue investigating, I'll understand. But I intend to keep on. After all, even if it was some nutter there's nothing to say he or she won't try again."

"Are you trying to frighten me?" Edwina's voice raised and all eyes in the shop turned their way.

"Certainly not. Although a flush of terror now and again does wonders for the complexion. No, I am simply reminding you that it isn't as if you have moved house since the strangler made the attempt." Beryl reached for a sandwich and bit into it. Marmite. More than just tea would take getting used to, she decided.

"I hadn't thought of that," Edwina said. "I bought a week's worth of advertising and this is only the fifth day, Who's to say even if the person in the garden last night has worked out whatever ailed him that there won't be another to take his place? There are a great many people out there who haven't been well in their minds since the war began."

"Cheer up, Ed. I'm sure you've been in worse spots before. I know I have. And think of the bright side."

"What's that?"

"You never feel quite so alive as when you are worried you won't be for much longer."

Edwina managed to down two more cups of sugary tea before they left the shop. Twilight was gathering about them and Edwina regretted not wearing a heavier coat. Up ahead the lights of the cinema marquee shone brightly. Polly Watkins stood at the entrance wearing a thin blue wrap, a frock and the sort of shoes Edwina deemed completely inappropriate for anything but a formal occasion. The lower classes were far too prone to overdress. Still, after all everyone had been through, such things seemed to matter so much less than they had before the war. Polly's hair was swept up off her neck and as they approached Edwina could see a blue scarf fluttering jauntily at her neck. Truly the girl was all dressed up.

Edwina watched as Polly furtively cast a glance at the cinema entrance. She looked up and down the pavement. A figure on the opposite side of the road called her name. She turned and the figure moved towards her. She looked at the cinema door once more then streaked round the back of the building. Edwina heard the figure call Polly's name a second time then slink back into the shadows. She felt her shoulders creep up round her ears. Beryl seemed to sense her unease and reached out to take her arm. She tucked Edwina's elbow into the crook of her own and began to whistle a tune that if Edwina had been forced to guess she would have attributed to a sailor on a third-rate ship.

"What's gotten into you, Beryl?" she asked.

"If you ever suspect you might be followed, make sure all possible eyes are on you. The person creeping up on you is not likely to make a move if you are making a scene."

As horrified as Edwina was to be seen weaving down the street like a drunken navvy, she was never gladder to be with her friend.

Chapter 11

"Beryl Helliwell found alive and well," Jack called down the street. "Takes up residence in idyllic English village." He waved the morning paper above his head and shouted the headline once more. He turned round to shout the news in the opposite direction then stopped and stared as a woman approached. There, right in front of him, at his very own corner, stood Beryl Helliwell. For a long moment he could not think, let alone speak. Finally, the worry she would think him a simpleton goaded him to recover his voice.

"You've been found, you know," he said, finally finding his voice. She leaned towards him. A heady mix scent of exotic spices and dusky flowers wafted towards him as she did so. He thought he had never smelled something so delicious in all his life. Not even a fresh tray of breakfast baps at Minnie Mumford's tearoom.

"Would you like to know a secret?" she asked. He nodded slowly as if he was doing so while several leagues under the sea.

"Are you sure I can trust you? You are a member of the press in a way, aren't you?"

"I promise. If you find out I've betrayed your secret you can feed me to one of those lions I've seen you pose with in the newsreels."

"Bravely spoken. I feel I can trust you." She leaned so close her breath tickled his ear. His knees wobbled and he clutched at his heavy bag hoping he looked worthy of her confidence. "I wasn't lost at all. I was hiding."

"Hiding. From who?" His heart thudded in his chest. It was all too thrilling.

"Everyone." She gave him an enormous smile and pried his fist from the strap of his bag. She placed a penny in it and held out her hand for a paper.

"Are you still hiding?" Jack looked up and down the street.

"Not anymore. I have things I need to do and it was time to get back to them. You seem like the sort of young man who knows what is what in his village. I think my friend Miss Davenport and I might have need of a bright boy like you with our mission. Do you think you would be able to show discretion if the need arose?"

"I'm sure I could, missus, if you'd tell me what *discretion* meant."

"It means not telling people things you were trusted not to reveal."

"So you mean don't act like Miss Rathbone at the post office?"

"That's it exactly. Do you think you could hold your tongue if need be?" Beryl Helliwell looked deeply into his eyes and his mind went blank once more. He was brought to his senses by a motorcar rumbling down the street. The driver slowed down, and then stuck out his hand for a paper. Jack concluded the transaction and she spoke again. "I shouldn't want you to make any promises you wouldn't like to keep."

"I would be more than happy to help you and Miss Davenport in any way you might need. And I promise I can keep my tongue. Even under torture."

"Let's hope it doesn't come to that. If and when I have need of you will I be able to find you on this corner?"

"Every day, rain or shine," Jack said, doffing his flat cap. "I'm here with the morning edition and then again with the evening newspaper. Or you can ask for me at the pub if it is near closing time. My mum usually sends me to fetch me dad." Jack grinned. Beryl Helliwell fished half a crown from her coat pocket and pressed it into his hand.

"I believe you are a man of your word. Consider this a retainer. Do you know what that means?" Jack wished he were the sort of man who could have said that he did know such words. But the truth was he could hardly read the headlines of the newspapers he sold. Still, the only way to learn new things was to admit you didn't already know them. He shook his head. "It is a sort of payment up front that the person who hires you can draw from if the need arises," she said.

"Like an advance?"

"Yes. But it is a commitment that also reminds us both that your loyalty is to me."

"It would have been even without the half crown, missus."

"I think you are going to be just the man for the job, Jack."

Beryl stopped in front of the butcher shop to look over the goods displayed in the window. Three wizened chickens and what likely would be claimed to be a ham hung from a pole. Beryl felt the offerings were at odds with the shop's sign proclaiming the establishment to be owned by one Sidney Poole, Purveyor of Fine Meats. She doubted the interior of the shop would yield a more inspiring inventory. Still, Edwina had insisted that there was absolutely nothing in the house to feed them if you didn't include a couple pots of raspberry jam put up before Edwina's mother died and a paltry three gherkins left bobbing in a jar.

Beryl pushed open the door and approached the large man dressed in a snowy white apron who stood at the back of the shop wiping a cloth over the top of the glass meat case with a broad hand.

"Good morning. Are you Mr. Poole?" she said as she peered into the case. It could not be said that Beryl was any sort of a cook. If the need to provide for her own nourishment arose she was perfectly contented with a bit of cheese and an apple. She had, on occasion, if the circumstances were dire, opened a tin of soup. She never bothered to heat it but rather preferred to consume it straight out of the can. Shopping for groceries was well outside her experience and in truth she had no idea whether what she was viewing in the case before her was the least bit suitable for Edwina's plans. She pulled an old envelope from her coat pocket, which Edwina had used to hastily scribble down a list.

"That I am. Anything I can get for you this morning, missus?" he asked.

"I wondered if you might have a small beef roast. Something suitable to serve three or four with a bit of bone in it for the dog?" Edwina's note had been quite clear on that. Crumpet must have a bone or there would be no peace at the Beeches.

"I expect I'll be able to find something for you. You're that American woman that's been missing for ages, aren't you?"

"I am a woman and I am an American. But I would take issue with the notion that I've been missing. I've known right where I've been all along." Beryl had no interest whatsoever in discussing her decision to eschew the limelight for some months. She couldn't really explain it to herself and thus had found it utterly impossible to make sense of for anyone else. Not only that, she couldn't see how it was anyone's business but her own if she had found herself in need of a break from all the frantic gallivanting. A butcher's shop was no place for self-reflection.

Mr. Poole snapped his fingers and pointed at her. "Beryl Helliwell. That's who you are. Staying up to the Beeches with

Miss Davenport. I've got just the thing for her. Now that I hear she's promptly settling her accounts once again." He dug round in the back of the case and hoisted a roast about the size of a loaf of bread up for her inspection. "How's this?" He turned it round for her to see a good-sized bone showing at the end.

"That will do nicely, I'm sure." Beryl hoped she was right about the roast. She consulted the list once more. "I'd like a chicken as well."

"I've just the one." Mr. Poole stepped to the window display and selected one of the paltry fowl hanging there. Beryl thought it unlikely such an unprepossessing bird would make much of a meal but she could hardly complain as she wanted to invite confidences from the butcher.

"That's lovely. Do you think the greengrocer across the street will have some sort of vegetable to go with it?"

"I'm sure they do. My nephew Norman stopped in this morning after he made a delivery there." Mr. Poole carried the roast to the roll of butcher's paper fixed to a dispenser at the far end of the counter. He spooled off a bit of it and neatly wrapped the roast, tying it up with a length of string. "Sprouts and parsnips I think he said."

"Is that the same Norman who used to work with Simpkins up at the Beeches before the war?"

"That's right. He's renting some land from the old Wallingford Estate now that the government has left off using all those girls as farmers. Making a real go of it, he is."

"You must be very proud of him."

"We are. Norman's been like a son to us." Mr. Poole shook his head and his extra chins wobbled. "No kiddies of our own you understand." Unlike Beryl, Mr. Poole seemed to regret his childless state. Beryl made a noncommittal clucking noise and returned the subject to produce.

"They must be fresh then, the vegetables?" she asked.

"Fresher than usual. Norman said he had a bit of a lie-in on account of his late night. He plucked those sprouts this morning as quick as he could but he still got in a couple hours later than is his habit."

"I thought farmers tended to keep early hours?" Beryl said. "Up before the birds and all that."

"He used to until recently." Mr. Poole lowered his voice. "It's that girl he'd been walking out with. Crazy for the cinema is Polly. She goes to the evening shows every chance she gets."

"Not really the right sort of a match for a farmer then, is she?"

"You put your finger right on it," he said, sliding the parcel across the counter. "Polly told him she wasn't interested in seeing him anymore on account of the hours he keeps. He's been staying up far too late trying to win her back. He looked positively done in when he was here."

"Have all his efforts paid off yet?" Beryl asked.

"Let's just say you'd best hope the sprouts are sweeter than Norman's temper this morning." Mr. Poole said. "Norman's the best sort of lad you'd ever want to meet. Whenever I think of how Polly's treated him it makes me see red." Mr. Poole wiped his hands on his apron, leaving reddish streaks all down the front. "He'd have been better off if she'd been lost to the influenza."

Chapter 12

By midafternoon Polly had still not arrived and Edwina was becoming a bit put out. Beryl could see from the set of her chin that she was worrying about it a good deal. She had looked much the same as a girl whenever something was on her mind. When taxed with it she admitted to being worried that Polly had said she would return to the Beeches but had no real intention of doing so.

"I'm afraid she has decided to teach me a lesson of some sort or other."

"You know there's no sense sitting round here and stewing about it. I say we head over to her house and ask her to her face." Beryl took Edwina by the arm and led her to the front hall. She plucked Edwina's third best hat from the hall tree and plunked it firmly on Edwina's head. "Where does she live?"

"She still lives with her parents at the far end of the village, on a lane branching off the road leading out of town. You would have passed it on your way here." Edwina wasn't sure she wanted to settle things with Polly. In her opinion it might be far better to simply ignore the whole thing. One didn't like to embroil oneself in unpleasantness if it was at all possible to avoid it. "It's quite out of the way now that I come to think of it."

"I can tell you are trying to wriggle out of your duties as an employer but I think it best you attend to this mess as soon as possible."

"I can't see why I should be involved at all. You're the one who offered her a position."

"I did so as a favor to you. Besides, it is your house. In any case, I shan't find it by myself if the house is as far out of the way as you are making it out to be."

"You managed to find your way to Nepal, Beryl," Edwina said.

"You assume a bit there, my friend. I found Nepal but I had been looking for Burma." Beryl gave her friend what she hoped was a winning smile and donned a hat of her own.

"I thought you had a faultless sense of direction," Edwina said. "The newspapers are always going on about it."

"What I have is a faultless sense of adventure and an enormous talent for making the best of things." Beryl draped a coat over Edwina's shoulders and propelled her towards the door. "Both of which I am attempting to share with you. Now lead on."

Sticking to the road would only make sense if they had taken the motorcar. As it was still out of commission Beryl had assured Edwina that she was delighted to see a bit of the countryside whilst they were at it. At the outset she insisted too much ease would make her stout if she didn't have a care and take some exercise. Crumpet naturally supported the notion of a good romp, and before long the three of them were clambering over a stile at the back of the property rented by Norman Davies.

"Are you quite sure this is the best way to go?" Beryl asked. She may have been known as an intrepid adventurer but she was not showing signs of it as the smell of the field dressing reached her nose. "You don't mean to walk across this muck, do you?" She looked down at the recently amended field with a scowl on her face.

"You said you wanted to experience life in a quiet backwater. Well, this is what it is like," Edwina called over her shoulder. "A bit of manure never hurt anyone."

"I don't believe my shoes would agree with you."

"What happened to your spirit of adventure?" Edwina asked.

"One of the keys to success when on expedition is to make sure to be kitted out in the appropriate gear. When you said we'd be cutting through a fallow field I had imagined stubble from a hay crop. Besides, I have rather a thing about shoes."

"I think this may be a wonderful time for you to show me how you make the best of situations," Edwina said, watching Beryl shake her shoe.

"If Polly doesn't have a car of her own it might explain why she never showed up for work today," Beryl said. "I'd be more than a little tempted to miss it if I knew I'd have to cross all this just to get started."

"I do wonder if she knew the field was going to be dressed when she suggested starting today."

"How much farther is it to Polly's parents' house?" Beryl asked. "It's starting to get a bit dark." Above their heads a flock of small birds wheeled and landed with ease in the uppermost branches of a tall tree.

"Three quarters of a mile, at least."

"Should we head back?" Beryl asked. "It is cocktail hour after all and I'm sure you'll be wanting one of your cups of tea. If we turn back now I might still be able to salvage these shoes."

"We'd be better off continuing on towards the Wallingford Estate. There is a road that runs back into the village from there. We could walk back on that instead of through the field." Beryl nodded and thus bolstered picked up the pace. Wallingford Hall stood on a bit of a rise visible a way off in the distance. Small cottages, empty save for one or two, dotted the edges of the rolling fields. As the gloaming enveloped them light winked on in the nearest cottage.

"Someone must live there," Beryl said, pointing to the flashing lights.

"Norman Davies rents that one."

"The sprouts and parsnips we had for luncheon must have been grown right round here," Beryl said. "I wonder if we'll see them."

"This is a fallow field. There are no crops planted here. That's why it's had the manure put down. He's preparing it for next year."

"What's that then?" Beryl asked, pointing at a fluttering bit of material waving in the breeze. "Does the farmer mark things off in some way?" She took a step towards whatever it was, her concern for her shoes forgotten for the moment.

"No. Not to my knowledge." A vague snatch of memory tugged at Edwina's mind as she thought the fabric seemed familiar, even in the low light. She felt her gait quicken even without the conscious decision to hurry. Surely the fabric was something unusual. They crossed the hundred yards or so at a swift pace and drew up sharply.

There was no doubt about what they were seeing. Polly Watkins lay on her side not a mile from her home, facedown in the field. Edwina recognized her clothing from the evening before. Wetness from the soil had seeped into her frock and Edwina ridiculously thought how well it would match Beryl's shoes. She must be suffering from shock to think such silly things. She wondered if Polly had slipped and become disoriented in the dark. Could she have died of exposure in the night? Her hair had, by and large, fallen from the cheap comb holding it in place. Edwina felt it made the girl look even more vulnerable somehow. She bent to turn her over, to raise her face from the muck, when she felt Beryl's hand restrain her.

"You mustn't touch a thing. We need to call for the police."

"Yes, of course. It doesn't seem right to leave her here though."

"You're absolutely right. I'll stay," Beryl said. "After all, you know your way round and I don't. Go telephone the authorities immediately. Take the dog with you. He'll only get into mischief here." Edwina nodded and then surprised herself by breaking into a run. She hadn't run in years. The soft muck of the field pulled at her feet with each step, hampering her efforts but not her determination. She was drawn for a fleeting moment to the lights in Norman Davies' cottage before chiding herself. He would not have a telephone. The caretaker at Wallingford Hall would be in and would let her use the one there. If it was still in service. She clutched her skirts in one hand and ran even faster.

Chapter 13

Beryl watched Ed disappear into the twilight. It was not the first time she had been alone to watch over a dead body. It was however the first time she wondered if the person whose vigil she kept had been murdered. Her heart hammered about in her chest. Not because she worried about coming under attack herself but because she suddenly wondered if Edwina would make it safely to call for help. Hadn't someone made an attempt on her life only days before? She told herself Edwina was far more capable than she looked. Besides, Crumpet was with her, and although he wasn't very large, Beryl had no doubt of his devotion to his mistress. She dug her hands down into her pockets to warm them and awaited her friend's return.

After a moment, despite her admonishment to Edwina, she couldn't resist confirming her worst fear. She pulled a small flashlight from her pocket. A torch Ed would be sure to call it, and flicked it on. She swept a bright, focused beam around Polly's body and then, before she could talk herself out of it, she bent down took a closer look at Polly's neck. No purple discoloration like the bruises on Ed's throat ringed the dead girl's neck.

Beryl found herself a bit light-headed. Not that she'd admit as much to anyone. To think something like this could have snuffed out her friend's life while she was pottering about in the guest room at Ed's house. But what did kill the poor girl? She held the beam of light steady and looked again. The hair on the side of Polly's head looked darker than the rest of it. It was matted, too. Beryl was sure it was not mud or muck she was seeing. She had seen enough bloody wounds to know the difference.

She straightened and looked out across the increasingly dark pastureland. It seemed an eternity before she spotted a play of lights making their way back across the field towards her. She let out a breath she hadn't realized she was holding. She waved her own flashlight about in wide, sweeping semi-circles to point the way. As they approached she made out two figures. The newcomer was taller than Ed and appeared to be a man. Crumpet had placed himself between Ed and her companion. Ed's face looked pinched. The shock seemed to have worn off a bit but sadness and that look of resignation everyone wore like a uniform over the past several years had taken its place. Beryl desperately wished she had not insisted they venture out to confront Polly. Or that she had not hired her back in the first place.

"This is Douglas Gibbs, the caretaker at Wallingford Hall. Thankfully he was in when I rang the bell."

"We've telephoned to the pub and asked for someone to locate my wife."

"Mr. Gibbs is married to Doris Gibbs, the village constable." Beryl heard a subtle change in Ed's tone that suggested she should keep what Ed had shared about her misgivings concerning the local bobby to herself. "A call to the pub is the fastest way to reach her. Not that she spends her time in there," Ed hastily added.

"Folks will run out and scour the streets until they find her. We never have things like this happen in Walmsley Parva. Polly will be sorry she missed the excitement," Mr. Gibbs said. He didn't seem to realize the irony of his words.

"Do you expect it will be long?" Beryl asked. "For her to get here, I mean?"

"I shouldn't expect so. Someone will have a motorcar and will drive the constable over to the big house."

"Should someone tell her parents?" Beryl asked.

"I think we should wait until my wife takes a look at her. She's a stickler for procedures is my Doris."

"They must be worried sick. I am certain she has lain here since sometime last night or the early hours of the morning," Beryl said.

"She was wearing that same outfit when we saw her go into the cinema last night," Edwina said. "Did you notice if she was with anyone then?"

"I heard someone call her name from the opposite side of the road. You did too, I thought."

"I heard it too but Polly didn't seem very interested in their company, did she? After all, she didn't call him or her over or even wave. She just hurried round the side of the building without a word." Both Beryl and Edwina cast a glance towards the small cottage with the warm glowing lights shining from the inside.

"Are you certain that is Norman Davies' cottage?" Beryl asked, dropping her voice to keep Mr. Gibbs from overhearing her.

"I'm afraid it is. You don't think he had something to do with this, do you?" Edwina asked.

"I've never met him so I am sure I can't say anything about his propensity for violence. I do know he was late getting those sprouts and parsnips dug, supposedly because, according to his uncle the butcher, he was having a lie-in."

"Do you think he was out here with Polly instead of home in bed where a good farmer would be?"

"His uncle mentioned he was distraught about the fact that

she threw him over and was doing whatever he could to convince her to take him back. Do you think he might have reacted poorly if it became clear to him she wasn't about to change her mind?" Beryl stole another glance at the nearby cottage. She thought she saw a curtain twitch in the window.

"I would have said I couldn't imagine such a thing until this week. But then I wouldn't have believed anyone who suggested someone would attempt to strangle me in my own garden either. At this point, I'm sure of nothing."

The moon had risen in the clear sky and revealed that the road was not as far from the field as Beryl had assumed. In fact, it was quite near to where the body was found. She and Ed had entered the pasture at a spot well away from the road but she realized they must have been traveling in a diagonal and had cut a long way off the journey. Still, it was easy to see the lights of an automobile arriving as it hurtled up the road and ground to a screeching halt when Mr. Gibbs waved his flashlight wildly.

Two figures got out of the car and Beryl heard the muffled sound of the doors shutting. The light had almost entirely faded from the sky and the chill of the night air seeped into her body. She wished she had dressed more warmly. Beryl cast a glance down at Polly's body once more and wondered at the way the girl had been dressed. Surely she could not have been planning to be out on her own in the dark without at least some sort of a wrap?

"So what have you found, Douglas?" A slim woman dressed in a dark jacket and matching long skirt addressed Mr. Gibbs. Her hat declared her to be a police constable even if her no-nonsense tone had somehow been unnoticed.

"It tweren't me, Doris. It were these two that found her." Mr. Gibbs flashed his light first on Beryl then on Edwina. "They can tell you more."

"You must be our famous visitor. The one causing all the chatter down at the pub and in the post office," Constable Gibbs said to Beryl. She turned to Edwina. "An attention seeker like her, I can imagine being involved in a thing like this. I should have thought you'd not be inclined to attract such notice."

"I hardly think it deliberate that we stumbled across a body out in a field while taking a walk," Edwina said.

"Where were you walking to?" Constable Gibbs asked.

"We were heading to see Polly, as it happens," Edwina said.

"Sounds to me like you were asking for involvement after all." Constable Gibbs turned her flashlight on the body. "So what have we got then? Douglas, train your torch right here." She bent over the corpse and with an effort rolled Polly's body onto her back. Beryl heard Ed gasp at the sight of Polly's mud-streaked face. The girl's eyes were half opened and the clear blue color of them against her dirty face made a grotesque contrast.

Constable Gibbs passed her flashlight over Polly's head then held it steady over the matted patch of hair Beryl had noticed. "Looks like she struck her head and knocked herself out. Dressed as she was she could have died of exposure even if there was no complicating injury inside her skull. Although Lord only knows what could have happened in there."

"Struck her head? On what?" Edwina asked. All four of them swept the area immediately around Polly's body for something that explained the injury. Mr. Gibbs stood and held his flashlight steady.

"What about that?" he asked. Constable Gibbs picked up a large stone the size of a baseball with her gloved hands. It lay just beside the body.

"I'd say that would explain it. She walked through here in the dark. Drunk as a lord, likely as not. She stumbled and fell. She struck her head and that was the end of that." Beryl heard a small hiss escape from her friend's lips. Edwina swept her light around them slowly then back again even more slowly.

"Have you noticed, Constable, that this is the only rock anywhere in this part of the field?" She turned the beam on the constable's face. "Are you not the least bit surprised that she should have the enormously bad fortune to happen to fall in the one place where she would deal herself a death blow?"

"You aren't trying to make this out to be something more than it is, are you?" Constable Gibbs asked. "You have a too much of a taste for the dramatic to suit me."

"It wasn't my intention to suit you. It was to once again point out that there might be more going on here than can be easily dismissed."

"Why was it you were going to see Polly?" Constable Gibbs fixed a gimlet eye upon Edwina and crossed her arms over her chest.

"She was engaged to begin working as a daily at the Beeches. She didn't arrive as agreed this morning and Miss Helliwell and I decided to walk over to her parents' house to ask her why she had not shown. Now we know why," Edwina said.

"Were you angry at her for not keeping her word?" Constable Gibbs asked.

"I was rather put out as it happened and did not want Polly taking it into her head to believe she could be so lax with her schedule if she wished to remain in my employ," Edwina said. "But I wouldn't go so far as to say I was angry."

"I told Ed we should have it out with her and should be sure the girl really wanted the job," Beryl said.

"So you planned to confront her? You wanted to engage in an argument with Polly?" Constable Gibbs asked.

"It wasn't quite like that. We weren't spoiling for a fight, if that is what you are implying," Beryl said. "Besides, it was all my idea and all my fault that we came out to speak with her. Ed was simply showing me the way to Polly's house."

"While I am certain neither my friend nor I killed this poor girl, I am equally certain it seems very peculiar that she would hit her head on the only rock in the field."

"You know as well as anyone that strange and unfortunate things happen all the time. I'll take a closer look once we've gotten her body inside and under better light. But don't go saying there is anything more going on here than an accident unless you hear me say so. I don't want another incident on our hands like that one with the missing Land Girl."

"Constable, there is something you should take into consideration when you are trying to decide what happened here," Beryl said. "Two nights ago someone attempted to strangle Ed with her own scarf in the garden of the Beeches."

Constable Gibbs stood and flashed her light into Edwina's eyes. "Why didn't you alert me when it happened?" she asked.

"I didn't want you to tell me I was being melodramatic about the entire ugly scene. Besides, I ran whoever it was off myself and have had no sign of trouble since."

"Until this," Beryl said, shaking her head at Polly's prone form.

"I wouldn't go assuming the two incidents had anything to do with one another. As I already said, it's more than likely the young woman tripped and the entire thing was an accident," Constable Gibbs said. "You've done your duty by calling for me so promptly. I thank you and suggest you leave the rest of this to those who really are in charge. Douglas and I will take it from here. After all, you no longer work on the Wallingford Estate and I expect you are rather cold. Clarence Mumford drove me over. I'm sure he'd be willing to drive you both home." Constable Gibbs turned away.

"I hope she plans to do a more thorough job this time than she did with the search for Agnes," Edwina said quietly to Beryl.

"Look," Beryl said, pointing to Norman's cottage. A tall figure stood silhouetted in the open doorway. "Someone seems curious about what is going on over here."

"He would be. No farmer likes to have uninvited guests trampling his fields even if he's got nothing planted," Edwina said. "We'd best get going before Clarence Mumford changes his mind about giving us a lift. I confess, I just want to get home," Edwina said.

Chapter 14

Clarence Mumford held the door of his motorcar for the two of them. Crumpet scrambled up into Edwina's lap and pressed his warm body against her own. She wrapped her arms around him to hold him in place as well as for the comfort his solid frame provided.

"There's a lap blanket in the boot if you've caught a chill," Mr. Mumford said. Their faces must have told him all he needed to hear because without waiting for an answer he opened the boot and pulled out a woolen blanket. He flicked it open with a snap and reached in to spread it over them, taking special care to tuck it in round Beryl. Edwina never could understand how Minnie Mumford had married such a thoroughly nice man. Perhaps it was her baking. Say what you liked about Minnie's snooping and her unbridled pleasure in gossiping with Prudence Rathbone, she did have a light hand with the pastry.

"It was definitely Polly Watkins you found?" Mr. Mumford asked as he climbed into the front seat and closed the door. "That's what they were saying at the pub when the call came in."

"I'm afraid it was," Edwina said.

"How did it happen? Do you know?" he asked. Edwina and Beryl exchanged a glance.

"Constable Gibbs is not sure as yet. I don't think she wants to say much until she knows for certain and has spoken to Polly's parents."

"Of course. What a terrible thing this is. A terrible thing. Such a lovely young lady," Mr. Mumford said.

"I didn't realize you knew her particularly well," Edwina said as the motorcar lurched forward and they jounced onto the hard packed surface of the road.

"She was the most regular customer the Palais had," he said. "Sometimes she used to get to chatting to me at the ticket counter if I happened to be the one attending it."

"Mr. Mumford owns the local cinema," Edwina said. "Polly was a very great devotee of the cinema then?"

"She was there several times each week. She certainly saw every new picture we brought in. Lately she's been there even more than usual."

"We both saw her just outside the cinema last night," Beryl said, turning to Edwina with a significant look. "You remember, Ed. It must have been the evening show since it started just after we'd finished our tea at the Silver Spoon Tearoom." Edwina felt a stirring of intrigue. Did that mean Beryl thought, as she did, that there was more to Polly's death than could be accounted for by an accident with an ill-placed rock?

"That's right, we did. She was all dressed for an evening out but she wasn't with anyone as far as I could see."

"Nor I. She was all alone. I'm quite certain of it," Beryl said. "You didn't happen to see her meeting anyone inside the cinema, did you, Mr. Mumford?"

"I'm afraid I wasn't working last night. I have been participating in an amateur cinematographer's troupe as a natural outgrowth of my cinema interests. We met last night for our weekly meeting. Then I went round the pub once I was done," Mr. Mumford said. "You could ask the ticket seller, Eva Scott, if Polly was alone. Or the projectionist. Walter has a good view of the seats from his vantage point. He surely could have said who comes and goes. Not that he'll want to talk to you though."

"Why not?" Beryl asked.

"He was terribly disfigured in the war," Mr. Mumford said. "He took the job because it is one he can undertake without having to see anyone. Or more to the point, not to let anyone see him. I almost never even see him myself."

Edwina thought of the staggering number of such young men since the outbreak of war. Tin masks with cleverly painted facial features were better than the horrors disguised beneath them, but many, if not most, men found it difficult to interact with others while wearing them. A tin mask could not change expression and most people found it difficult to converse with those wearing them. She could well understand why a young man with such an injury would choose an occupation that would shield himself and those around him from the inevitable awkwardness that would arise.

They travelled the rest of the way in silence, only the occasional crunch of something beneath the tires making any noise. Crumpet got to his feet and pressed his nose against the window as Mr. Mumford pulled up in front of the Beeches, right next to the door. The light over the front step shone brightly and Edwina was glad of that small sense of security it afforded. Beryl hurriedly pulled the blanket from their laps and nearly knocked poor Crumpet over.

"Such a shame," Mr. Mumford said again as he held open the door and took the blanket from Beryl's outstretched hands. "Do let me know if there is anything either I or my wife can do for you ladies." He lifted his hat and waited until they had let themselves into the house before reversing the motorcar.

*   *   *

The fire had burnt down to cinders but with a bit of prodding on Beryl's part a good flame licked the inside of the fireplace in just moments.

"Just something I picked up during my travels," Beryl said, standing back to survey her handiwork. "I don't suppose either of us has much of an appetite after what we saw, despite all the traipsing round?"

"I promised Crumpet that bone from the leftover roast. And I could do with a cup of cocoa," Edwina said. "Shall I fix one for you, too?"

"Only if by cocoa you mean a double Scotch, neat." Beryl said.

"I am not even sure exactly what you mean by neat. I assume it is some sort of Americanism. You know where to find the drinks cupboard." Edwina returned a few moments later with a steaming mug in her hands. Beryl had taken the opportunity to change into a marabou-trimmed dressing gown and velvet turban. Her feet, propped on the ottoman in front of the fire and clad in a pair of thick socks did little to finish off the ensemble in style. Beryl swirled the glass in her hand and took a long sip before acknowledging Edwina's return.

"You've got that look on your face, Ed, that you used to at school every time you were wrestling with whether or not to confess your sins to the headmistress. What's wrong?"

"Besides stumbling upon a dead girl?"

"That goes without saying." Beryl raised one wool-covered foot and pointed it nimbly at Edwina. "It's no sense denying it. You'll tell me in the end and we are both too tired to dance round it."

"I can't help but think that if we hadn't put out the story that we were investigating something amiss in Walmsley Parva Polly would not be dead."

"You can't go blaming yourself for what happened to Polly."

"Why not? Aren't we in agreement that it is far less likely that Polly died as a result of an accident than that she met with someone who wished to do her harm?"

"Certainly we are. Constable Gibbs' assertion that she hit her head on that rock is utterly absurd," Beryl said. "But that doesn't mean her death has anything to do with you or me."

"But how else would you explain it? You arrived. We started a rumor. Someone tried to strangle me and then no sooner did you hire Polly to work here than she's killed."

"Those things are all true and some of them may even be connected but there is nothing to say one led to the next and then to the next. And even if it did, you aren't at fault for what happened to Polly."

"Then why do I feel so guilty?" Edwina asked.

"It's just your nature. I actually think you have an overinflated sense of your own importance. There could be dozens of unrelated reasons that someone wanted her dead. Dozens of suspects could be lurking about your beloved village as we speak."

"Like who?" Edwina shifted in her seat in the wingback chair.

"Norman Davies springs quickly to mind," Beryl said. "After all, he was her jilted sweetheart who just happens to live a stone's throw from where her body was found."

"A very poor choice of words, Beryl." Edwina blew with a bit more vigor than necessary on her cocoa, slopping a bit of it over the side and down onto her lap.

"But telling, wouldn't you agree? Simpkins says young Norman was determined to win Polly back. Do you think it was him calling to her last night from the shadows outside the theatre?"

"I suppose it could have been," Edwina said. "Do you really think it might have nothing to do with us asking around about Agnes?"

"I won't insult you by saying there is no chance we've

opened a can of worms but I will say there are a couple of other possibilities that spring to mind."

"Besides Norman?"

"Certainly." Beryl held up her hand and began to count off on her fingers. "There's anyone who had something to hide at the Wallingford Estate, there's anyone whom she cleaned house for as she'd have access to secrets hidden in their homes, and let's not forget Sidney Poole who was righteously angered on behalf of his nephew Norman. Lastly, I have a bad feeling about that oily Mr. Mumford." Beryl bushed her fingertips against her dressing gown as if to wipe off something distasteful.

"Mr. Mumford is a very pleasant man." Edwina was shocked. "I haven't the slightest idea what you are talking about."

"I found nothing the least bit pleasant about his octopus impression he rendered while adjusting that lap blanket of his."

"Octopus impression? What are you going on about?"

"His hands were absolutely everywhere at once. I have never been so thoroughly and unsolicitedly tucked in in all my life." Beryl took a long swallow of her drink. "And that, my friend, is saying something."

"Are you implying he took liberties with your person?"

"I'm implying nothing. I am flat-out saying that he used his pleasant demeanor to put his mitts where he shouldn't have. In my experience men who do that so boldly to one woman are doing it to a great many of them."

"I've known Mr. Mumford for years and have never been the recipient of such unwanted attentions," Edwina said. She was shaken to the core. First a dead girl and now a hero shown to have feet of clay. What was the world coming to?

"I expect he thinks too much of your good opinion to disrespect you in such a way, Ed. Consider yourself lucky to be armed with such shining character."

Edwina was not entirely sure she had been complimented. Beryl meant it as such but there were times, especially since so much had changed during the war years, that she felt a restless urge to throw off convention and have a few adventures of her own. Perhaps that was why she had been so easily convinced that Beryl had not done such a very bad thing in lying about their involvement with a fictitious intelligence agency. The more she thought about it the more convinced she became that she had been led off the straight and narrow by the call of adventure. She was surprised and even a bit proud of herself as the thought took hold. She was lost in such surprising thoughts when Beryl spoke once more.

"Why do you think Constable Gibbs was so disinclined to believe Polly's death was anything other than an accident?"

"Doris Gibbs was one of the people who didn't much approve of the girls from the Land Army. It was one of the reasons she didn't put forth any real effort into the search for Agnes Rollins."

"Why didn't she approve of them? I would have expected as a rare female police officer herself, she would have been more supportive of other women in non-traditional jobs than most people."

"I would have thought so too but that wasn't what ended up happening. Doris felt that women had to be even more pristine in their character than men to earn the respect of their positions and she was not about to let immoral behavior from other women in uniform drag down her reputation or her chances of keeping her post when the war ended."

"What sorts of immoral behavior was she concerned with?"

"Girls with khaki fever. She had an especial horror of girls known to put themselves in compromising positions with the soldiers." Edwina felt herself blush even from mentioning such a topic. "She kept a list of girls in the town she thought were already of soiled character or those in danger of losing their reputations. She warned them off the streets and marched them back to their homes."

"Was Agnes on her watch list?" Beryl asked. "Is that why she never investigated her disappearance thoroughly?"

"I suppose that could be the reason."

"Do you think she may make no more effort on Polly's behalf for the same reasons?" Beryl asked.

"I think it is quite possible. After all, she didn't think much more of Polly than she did Agnes. She certainly wouldn't have if she discovered Polly threw over a well-liked young man like Norman Davies. And started spending so much time at the cinema."

"Your constable doesn't approve of cinema attendance either?"

"She has mentioned her belief that excess time spent there leads to every sort of vice."

"So there isn't much chance she is going to give this a thorough look, is there?"

"I very much doubt it."

"Did you notice Polly's shoes?" Beryl asked, looking at her own feet. Really, the woman was quite obsessed with footwear.

"They matched her dress, wouldn't you say?"

"They did," Beryl said, draining her glass and thumping it down on the table beside her.

"Polly didn't seem to me to be the sort of girl who would put her finery in jeopardy by tramping through a manured field with it."

"So?"

"So if Polly had planned to walk home through that field, don't you think she would have thought to bring a change of footwear to save her party shoes from being ruined?" Beryl asked.

"I suppose she would have done," Edwina said. "But where were they? I didn't see any boots or any other shoes lying around for that matter."

"Exactly. Which means either her change of shoes went missing somehow or she didn't go through that field by choice."

"You think someone forced her to go through the field?"

"When we got into Mr. Mumford's car I was surprised at how close the road was to where Polly's body was found. Someone could have driven her as far as that and then carried her body to the spot where we found it."

"Why should anyone want to do that?"

"Maybe to make it look as though Norman Davies were involved. Maybe to make you wonder if her death had something to do with your questions about Agnes and the Wallingford Estate. I think we should mention it to Constable Gibbs."

"I'm not certain Doris would appreciate our interference," Edwina said. "She didn't take kindly to me questioning her about the way she handled the investigation into Agnes' disappearance. It isn't likely she'll be any happier about suggestions when a body is concerned."

"She didn't prove to be an enthusiastic investigator in the past. If she declares Polly's death an accident I think we ought to keep looking into it ourselves."

"You mean you wish to investigate Polly's murder?"

"I believe we should look into the whole of it, lock, stock, and barrel. We still don't have any more of an idea who tried to strangle you than we ever did. Agnes is still unaccounted for and Polly is dead. If Constable Gibbs doesn't launch into an enquiry of her own I say we dive right into the breach. What do you say?"

As sordid as it was, Edwina felt that faint tingle of anticipation once more. It was wrong. Very wrong indeed of course to find any pleasure whatsoever in a tragedy that befell another. Especially one so young as Polly. Then again, what was life if you found little reason to climb out of bed in the morning? If you felt numb to the song of sparrows and the smell of wood smoke curling from a neighbor's chimney on a crisp autumn morning? Was it really so awful to wish to feel alive again?

"All right, I agree. But only if we find Constable Gibbs has decided not to investigate."

"How will we know if she has determined Polly's death was an accident?" Beryl asked.

"The way everyone finds out anything in Walmsley Parva. We visit Prudence Rathbone's shop tomorrow afternoon."

Chapter 15

Prudence Rathbone was in her element. Never in all her born days had she experienced a week filled with such excitement. Not when war had been declared. Not when the armistice had been announced. Not even when beloved King Edward VII had passed on. First Beryl Helliwell appeared without notice in her shop and now there was the news of the death of Polly Watkins.

Prudence felt her position in the community acutely at such times of crisis. Especially when waves of information broke across Walmsley Parva like the wake from a great battleship. It was her duty, she knew, to put her fellow villagers' minds at ease by providing them with the answers to the questions they hadn't even known to ask.

As one would expect from a gentlewoman of her good standing, Prudence would never frequent the pub. If it hadn't been for Minnie's less than exacting standards where the niceties were concerned, Prudence might have been amongst the last to know what had happened. Minnie's insistent knocking dragged her from her bed where she had tucked herself up with a steaming cup of Horlicks and a deliciously scandalous novel she had ordered through the mail under a name not her own. As the postmistress she enjoyed the privilege of postal privacy unknown to all others in Walmsley Parva. She knew better than anyone how tongues in the village tended to wag.

Once Minnie had delivered the news and the admonition to be sure to lock her doors and not answer to anyone, Prudence had started in wondering who could have possibly done such a thing. The obvious conclusion was Beryl Helliwell. After all, rumor had it that Edwina Davenport had suffered an attempt on her life only hours after Beryl's arrival. Prudence had it on good authority that Beryl had been to speak privately with Polly at the solicitor's house. Add to that the fact that Beryl and Edwina supposedly stumbled upon Polly's body in a field that they had no reason to be traipsing across. Prudence's long nose had twitched deliciously as she watched Minnie's face when she suggested that Beryl Helliwell might be responsible for all the goings-on. For all they knew the agency that Beryl worked for had trained her as an assassin.

Bearing all that in mind, she had risen early, dressed in black, and packed a white paper box with an assortment of licorice and lemon drops. Tucking it under her arm she had congratulated herself on being a generous enough sort of person to not mind going to the expense of hiring a cab. Michael Blackburn managed to get her out to the Watkins house to deliver her condolences and to collect any available information before the rest of the village had cracked open their morning newspapers.

It had been a bit awkward perhaps that the Watkins were not as grateful of her attentions as they might have been. Perhaps she should have offered them chocolates but it wasn't as if they were regular customers, now was it? Prudence told herself the bereaved were always unpredictable and the rest of the village had a right to know the sort of danger they might be in from a violent criminal.

Things had gone more smoothly when Constable Gibbs had entered the post office midmorning to collect her post. The constable had long relied on Prudence for information crucial to her peacekeeping efforts in the village and the two enjoyed a cordial relationship. A friend would do nothing less than enquire as to the progress of so arduous a task as the investigation into an unexplained death. Prudence kept a box of butterscotch disks on hand as added incentive if the constable seemed reticent. Butterscotch disks was the way Prudence had learned the name of the person responsible for stealing ladies undergarments off the washing lines two years previous. She could hardly expect less of them as time went by.

Prudence had already told half the village the news by the time Beryl and Edwina wandered in to enquire after some peppermints for Beryl and a bottle of mucilage glue for Edwina.

"How well the pair of you look considering the horrors you must have felt last evening," Prudence said, punching the enameled keys on the large brass till. "I'm sure I would still be abed clinging to a hot water bottle if ever I had such a nasty shock." Prudence hoped her tone clearly conveyed her disapproval of their callousness. It spoke very ill of them both that they were seen outside of the Beeches after such a discovery. It shored up her already firm conviction that one, the other, or both of them were somehow involved.

"One must go on, no matter what, don't you think, Miss Rathbone?" Beryl asked. "Even when confronted by a murder." Beryl turned to Edwina and the two of them nodded knowingly. Prudence felt thrilled right down to her very soul. The idea that she knew something two of the King's own valued secret agents did not warmed her like nothing had in years. She fairly bubbled over with the news.

"But it isn't murder, now is it?" Prudence slowly selected Beryl's change from the drawer. "Constable Gibbs brought the news herself this morning. I'm surprised she didn't stop to tell you since you are all investigators." She dropped the coins into Beryl's outstretched hand.

"As I am sure you will agree, one of the great strengths of the British people is a clear understanding of one's place. I'm sure Constable Gibbs would never have gone so far above herself as to consider imposing upon loyal and devoted servants of you know who," Edwina said. "I am most grateful to the constable for not placing us in such an awkward position. But rest assured, if our nation would be best served by us becoming better informed on this matter, we will not hesitate to do so." Edwina turned on her heel and strode out the door. Beryl gave Prudence a bright smile just like the ones she always displayed in the newspapers, reached for her parcels, and followed her friend out into the street without another word.

Beryl waited until they were out of the reach of Prudence's prying eyes before turning to Edwina in amazement. "You were magnificent in there. After all your talk about not being able to hold your head up in the village I wondered how you'd manage Prudence, but I couldn't have done it better myself."

Edwina waved her hand in front of her face as if to dismiss the compliment.

"The important thing to consider is that Constable Gibbs has determined not to investigate," Edwina said.

"You're right, of course. Where do you suggest we begin?" Beryl asked.

"We will accomplish twice as much if we question people separately," Edwina said.

"Agreed. But where to start? You're the expert on Walmsley Parva."

"I think I should pay a call to Polly's family to offer my condolences and then just happen to stop at Norman Davies' cottage since I would be passing so near it would be a deliberate snub not to stop in."

"How very underhanded you are, Ed," Beryl said. "I think I will pop into the cinema and satisfy my curiosity about Mr. Mumford and his claims that Polly was an avid patron of his establishment."

"I do wish you had a perpetrator you preferred to Mr. Mumford. I still think he's a lovely man."

"Why don't you reserve judgment until we've both made the rounds. Shall we plan to meet back for teatime at the Beeches to compare notes then?"

Edwina nodded and Beryl watched as her friend hurried off down the high street towards the far edge of the village. A little voice in the back of her head told her to hope she was not seeing the last of her. Filled with a sense of excited urgency she set off for the Palais.

Chapter 16

The cinema opened for the matinee at two in the afternoon. Edwina had agreed that it would be best if only one of them approached Walter Bennett, the projectionist. If he were as leery of interacting with others as Mr. Mumford had said, just one visitor would be too many. Two would likely send him into hiding.

It took her rather longer to walk to the cinema than she would have expected. While she wouldn't have admitted it for the world, the walk last night had tired her out completely and had left her more than a little sore from all the walking on uneven ground and standing out in the cold and damp. There were no two ways about it. She was becoming soft. Perhaps a course of exercise was in order. Maybe she would be wise to set up a sort of camp in the garden to re-acclimate herself to the perils of sleeping rough. She had a reputation after all that she was not eager to relinquish.

She stepped into the warmth of the lobby and made straight for the posters on the wall. She lingered in front of each, giving the girl dressed in a pinny and wandering around with a carpet sweeper time to fully work up her curiosity. By the time Beryl turned to face her, the young woman had abandoned all pretense of minding her own business and was instead staring goggle-eyed at Beryl and her ankle-length, mink coat. Beryl turned on her best public smile and crossed the plush carpeting to the ticket window.

"You're Beryl Helliwell," the girl said. "We showed newsreels of your balloon takeoff. And your trans-Atlantic flight attempt."

"And you're Eva Scott." If anything, the girl's eyes bulged even farther out of her head.

"How do you know my name?" she asked.

"Your employer told me your name when he described you as someone who would know all about the comings and goings in the cinema."

"Are you here to see one of the pictures?" Eva asked. "I can tell you all about all of those."

"I'm sure you could and I am ever so obliged but what I need is a bit more specialized knowledge than that. After all, I can read about the movies on the posters on your wall. What I want is something only you would be able to tell me."

Eva bobbed her head up and down. "I'll help any way I can. What do you need?"

"I wanted to know if you sold a ticket to Polly Watkins for any of the shows two nights ago?"

"Polly Watkins? The woman that was found dead up on the Wallingford Estate?" Eva asked with a squeak.

"Yes. Did she attend a show the night before last?"

"Do you want to know if she attended a show or if she bought a ticket?"

"Aren't those the same thing?" Beryl asked, her curiosity aquiver.

"Not necessarily." Eva clucked her tongue like an old woman. "Some girls seem to rate special privileges."

"Was Polly one of those girls?" Beryl asked. Eva hesitated. "She was quite pretty."

"Her looks were part of it but so was her manner."

"Let the right sort of people know she'd welcome some attention, did she?"

"That's just it. She never missed an opportunity to advertise her willingness to be friendly," Eva said. "If you understand my meaning." Beryl nodded sagely.

"So did someone else pay for her tickets to the cinema or was she simply let in for free?" Beryl asked.

"Some of each. She had a local lad she used to walk out with and he bought tickets for them both from time to time."

"I understood Polly was far more regular in her attendance than someone who came from time to time."

"That is true. A real enthusiast she was."

"So I bet you know who gave her the nod to get in for free and I bet it wasn't you." Eva looked around and when no one else appeared in her line of sight she leaned towards Beryl and lowered her voice.

"My mum will be ever so cross if I lose my job."

"I promise I won't say a word. Your employer has none of my esteem and you have my sympathy. The man is not really a gentleman, is he? I assure you I shan't be shocked by whatever you have to say."

"Mr. Mumford lets some women and girls into the shows without a ticket. He told me if someone comes to the ticket window and tells me they were actresses invited by him I was to let them in for free."

"Did he say why?"

"He told me he wanted the actresses from his cinematographer's troupe to have as many opportunities to study the professionals as possible."

"He did, did he? Did you believe him?"

"Not hardly. I asked, all innocent-like if he meant Mrs.

Mumford, too. He said certainly not to tell her as she didn't look as kindly on his participation in the group as he would like." She gave Beryl a knowing look.

"Have there been a lot of actresses in here asking for free admittance?"

"I've had the job for at least three years and in that time I'd say there have been upwards of a dozen," Eva said. "Polly Watkins was one of the latest of them."

"Did you recognize any of the other so-called actresses?" Beryl asked.

"There used to be more of them when the Land Army was here. All sorts of girls from the Wallingford Estate used to watch the shows for free." Eva bit her lip like she was thinking.

"How about that young woman who went missing? Did she ever come in here and watch a show for free?"

"I believe she did but I don't remember for certain. It's been some time since she disappeared."

"Anyone else you recognized?"

"Nurse Crenshaw, if you can believe it. She was the one who was a regular just before Polly started coming in every time there was a new show."

"Did Polly come in for a free show two nights ago?"

"She didn't come to the ticket window. But I saw her outside looking in not too long before the evening show started." Eva shook her head. "Dressed up like she was trying to impress someone, she was. My mother would never let me out of the house in the sorts of things Polly Watkins wore."

"Your mother must love you fiercely," Beryl said. "Although such attention is not always easy to bear." Not that Beryl had any firsthand experience with such things. Her own mother had sent Beryl to boarding schools just as soon as it could be said she had outgrown her nanny. Still, she had heard tell that many mothers possessed a fiercely protective nature.

"She means well. I suppose with what happened to Polly I

appreciate her more than I did. People are saying if Polly's parents had been a bit more careful she might not have ended up like she did."

"Anyone in particular saying that?"

"Just about everyone. People are saying she must have caught the attention of some lunatic skulking around the village. You have to expect problems when you run around showing yourself off like some sort of exotic bird."

"I was just leaving Mrs. Mumford's tearoom about the same time Polly was looking in the window here at the cinema. I thought I heard someone calling her name from across the street. Did you happen to see anyone near her?"

"No, I didn't. The street was very quiet for most of the show. Hardly anybody about until I saw you drive by at about the time the show let out," Eva said. "Your motor is easy to notice, isn't it?"

"You saw my car on the road? Are you sure?"

"It must have been yours. It's the only one like it in town."

"You are sure you saw me driving it?"

"Well, no, not exactly. But it is yours. Besides, you drive awfully fast and the motorcar was hurtling down the road at top speed."

"Do you remember which direction the car was headed?" Beryl asked.

"Out of the village. Off towards the Wallingford Estate," Eva said. "Don't you remember where you were going?"

"A little known side effect of travelling at high rates of speed is that they can result in temporary memory loss. I appreciate you helping me to fill in some embarrassing gaps in my evening." Beryl laid a velvet-gloved hand upon Eva's arm. "I can trust you to keep my little slip-up to yourself, can't I? I shouldn't like such a thing to become common knowledge. It might discourage progress in the entire automotive industry."

"Of course, Miss Helliwell. You can count on me." Eva

positively glowed. Beryl flashed her a million-pound smile and strode out the door. She stopped on the sidewalk and looked towards the Blackburns' garage and wondered how difficult it would have been for someone to steal her car from within its walls. Or if Eva's sighting of her vehicle laid the blame for its use on one of the Blackburns. She had offered for them to take it for a drive. She had to wonder too whether or not it had been used in what had happened to Polly.

Chapter 17

So many people filled the Watkins' small cottage, Edwina was able to quickly make her excuses and leave Polly's grief-stricken parents in the care of their well-meaning relations. If Edwina hadn't known better she would almost have said some of those relations were enjoying themselves on account of the novelty of it all. It was with a great sense of relief that she saw herself out and made for Norman Davies' cottage, an easy and pleasant twenty-minute walk away.

Edwina had dressed for the weather and for the fields and found her spirits rising despite the fact that her mission was born out of tragedy. Beryl had been right; it felt extraordinarily good to put Prudence in her place for once and to have something to occupy her time besides sorting jumble sales or arguing with Simpkins over the placement of spring bulbs. Which reminded her, she would need to speak to him about her stick pile when next he showed up at the Beeches. Simpkins' work habits made Polly's look as regular as a well-oiled clock.

The field looked as unlikely a place for a body to turn up as Edwina could imagine. As she approached the spot where Polly's body had lain she considered again the question of Polly's walking shoes. Or for that matter, the question of Polly walking at all. She had been a silly girl in many ways but she had not been frivolous with her money. In fact, Edwina had the distinct impression she was planning for a large purchase from the way she had asserted herself over her wages when Edwina had been forced to dismiss her.

It heated her face just calling the incident to mind. Polly had looked at her with more pity upon her face than anger the day she put her cheaply shod foot down and announced she would not return until she was paid her back wages. She had things to pay for she had said and as much as she liked obliging Edwina she simply could not continue to do so when there were other ladies in Walmsley Parva with ready money who kept at her to come to work for them instead.

Edwina shook herself a bit. The best thing she could do for Polly now was to keep asking questions until the truth of her death was uncovered. She was determined not to allow another girl in the village to end up with as little justice as had been served for Agnes Rollins. Edwina swept her gaze over the field as she made her way between the place she'd discovered Polly's body and Norman's front door. Polly's walking shoes were nowhere in sight. Edwina felt more worried than ever for Norman. Beryl's theory that someone wanted it to look as though Norman was involved in Polly's death seemed all the more sensible as she noted the scant distance between the two points.

Norman opened the door and came out onto the stone stoop as soon as Edwina landed the first rap upon the wooden door. His face looked grey even in the bright daylight and his shirt-tails flapped in the breeze. He clenched his bare toes against the stone surface of the stoop and Edwina thought for a flicker of a moment that perhaps it had not been wise to come to call without Beryl. Or at the very least Crumpet. He wasn't large but he was loyal and Edwina realized she would have been very glad of an extra set of teeth she knew to be on her side.

"Rumour has it you're the one who found Polly," Norman said.

"I did. And very sorry I was to do so. Such a loss."

"You're sorry to be out your maid, don't you mean?" Norman said. He turned his back on her and stepped into the cottage. Edwina glanced back over her shoulder then decided that since she had come this far she would risk going in after him. Norman was not the most prepossessing of men but she had not often known him to display a violent temper. She stepped in after him and noted the heavy scent of spirits. A bottle lay on its side on the wooden table in the center of the dimly lit room, its contents darkening the stone flags of the floor.

"I'm not here about my own connection to Polly, but yours. I am sure you are badly grieved by what has happened and I wished to convey my deepest sympathies."

"Why should you do that? I had no claim on Polly anymore." Norman dragged out a chair from beneath the table and sank into it. Edwina helped herself to the only other one and folded her hands in her lap.

"It was commonly thought in the village that you and Polly were walking out together. I assumed you would be devastated by this news."

"Polly and me stopped courting a few weeks back. She said life with a farmer wasn't what suited her anymore and that she had bigger plans for herself than collecting eggs and praying for a good summer. She said she'd had enough of all that when she worked in the Land Army and wasn't about to do it again."

"So she broke things off with you because you rented this place?"

"That was what she told me but I think that was just an excuse." Norman gripped the arms of the chair so hard his knuckles whitened.

"Why did you not believe her, Norman?" Edwina asked. "If I recall, Polly was never the most enthusiastic Land Girl. Not like Agnes Rollins and some of the other women." Edwina kept her gaze on his face as she said Agnes' name. She noted a tightening between his brows when she said the missing girl's name.

"I think she had found someone else. Someone who she could be proud of instead of a man who spent the whole war on the farm where he saw nothing more dangerous than a cow who kicked when you milked her," Norman said.

"Why would you say that? Polly understood as well as any of the Land Army women how necessary agricultural workers were. I can't imagine she would have held the fact you were needed here against you. And I certainly don't think it meant she had a new man in her life," Edwina said.

"I followed her. I know she was with someone else," Norman said. "She used to get all dressed up in her finery and head to the cinema every chance she got. I took her there myself whenever I could make the time and had the spare money but it was never often enough for her."

"Were you at the cinema two nights ago perhaps?"

"Why do you want to know?"

"Because I saw her outside of the cinema before the evening show began. Someone called out to her but she didn't answer. I wondered if it were you in the shadows."

"What if it was?"

"If you still cared for Polly at all you will be as eager as anyone to find out what really happened to her. If you were at the cinema and didn't do something rash and regrettable you may have seen something that could help with the enquiry into her death."

"I thought the investigation was over. Polly's parents told me Constable Gibbs was satisfied that Polly tripped and hit her head."

"You know that field better than anyone else. How stony is it out there?"

"It isn't. That's one of the reasons I decided to do whatever it took to rent it. The soil is friable and almost entirely free of stones. It's perfect for crops."

"Then you must understand my reluctance to agree with Constable Gibbs. I think it very unlikely that Polly would have died by striking her head upon a stone in that particular field. Which brings us straight back to what really befell her." Edwina looked over her spectacles at him. "So, were you watching her at the cinema the night before last?"

Norman nodded slowly. "I was. I couldn't think straight ever since she told me she was done with me. I've been up late, can't awaken early. I can't concentrate on my work at all." Norman drew in a ragged breath. "I just thought if I knew for sure that she was with someone else I could let her go. If she seemed happy."

"So you were the one in front of the cinema."

"I'm not proud of it, but I was. I called out to her and she ignored me. I told myself maybe she didn't hear me so I raised my voice." Norman bent his head. "She looked straight at me then turned her back and ran round the side of the cinema like she needed to get away from me. Like she wanted to avoid me at all costs."

"Did you follow her?"

"God help me, I did. I just couldn't believe she would snub me like that. After all the time we were together. So yeah, I followed her clear round the back of the Palais. She went right up to the back door and pounded on it like she knew someone would answer."

"Did someone open the door?"

"Right quick like they did. I'd be willing to bet anything you'd wager that he was waiting for her on the other side of the door."

"Who was waiting?"

"That poor sod with the tin mask. Walter Bennett."

"The projectionist?" Edwina was stunned. Walter Bennett

was a recluse. No one in the village knew much about him at all. He had arrived before the end of the war and had wanted nothing more than to be left in peace. He lived in a cottage on the side of the Wallingford Estate closest to the village but he still was rarely seen. He even had his groceries delivered. He spoke to no one as far as she knew. The idea that he would have been waiting for Polly seemed preposterous. She looked pointedly at the bottle of spirits. Norman seemed to hear her thoughts.

"You could have knocked me over with a baby's sigh when I saw him standing there. He actually reached out and pulled her into the back room of the cinema by the arm. Not that she looked like she minded."

"Did you not think to go in after her? To be sure she had wanted to be pulled into the cinema? After all, she ended up dead not long afterward."

"You don't think I haven't spent every minute since I heard the news wondering if she would still be alive if I had swallowed my pride?" Norman's voice grew husky and Edwina felt a cold dread that he might begin to cry.

"I'm sure it has been terrible for you." Edwina meant it. How he must have suffered playing his choice over and over in his mind.

"I didn't have any money to buy a ticket, you see, and I did try the back door but it was locked up tight. I wasn't about to go in and admit to the ticket girl than I hadn't even the cost of a ticket in my pocket. I was humiliated enough by the look on Polly's face. I wasn't going to put myself through that with another girl and whichever folks from the village who happened to be there, too."

"I've chided myself for not following her round back of the building when I saw her, too. You mustn't judge yourself too harshly." Edwina thought of something else. "Did you wait to see her come out again?"

"I tried to wait up for her. Truly I did, but it was cold and dark and I was already dead on my feet. I had a long walk home and no supper awaiting me neither." Norman most definitely looked like he might burst into tears. "After a couple of hours leaning against the back wall of the Palais I couldn't take it anymore. I just up and left her there."

"Did you see anyone else there? Did anyone see you leave?"

"I saw the lights from a couple of vehicles pass down the street but I never saw the motorcars themselves. As far as I know, no one saw me. Why would they? No one had any business at the back of the cinema at any time of the day but certainly not in the evening when a show was playing inside."

"What about after you started walking home? Did you see anyone then?" Edwina asked.

"No. I cut through the fields like you must have done when you found my poor Polly. And before you ask, I doubt anyone saw me either."

"Did you not notice any lights along the road running up to the Wallingford Estate?" Edwina thought again about Beryl's assertion that Polly's shoes were too clean to have traipsed through the field. A car would have explained how they stayed that way.

"I didn't notice any lights of any kind until I saw what turned out to be your torches when you discovered her. Now mind you, I started in trying to drown my sorrows just about as soon as I reached home." Norman sighed. "Like a dog licking its wounds. If it weren't for my worries about vandals in the crops I would have ignored you being out there, too."

"You didn't run across any of Polly's walking shoes anywhere along the way, did you?"

"No. No shoes at all. Why do you ask?"

"Polly was wearing a pair of dress shoes when we found her. I don't think she would have planned to walk through the field in them."

"I'm sure she wouldn't have. Polly was proud of her appearance. Besides, she would have known I had dressed the field. The scent would have been impossible to ignore, even from her parents' place. Whenever the wind shifted they would have smelt it. Polly would have taken the road."

"You didn't see her body in the morning just lying out there?"

"I wouldn't have done. I was busy all day out in another field digging and harvesting. Not to mention I had been in the village in the morning delivering veg to my uncle. It takes ages to get there and back with the speeds old Joe will move." Norman let out a slow sigh. "I just wish I could have been some sort of help to her."

"You have been a help, Norman. However you left things I imagine Polly would have been proud of the way you've spoken up for her and tried to help make things right." Edwina rose. "I had best be getting along home. I suggest you try to eat something. You can't bring Polly back but you won't be happy if you can't get those fields ready for winter. It will be here before you know it."

Chapter 18

The garage bay still held her car but neither mechanic was in view when Beryl stepped into Blackburn and Blackburn looking for Michael. At the back of the garage she spotted a wooden door with a grimy windowpane. She approached and listened for sounds from inside. The distinct squeak of chair castors in need of oiling reached her ears and she rapped upon the glass.

"Come in," called Michael's booming voice. Beryl looked at the bench beside the door and without really questioning why she did so, she picked up a spanner and slipped it into one of her deep coat pockets. One could never be too well prepared when entering a possible enemy's den. She checked to be sure she felt her smile slip into place then turned the knob.

"Mrs. Helliwell, what brings you back by? Are you checking up on our progress with your motorcar?" Michael stood as she entered and gestured to the chair opposite him across a wooden desk that had seen better decades. She liked her chances. Michael's desk sat between him and the door. Likely, no matter how unpopular and impertinent her questions, she could get out of the garage before any real harm could reach her. She eased down into the chair and leaned back as if she had all the time in the world for a chat.

"As it happens, I did want to ask you about my car. I wanted your expert opinion about how it handles out on the open road."

"The open road?" Michael reached into his pocket and pulled out a cigarette pack. He tapped on the pack and held it out to Beryl.

She shook her head. "Thanks, but I prefer my vices to be of the liquid variety." She waited for him to strike a match on the bottom of his heavy work boot then asked again. "I meant two nights ago in the late evening. Personally, I love driving in the dark. It helps me to think when there is nothing but me and the open road."

The door to the garage opened once more and Norah appeared in the threshold.

"Hello, sis. Miss Helliwell and I were just discussing the joys of night driving," Michael said. Norah crossed the room and came to lean up against the desk, crossing one trouser-clad leg over the other.

"I can't say I have much of a taste for the dark," Norah said. "I prefer being able to see a good long way ahead of me. You feel just the same, don't you, Michael?" Norah turned to her brother and Beryl had the distinct impression that she was coaching him as to what to say.

"After spending so much time in the trenches I like to have my eyes where I can see things."

"I see what you mean. I just wondered how the car was coming along. Someone said they saw it out two nights ago for a run and I hoped from what you said when first we met that that meant it would have been ready by now. I've missed driving her rather terribly."

"One gets used to the luxury of driving quite quickly, I

think," Norah said. "Or at least one comes to prefer riding to walking almost as soon as one can choose."

"Edwina and I quite missed the opportunity to take the car the other night." Beryl paused. "I'm sure you're heard about what happened?"

"We try not to get involved in village gossip. I find it's bad for business to take notice of such things." Norah shook her head at Michael ever so slightly.

"But you have heard about Polly Watkins?" Beryl asked.

"It's got nothing to do with us, does it, Michael?" Norah got up and went round the desk to stand beside him. She placed a hand on his shoulder. Beryl wondered if Norah was worried she might mention Agnes Rollins and wanted to be there to calm her brother should he become agitated. She slipped her hand into her pocket and wrapped her fingers around the comforting heft of the spanner.

"I should think in a small village like this where everyone knows each other that a murder would be cause for anyone to take notice," Beryl said.

"Constable Gibbs said it was an accident," Michael said, looking up at Norah. She nodded down at him reassuringly. "No one said anything about a murder."

"I believe I just did. Which is why I was asking about one of you taking my car out for a run. Someone said they'd seen it on the road at about the same time the last show of the evening finished up at the cinema up the street two nights ago."

"The person must have been mistaken. Your automobile was safe as houses here in the garage." Norah said. "Michael and I were home together all evening after we closed up here."

"Is that so?" Beryl asked, turning to Michael.

"If Norah says so, who am I to disagree?" he said.

"It is a rather a distinctive-looking conveyance. I shouldn't have thought it was an easy thing to mistake."

"Who, if I may ask, told you they had seen it out?" Norah asked.

"I'm afraid I cannot give out that sort of information during the course of an investigation." Beryl straightened her shoulders and shook her head in a way that she hoped looked convincingly final.

"Well, whomever says they saw it out either needs a new pair of spectacles or happens to be lying. We don't want to sound uncaring but we hardly knew Polly to speak to and we've had more than enough involvement with lives snuffed out at too early an age to want to dwell on one so loosely connected to us."

"I suppose someone else might have let themselves into the garage and taken it out without our knowing," Michael said.

"Don't you lock the garage at night?" Beryl asked.

"We do, but there isn't any reason someone might not have pried the lock open and let themselves in. Your automobile would be very tempting for a lot of the young lads round here," Norah said.

"Not just the young ones either. That Norman Davies stopped in after delivering a load of veg to his uncle the other morning. He said a vehicle like yours would make a lot of his problems disappear," Michael said.

"What do you think he meant by that?" Beryl asked.

"He was later than usual dropping off his produce. I figured he meant that he could transport things from the farm to the town in a motorized vehicle a lot more quickly than he could by using a pony and a wagon," Michael said.

"Have you any reason to suspect that this is what happened? Was the car in different condition when you arrived yesterday morning than when you left it the night before?" Another flicker passed between the pair of them and Beryl felt she would have much to share with Edwina when they reconvened at the Beeches.

"No. I can't say that there was anything amiss. It was just one possible explanation for what your witness saw, not an accusation by any means," Norah said. "As I'm sure you noticed, we are still finishing up with your motorcar. If you would like to have it back tomorrow we should really get back to work."

Beryl stood. "Thanks for your time. I look forward to having it back as soon as possible. If either of you think of anything out of the ordinary or anything connected to Polly I would appreciate you letting me know straightaway."

Beryl was quite certain she heard a joint sigh of relief as she closed the door behind her. She stood listening at it for a moment hoping to overhear something that cleared up the fact that Eva insisted she had seen the car out on the street. When nothing was forthcoming she stepped over to the bench and returned the spanner to the workbench as silently as possible. She stepped out into the bright sunshine and quickened her steps for home.

"So what did you find out?" Edwina asked as soon as Beryl entered the hall. Edwina helped her out of her coat and hung it for her and raced ahead to the sitting room where a fire and a snifter of something amber colored and alluring sat next to a half-filled decanter. Beryl flopped into the chair and cradled the glass in both hands. She was delighted to see Edwina looking as animated as she herself felt. What a change only a few days could make. Then Beryl thought the same could have been said for Polly Watkins and she lost a bit of her sparkle.

"I had a most informative day. It turns out Polly was on a special list of young ladies that Mr. Mumford provided with free access to the cinema."

"Why ever would he do favors like that?" Edwina asked. Despite their age, her friend was still so innocent in many ways,

Beryl thought. It was almost a crime to disillusion her. But one had to accept that in the course of an investigation nothing could be held sacred.

"He was hoping they would extend favors of their own in his direction I expect."

"Where did you hear such a nasty rumor?"

"From Eva, the ticket girl at the theater. She said quite a number of girls and women were extended that privilege in the three years or so that she had been working there. The interesting thing was that she thought maybe Agnes had also been one of them. Nurse Crenshaw definitely is."

"Nurse Crenshaw?" Edwina's teacup shook in her hand. "And Agnes. Still, I suppose Eva would be in a position to know about it if anyone would. Did Eva tell you anything else worth knowing?"

"She did. She said she saw my car racing down the road past the cinema at around the same hour the last showing of the night would have let out."

"Really?"

"Really. I went straight over to the garage to ask the Blackburns about it but they both denied driving it. They suggested it might have been local men or boys who couldn't resist taking her for a run."

"Did they say who could have done so?"

"One of them mentioned Norman Davies as a possibility. Michael said he was admiring the motorcar the morning he came in with the late produce run."

"He never mentioned to me that he stopped in at the garage. He made it sound as if he were hard at work all day long either in the fields or doing the produce delivery."

"What else did he have to say for himself?"

"He said he had no idea how Polly came to be found in the field. He also said that he was the one we heard calling her name in front of the cinema."

"Did he say why she didn't respond to him?" Beryl asked.

"According to Norman she had been giving him the cold shoulder for weeks and had finally told him she no longer wanted to go walking out with him."

"That fits with what we had heard from others about her throwing him over. It wouldn't be the first time that a young woman was killed by a man that said he loved her," Beryl said. "I suppose he told you that he was still desirous of her company?"

"He said he was trying to win her back, which is why he was following her."

"Did you believe him?"

"I believe that he loved her and wanted her back but I am not sure he wasn't consumed by a jealous rage. He says he had suspected for some time that she had found another man and he was following her in part to confirm that he was right. It seems the night she died he got his answer."

"Really? How so?" Beryl took a sip from her glass and stared over the rim.

"Polly went round the back side of the cinema and he followed her there. He saw her bang on the door and then the projectionist let her in," Edwina said.

"The mysterious projectionist. That explains why such an avid film enthusiast would stop taking advantage of Mr. Mumford's offer of free entrance to the shows. She was getting another man to let her in for free," Beryl said. "What do you know about the projectionist? Is he a local man?"

"Not at all. He arrived in Walmsley Parva one day out of the blue. Prudence managed to winkle out of him that he wanted to make a fresh start in the English countryside after picturing it for so long while he was down in the trenches. She must have given him quite a grilling because no one has really laid eyes on him since. He stays entirely out of village life," Edwina said. "You know there is nothing to prove Polly spent time with him after she entered the building. He doesn't seem the sort to be chatting with strange young ladies."

"There is only one thing to do. We shall have to ask him." Beryl refilled her glass from the crystal decanter and inhaled the rich scent. The day had been the best she'd had in some time. Something about this sort of adventure suited her down to her boots. Which reminded her.

"Did you ask Norman about Polly's shoes?"

"I did. He said she never would have worn her party shoes to walk across the field. Especially since she would have known he had recently manured it. In fact Norman said she would have been able to smell it from her parents' house and would have known not to risk her shoes."

"So her shoes are missing. If we find them we may find who killed her," Beryl said. "Did you think to ask him about any vehicles in the area that night?"

"I did but he said he had been drinking heavily from the moment he arrived home and he didn't see or hear a thing until he spotted our torches so close in the field. He worried about vandals in the crops enough to rouse him from his stupor."

"Could he have been drowning his sorrows to such an extent to try to forget what he had done to Polly?"

"He might have done. I hate to think so, but someone killed her. He is probably the strongest suspect.'

"Who knows what tomorrow will bring, Ed? I suggest we do the same tomorrow as today and separate. Although I did wonder for a moment or two at the wisdom of that. I actually slipped a spanner in my coat pocket before I went in to question Michael and Norah Blackburn."

"A spanner?"

"It's a very effective weapon, Ed."

"Please tell me you've never used one yourself for protection?" Edwina's teacup chattered in its saucer once more.

"You recall me mentioning that unsavory bedtime reading material preferred by my former husband?" Edwina nodded. "It was included in a chapter concerning violence and the motorcar." If Edwina's teacup could be trusted she was soothed by the answer. Beryl saw no reason to upset her further with the truth.

"So where do we go from here?" Edwina asked. "Who do we question next?"

"I think I ought to have a word with the projectionist. I think you should go to speak with your Mr. Jarvis." Beryl fixed a gimlet eye on Edwina's face for signs of interest.

"He's not my Mr. Jarvis. Why on earth would you say a thing like that?"

"If he isn't, I dare say he'd like to be. Have you seen his collection of watercolors?"

"I've accompanied him from time to time on his en plain air ventures. He does rather tepid landscapes. I try to encourage him, but to be honest I doubt he will ever set the artistic world ablaze. Why do you ask?"

"No reason. I just noticed his collection when I was at his house to speak with Polly about returning to work here. If you call on him at his house you should ask him to show them to you."

"What is it you think I should ask Mr. Jarvis as concerns the case?" Edwina said.

"We need to know if Polly was acting differently than usual. If so, Mr. Jarvis might have noticed something and would tell you about it."

"I could stop in tomorrow at his chambers. I haven't been there in some time and I do like to visit the place from time to time. It holds many pleasant memories for me."

"It was your father's office too, wasn't it?"

"It was. Mr. Jarvis was the junior partner in the firm until he took sole ownership upon Father's death. Father wanted Fred to follow him into the law but he had other plans." Beryl knew more from what had not been said over the years than from what had, that Frederick Davenport had been a bit of a disappointment to his father. He wasn't a serious sort of person like his older sister. If life were different, Edwina would have been the far better choice to follow in her father's footsteps. In fact, Beryl seemed to remember the question of Edwina attending university with an eye towards joining her father's firm.

Mrs. Davenport had put an end to that scheme almost immediately. No daughter of hers was going to make such a bluestocking spectacle of herself. What was next? Agitating for the vote like those Pankhurst women was not what she had planned for her only daughter. In the end Mr. Davenport had looked outside the family for a protégé and had found one in Mr. Jarvis. Fred joined up as soon as war was declared and for some time it looked as though he had finally found his calling as a soldier. But his luck ran out not long before Armistice when his trench collapsed upon him and he was smothered to death. Mrs. Davenport died herself not long after, leaving Edwina with death taxes, a large house, and no family at all.

"Then by all means stop in and ask about Polly at his office if you think it best. I am sure you will be more than welcome wherever you chose to hunt him down." Beryl forced herself not to wink. Edwina would assuredly not approve of winking.

"I can't imagine why you keep saying such silly things. You only met Mr. Jarvis one time and then very briefly," Edwina said, two spots of color heating up her pale cheeks.

"May I remind you I also only met Mr. Mumford very briefly and I took an accurate measure of him? I happen to be an expert in the male mind, and while I don't like to make it sound like a criticism, Ed, you, simply put, are not."

"I cannot imagine why I'd want to be."

"I'm not suggesting that you should. It's nasty business really and one you might be glad to be well shot of, with occasional exceptions like your Mr. Jarvis." Beryl put her glass down on the table and stretched her long arms above her head. "Time to head for bed. If tomorrow proceeds as I hope it does, you shall need your beauty sleep."

Chapter 19

First thing that morning Norah had telephoned to say she could return Beryl's motorcar by midday. Crumpet danced around her feet as Edwina opened the door of the cooker. The roast chicken was coming along nicely no matter how Beryl had complained of its size. A tantalizing scent of savory vegetables mingled with the fragrance of the bird and filled the kitchen with its aroma. She hummed to herself just under her breath. It had been far too long since Edwina had had anyone to cook proper meals for and she hadn't realized how much she had missed it. After Father died she and Mother had developed the habit of taking most of their meals in the kitchen. As her mother's health failed she preferred a tray in bed. By the end her mother hadn't any appetite no matter what she prepared.

She closed the oven door and passed through the butler's pantry to the dining room. In just a few trips she had the glasses and plates set out and the candlesticks and a vase of Michaelmas daisies placed on the table. It had been so long since she had bothered Edwina had almost forgotten how the walnut paneled room looked with the table laid.

She stepped back and admired the results. Edwina had even had time to polish her mother's prized silver carving set that morning. She laid the knife and fork at the end of the table just as she heard the crunch of gravel in the drive. She stepped to the window and watched as Norah hopped out of Beryl's motor-car. From this distance there was no sign any damage had ever been done to the bonnet. Crumpet fled down the hallway barking when the sound of knocking landed upon the front door.

Beryl presided over the luncheon in such a way as to make Edwina almost forget the purpose was to conduct an interview. Between forkfuls of roasted potatoes and sweet parsnips her old friend managed to regale them both with the comic details of an expedition to Nepal. She worried that the meal would be over before anything was said and that they would be no closer to discovering what Norah had to say about her brother. She was very curious as to how it would tally with what the doctor had confided when Edwina had consulted him about her bruised neck.

"These potatoes are first rate, Ed, but they would be even better dressed with yak butter," Beryl said, waving her fork laden with a speared piece of potato in Edwina's direction. "I don't suppose they've got any of that at the local shops, have they?"

"Things became quite dire during the war years but I am proud to say we were not reduced to relying on yaks for our dairy products." Edwina was rather pleased for the opening in the conversation to introduce the topic. "Thanks to the efforts of women like Agnes and the other Land Army women, we could depend on fine British cow's milk." Beryl nodded and placed her fork down.

"You have some things to tell us about Agnes too, don't you, Norah?" she asked.

"I have more to say about Michael really. Since you're determined to look into the whole business I expect you're likely to hear how he was and to wonder if he had anything to do with what happened."

"Why don't you tell us what you think we should know?" Edwina asked.

"I'm afraid any problems that arose were my fault. After all, I gave Agnes the suggestion."

"Which suggestion was that?"

"I told you I used to do repairs on the machinery from time to time at the Wallingford Estate," Norah said to Beryl. The older woman nodded. "Once when I was there I got to talking with Agnes. She said she loved reading and wished she had some more books to read. I told her there were plenty at the hospital. I said they'd been part of the library on the estate when Lady Wallingford turned the whole thing over to use for the war effort."

"What does that have to do with your brother?"

"I'm getting to that bit," Norah said. "Agnes said she wouldn't feel right about borrowing books from the hospital when so many of the patients couldn't read them."

"The gas?" Edwina asked.

"That was part of the problem. A lot of the men at Wallingford couldn't see, at least until their eyes healed from the blistering. But there were others that just didn't seem to see anything even though their eyes had not been injured. I suggested Agnes would be a real help if she read aloud to the soldiers who couldn't read to themselves."

"Was Michael one of those soldiers?"

"He was one of the ones who had what they called the thousand yard stare. I spoke to him and sang to him and held his hand but nothing got through. It was like his spirit had lifted up and out of his body and only a husk remained." Norah dabbed at her eyes with her serviette. "But slowly he seemed to respond to Agnes' voice reading to them. She found a copy of

Tarzan of the Apes, which Michael had read over and over as a youth. She used to sit near his bed and she read it to him. By the beginning of the second book Michael was looking around and starting to respond to noise and light. By the time she had moved on the third book, *The Beasts of Tarzan,* he was making conversation and almost seemed back to his normal self."

"So what was the difficulty?" Beryl asked. "It sounds like Agnes was a godsend."

"I thought so, too. I still do. Michael believed he owed his recovery entirely to her. Dr. Nelson told me he thought that explained what happened next."

"Which was?" Even as she asked, Edwina wasn't sure she had the stomach to hear whatever Norah was going to share. She had heard far too many sad stories of lives run off the rails to have the heart for another one.

"Michael became possessive of her. He didn't want her to read or even talk to any of the other men. He certainly didn't want her to show any interest in them. He would spend all day asking where she was and when she was coming to visit next. The doctor and the nurses and even I tried to explain that Agnes had other duties to perform and she wasn't able to devote herself exclusively to entertaining him."

"How distressing," Edwina said.

"It really was. He kept saying he knew the others were no good for her and that she should be careful. I think she was quite uncomfortable with the situation because her visits got further and further apart. In the end the doctor suggested it would be better if she simply stopped coming."

"How did Michael react?"

"At first he was quite melancholy. As I remember it, he retreated back into himself for a bit. But by the time she went missing he seemed back to his old self once more," Norah said. "He's finally adjusted to the loss of his arm and has gotten on with his life. I think it was just an unfortunate fixation and one that has passed. But I'm sure you can see why I don't want you to bring Agnes up with him."

"We shouldn't like to set him back in any way. He's a very pleasant young man and we need all of those that we can come by," Edwina said.

"Not to mention he's a very fine mechanic," Beryl said. "I do have one question though. Did anyone ever question Michael about Agnes' disappearance at the time? Did he even know she had gone?"

"The doctor wouldn't allow it. He said his loyalty was to his patients and that their needs came first. In fact he wrote to me to assure me that whatever had happened with Agnes would not be brought to Michael's attention," Norah said. "It must have worked because he improved quite rapidly after she was gone."

"And he never asked after her once he was fully recovered?" Beryl asked.

"He never asked and I never offered any information. I expect he assumed she left Walmsley Parva when her commitment to the Land Army was fulfilled. They only signed up for a year, I believe." Norah turned to Edwina.

"That's right. Although some of them signed up again," Edwina said.

"All I know is that I heaved a huge sigh of relief when I realized she was gone. He still has his bad days but nothing like he used to. Which is how I intend to keep it. I've told you all I know and would be most grateful if neither of you did anything to jeopardise his peace of mind."

"I think we've heard enough, don't you, Ed?" Beryl said.

"Absolutely. I hope all this sad talk of the past hasn't spoilt your appetite. I've made an apple tart for pudding." Edwina didn't wait for an answer but rather pushed back her chair and left the room.

* * *

Beryl offered to drive Norah home after each of them had enjoyed their fill of tart and had taken a brisk walk around the garden to settle all they'd eaten. Norah refused, saying she could still do with a good deal more exercise than a stroll. Once the door was closed behind her Beryl took Edwina by the arm and steered her to the parlor.

"What do you think of that?" she asked.

"I think if Agnes' body had turned up instead of Polly's, Michael would have easily been the first one to look at as having killed her."

"He certainly seems like a strong suspect. Fixated, unstable in his mind. Jealous." Beryl drummed her fingers on the side table. "But you know, there is another possibility as well."

"Besides her not being dead but merely missing?"

"Yes. Assuming she is no longer amongst the living, we have another possible suspect."

"Who?"

"Norah herself," Beryl said. "She is remarkably protective of her brother and was very clear about the fact that she was delighted for Agnes to have had no further contact with Michael."

"But to kill her? Doesn't that seem a bit extreme?"

"Can you think of a better way to be sure Michael would never see Agnes again?"

"No. I'm afraid I cannot."

"Do you know of any reason either of them might have had reason to do away with Polly?" Beryl asked.

"I shall have to think about it a bit more and ask some more questions. Hortense might have a better idea than I do about Polly's friends during her time in the Land Army."

"I believe we have already established that you are the best person to charm information out of Mr. Jarvis," Beryl said. "Which leaves me with the formidable matron, Hortense Merriweather."

"I do wish you'd stop saying such things about Mr. Jarvis. I will find it impossible to question him properly if you don't leave off with your insinuations."

"I cannot help that I see something that ought to have been obvious to you for eons," Beryl said. "I suggest you wear your smartest hat."

Chapter 20

Hortense lived close enough to the Beeches to make it difficult to justify taking the car but Beryl simply couldn't resist. Although she tried to convince herself she could use the exercise it was to no avail. She was behind the wheel and rolling through what she had come to think of as the heart of the English countryside. It was the quality of the light, she decided as she asked herself what set this rural scene apart from that of other places. Surely it was that rather than the lumbering herds of wooly sheep dotted the rolling hills and a swiftly running creek gurgled alongside the road. Norah was correct; the vehicle was indeed as good as new. Beryl's mood lifted higher and higher with each bend in the road. How she loved to feel the wind whipping through the open window as she tooled along the narrow country lanes.

Before she knew it the crooked wooden sign indicating the turnoff for Hortense's lane appeared in her windscreen. Beryl yanked on the wheel and jounced almost immediately to a stop in front of a thatched cottage fronted by a garden brimming with bronzed foliage and bare-twigged shrubberies. What would it be like, she wondered, to stay in one place long enough to recognize how much a tree had grown or whether or not it was a better year for fruit than the last had been? Edwina would know those things and more about her beloved Walmsley Parva, Beryl thought as she slid from the seat of the car and stepped onto the cobblestones that paved the lane. Not much space to leave a vehicle here. There was just enough room for another to pass if the driver was extraordinarily careful.

White curtains twitched at a front window and Beryl was sure she had found someone at home. She stepped to the door and rapped upon the shiny brass knocker shaped like a ship. The door swung open without the faintest of squeaks and a sturdy woman with decidedly grizzled hair looked out at her through thick spectacles.

"Hello, I'm Beryl Helliwell. I hate to disturb you but my friend Edwina suggested you might be able to shed some light on a question that has come up."

"I've already told Edwina everything I know about that Land Army girl disappearance. I have a great deal to accomplish today and very little patience for wild-goose chases." Hortense stood blocking the door, her arms laced across her prow of a bosom.

"Edwina said you ran a tight ship when you were the matron at the Wallingford Estate. High praise from a woman like her who is also known for not suffering fools gladly." Beryl looked at her carefully, searching for signs of thawing. Sure enough, Hortense took a step back and motioned for her to follow. She entered a low-ceilinged sitting room off the hall and gestured to a stiff-looking chair covered in faded, threadbare upholstery. Beryl lowered herself into it as though slipping into a boiling hot bath. Despite her care, prickles of horsehair prodded her backside straight through her clothing. She wondered if discomfort of her unexpected guests was a way Hortense kept to her schedule. Beryl certainly had no intention of staying any longer than she must.

"What's this all about? Why are you and Edwina so interested in Agnes and the goings-on at the Wallingford Estate at this late date?" Hortense asked.

"Edwina was attacked in her garden four nights ago as soon as it became common knowledge that she was investigating some underhanded goings-on in Walmsley Parva. I asked Polly some questions about Agnes and shortly after that she ends up dead. We think there is a connection."

"What does Constable Gibbs have to say about it?"

"About as much as she did about Agnes' disappearance. She thinks nothing nefarious explains either incident. A most narrow-minded view in my opinion," Beryl said. "I understand it is common knowledge that Constable Gibbs was inclined to take a harsh view of the Land Army women and what she presumed to be their rampant lack of morals. In light of her prejudice, Edwina and I have decided to look into the matter ourselves."

"In that case, I suppose I could answer a few questions. After all, I never did agree with the constable about my girls," Hortense said. "What is it that Edwina wants to know then? And why did she send you instead of coming herself?"

"Edwina was unavoidably detained this afternoon and as she had told me quite a lot about you, I wanted to make your acquaintance myself. It is a pleasure for me to meet other people who knew Edwina as a young woman. You've known her most of her life, haven't you?" Beryl shifted slightly in the chair and felt another jab in her tender nether regions.

"That's true. Our parents moved in the same social circles and we were placed in each other's path over the years for parties and dances. That sort of thing. We haven't seen as much of each other as adults as so often happens when one person marries and the other does not."

"Edwina tells me that renewing your acquaintance was part of the appeal of her decision to volunteer as the Land Army Village Registrar," Beryl said.

"That is very kind of her to say, I'm sure. Edwina was a remarkable help with keeping track of which girls went where and when. She has a marvelous memory for all that sort of thing as well as being a dedicated record-keeper. We were very fortunate to have her."

"It was about some of the workers at the Wallingford Estate that I wished to inquire. Do you happen to remember Agnes Rollins reading to the men in the hospital wing of the estate?" Beryl asked.

"I believe she did, yes. She asked my permission to do so, if I am properly recalling things."

"Did you grant it?"

"I think I told her it was a kind thing she was offering to do and that it did her far more credit than the sorts of things many of the other girls got up to of an evening when they thought I didn't know what they were about." Hortense tut-tutted loudly.

"So there wasn't any trouble with Agnes spending time with the soldiers? No unwanted attachments? That sort of complication can arise very unexpectedly."

"She did have a bit of trouble with Michael Blackburn in just the manner you mean. But maybe you knew that already and just want to know if I know?"

"Right you are, I'm afraid. I had heard about Michael's unwholesome attention towards Agnes. I did wonder how tight your ship really was."

"I shouldn't have presumed to call it watertight, but I think I had a good notion of where all the leaks were." Hortense nodded to herself. "I prided myself on applying pitch to any such breaches with a thick brush."

"Was Polly one of the leaks?"

"I wouldn't have said that so much as that she tended to forget herself, to aim above her station in that dreamy way of hers. Most of the other girls were from the cities and much larger towns. They had no idea what they were getting into when they signed up. The silly girls happened upon a rally in a town square and felt called to a patriotic duty or they went looking for a bit of excitement far from home and they plunged in without thinking too much about it. For them it was a thing they did during the war and nothing more."

"But Polly was different, was she?"

"Polly was trying to escape the drudgery of going into domestic service. She didn't want to spend her life answering to the beck and call of her betters but she didn't want to leave her family and her sweetheart for a job in the city like at an armaments factory. She wasn't smart enough to be a nurse. So she followed that sweetheart of hers, Norman his name was, to the Wallingford Estate instead. Considering how unsuited she was to being a servant, it was a wise decision."

"You were familiar with her work as a maid?" Beryl asked.

"She came here as a daily twice a week. Recently I was forced to ask her to leave my employ and not to return."

"Edwina mentioned she wasn't the most enthusiastic worker."

"None of them are anymore. Servants have always been a tiresome and inferior race. No, it wasn't her laziness but rather the fact that she was a thief that finally forced me to take action. I am certain she took my mother's engagement ring. She denied it, of course, but who else could it have been?" Beryl had the impression that Hortense was the sort who always thought of the domestic staff first anytime she needed someone to blame. Still, Hortense's allegation tallied with the rumors about Polly that Edwina had mentioned.

"You said she came to the Land Army following after her young man? Did she like the work there?"

"Not that I ever noticed. I shouldn't have been surprised if the biggest reason she joined up was to keep an eye on Norman."

"Why would she need to do that?" Beryl asked. "I thought they were quite a devoted couple at that time."

"She was devoted. He was one of the only young men in arm's reach surrounded by sophisticated, educated women willing to do their bit for King and country. Polly had good reason to be jealous."

"Anyone in particular that she feared might turn Norman's head?" Beryl asked.

"Agnes, for one. I used to see them talking behind the barns. I think the interest was only on his side though."

"Why would you say that?"

"He had her by the arm once and I was surprised to see that she was determinedly tugging it away. When he saw me he let her go. I noticed her rubbing her arm like it was injured."

"Did you ever see that sort of problem between the two of them again?" Beryl asked.

"I can't recall ever seeing any more arguments or physical exchanges. They never did seem to me to be friends though," Hortense said. "In fact, now that I think of it, if pressed I'd say he went out of his way to avoid her after the exchange I witnessed. It wouldn't have been easy though. The estate was not such a large property that workers could avoid each other with ease."

"Was there a similar coolness between Polly and Agnes?"

"Not that I was aware of. They talked to each other and worked together every day. Perhaps it was a question in Polly's case of keeping her enemy closer. If she were with Agnes then Agnes couldn't be alone with Norman." Hortense looked up at the clock chiming on her mantlepiece. "As I am quite certain there is nothing else I can tell you I really must get on with my day. The jumble sale won't set itself out you know." Hortense rose and stood over Beryl until she also got to her feet.

"If you think of anything else, I am sure Edwina would love to hear from you."

"You can tell Edwina that if she wants to speak to me about Agnes, Polly, or anything else for that matter, she can drop in at the village hall and do her bit for the jumble sale. Like I told her before, it is impossible to get good help. Now with Polly dead there is even one fewer person to help with the job."

"Did Polly help with the sale? I had understood her to be more of the sort of girl who was up for parties and the cinema than good works in the community."

"You are correct about that, most assuredly. It was rather tedious but I told her it was her obligation as someone in my employ to provide whatever assistance I required of her. She wasn't happy about it but she acquiesced in the end." Hortense headed for the door. "Those in the serving class always do in the end."

"Did she continue helping out after you dismissed her from your service?" Beryl asked.

"Of course not. What little influence over her I held disappeared the moment our arrangement ended. There is no sense of community instilled in a girl like Polly Watkins. None whatsoever. Now, if there is finally nothing else?" Hortense went to the door and yanked it open as if it had done her a personal affront.

Beryl knew when the time had come to take a hint. With little by way of good-byes she hurriedly took her leave. Edwina had not said Hortense was a close friend and Beryl had wondered at that since they had been thrown together so much as children. From their time together as girls Beryl knew Edwina did not share Hortense's views on differences between community members based upon class. After all, Edwina had seemed to enjoy having Norah for luncheon. Beryl couldn't imagine Hortense happily allowing a mechanic to sit down to the table with her. She thought about Hortense's words all the way to the cinema.

Chapter 21

If she were to be honest with herself, Edwina was soundly discomfited by Beryl's insistence that Charles held her in any particular regard. Despite her reluctance to visit Charles Jarvis, Edwina told herself it was her Christian duty to follow through on Polly's behalf, no matter where the investigation might lead. Even if it were true that Charles held a certain tendresse for her, the use of feminine wiles offended Edwina's sense of fair play. Besides, she was terrible at employing them. The few times she had attempted to do so during her extreme youth had proven disastrous and memorable. One incident involving a picnic hamper and a rowboat had proven so embarrassing that for more than a year all her mother had to do was to mention the word *sandwiches* and Edwina fled the room. In an effort to dissuade any increase in any interest he may have had for her, Edwina selected her third best hat from the hall tree and stuck it on her head with scarcely a glance in the mirror.

Her thoughts plagued her all the way to Charles' chambers. She was not a girl any longer, she chided herself as she lifted the latch on the door to the solicitor's office. Besides, she had been a part of that particular establishment far earlier than Charles himself had. After all, he became her father's junior partner years after she had spent her girlhood holidays sprawled across the oxblood leather couch in the waiting room reading law books her mother would not have approved of had she known.

She took a deep breath and the image of her father with his muttonchop whiskers and baritone voice seated soothingly behind his vast mahogany desk appeared in her mind's eye. She knew how lucky she had been and the losses she had felt were all the more acute because of it. Charles' secretary, a solid, woman with a cheerful disposition, welcomed her as she entered and said her employer was in and would be delighted to see her, as always, she was sure. Wouldn't Edwina come right through?

Charles stood up, nearly knocking over a bottle of ink when Edwina entered. "I was planning to call on you at the Beeches before the day was out. I've heard the news about Polly Watkins and also that you were the one who found her. Along with that friend of yours. What is her name?" Charles squinted as if he were searching his memory. It was a singular moment. Charles never forgot anything important and Edwina had yet to meet anyone who did not think Beryl made a lasting impression.

"Beryl Helliwell. She's quite a famous adventuress. I'm sure you've heard of her," Edwina said.

"If you say so. I can't say I've paid much attention to adventuresses or Americans either for that matter." Charles came round from behind his desk, a more modest version than her departed father's, and offered her a seat. He waited for her to settle herself and then sat in the visitor chair beside her. "Now tell me, how are you really?"

"I'm absolutely fine. It was a shock, of course, to find a body, but I wasn't the one injured so I have no cause for complaint. I seem to have bounced back well enough," Edwina said. "I came to ask you some questions about Polly. I know you have been on better terms with her than I of late."

"She was at my house doing the cleaning the the same day she died. I was absolutely stunned to hear she had died so unexpectedly." Charles tented his fingers and leaned back in his chair. "It shouldn't have been so shocking after all the young people who were fine in the morning and gone by the afternoon from flu but there's been no sign of that long enough so as to get complacent again."

"I know just what you mean. If I had come across some elderly tramp that had fallen down for excess drink or even an injured former soldier who had done himself a mischief I would naturally have been startled, but I wouldn't have been so shocked. How did she seem to you that day when she was at your house?"

"She was much as usual." Charles looked down at his feet stretched out in front of him. "One doesn't like to complain but . . ." His voice trailed off.

"But she wasn't a very ambitious girl."

"Not where the cleaning was involved, no," Charles said. "She seemed glad to be adding the Beeches back to her roster of cleaning jobs though. I gathered from a few hints that she dropped that she was saving up for something special and a few extra shillings would be quite welcome."

"Beryl mentioned the same thing. Had you any idea what the money was for?"

"I didn't pay any attention to her chatter generally. In fact, I tried to avoid being home when she was here. I told her I didn't want to be in her way, but the fact was I could only listen to so much about one film star or another. She had been even more verbose of late. I think she'd seen every film that had come through the local cinema."

"I have reason to believe you are right about that." Edwina still couldn't quite credit what Beryl had told her concerning Mr. Mumford. He did have such a kind way about him. "So nothing but film stars and tittle-tattle from Polly called your attention?"

"She did ask me something a little different a week ago or so," Charles said. "I don't suppose it falls under client confidentiality even though it was a legal question as she didn't ever ask me to represent her interests." Edwina's ears pricked up.

"What did she ask you about?"

"She wanted to know how long something could be considered a crime. She asked if there was any possibility that someone could be prosecuted for something that had happened during the war years. Naturally I asked for specifics. I am loath to offer legal advice with so few details."

"Did she give them to you?" Edwina felt herself sliding to the edge of her seat.

"She refused to say anything specific. She became quite agitated when I said I didn't feel comfortable advising her with so little to go on. In the end I relented because she was so insistent. I told her it depended entirely on the sort of crime committed and that there were different statutes of limitation on crimes based on the severity."

"Do you remember if she asked for any examples or if she seemed particularly interested in any specific piece of information?" Edwina asked.

"She asked if anything criminal had no limitation. I told her murder would always be held to account. She asked about military law and what constituted treason. I told her that military law was not my specialty, especially as concerned wartime. That was the end of the discussion."

"Did she seem encouraged or discouraged by your response?"

"More disappointed I think that I couldn't tell her exactly

what she wanted to know without her sharing confidences. I offered to take her on as a client for no charge if she felt she needed legal counsel but she said she would take care of the matter herself."

"Did she ever mention it again?"

"She didn't. And I didn't like to ask. I thought of it several times over the week or so since she brought it up and then it did occur to me again after I heard she had been found dead. I couldn't help but wonder if I had pressed her to confide in me if she would still be alive."

"She was young, but she was an adult, Charles. Both you and I know Polly could not be convinced to do anything she wasn't inclined to do."

"It is very kind of you to say so and your words relieve my mind a bit. As did hearing that Constable Gibbs has determined Polly simply met with an unfortunate accident."

Edwina looked at Charles. He was a nice man in many ways but he struck her as being entirely devoid of an imagination. She rather enjoyed shocking him from time to time with the odd suggestion that rousted him from his comfortable and stodgy ways.

"That's exactly why I am here, Charles. Beryl and I are completely convinced that Polly did not meet with an accident at all, but rather that someone deliberately killed her." As if on cue Charles' mouth flapped open and a strange gargling sound bubbled up out of his throat.

"You think she was murdered? Here in Walmsley Parva?"

"Why not? Someone made an attempt on my life the day Beryl arrived—in my own garden. It seems to me it wasn't so very outrageous for a young woman walking alone at night to meet with danger. It appears the village is not as safe as it once was."

"Did you report what happened to the authorities?"

"I did not. If Constable Gibbs was not inclined to investigate an actual murder, I hardly think she would have been more enthusiastic about getting to the bottom of an attempted one."

"Have you considered someone may make another attempt on your life?" Charles leaned across the narrow space separating their chairs and made as if to take her hand. She stiffened like a vole sensing the shadow of an owl and he dropped his hands abruptly and clutched at his armrest instead.

"Of course I had considered that, Charles. I won't be able to feel comfortable in my own home until the matter is resolved." If there was one thing Edwina detested it was being spoken to as though she hadn't a brain in her head.

"I suppose that adventuress woman of yours talked you into getting involved in something as potentially dangerous as this." A pained look flitted across Charles' face. Edwina wondered if his digestion was troubling him.

"It wasn't just Beryl. Constable Gibbs' refusal to see sense when she declared Polly's death an accident is what convinced me to take part in looking into this matter."

"I had heard the rumors bandied about by that Helliwell woman that you are a pair of secret investigators. You were putting yourself in harm's way before Polly was killed."

"I thought you took no notice of anything to do with adventuresses or Americans," Edwina said. Charles shuffled his feet.

"What would your mother say?" Charles asked. It was very low of him to bring up her mother, and not worthy of a gentleman. Edwina felt the interview was at an end.

"Fortunately, Charles, I needn't ever know." Edwina stood. Still, the interview was not a waste no matter how unpleasantly it had ended. She could hardly wait to get home to share with Beryl what she had learned. "I'll take my leave of you, Charles. I appreciate your time."

"Don't let's leave off like this." Charles said. "I confess that while I may have overstepped propriety, I am simply worried about you now that there is no one to take care of you."

"As I've told you on more than one occasion, I am perfectly capable of looking after myself." With that, she walked briskly out the door, banging it shut with enough verve to let the secretary know the tenor of the interview. Really, Charles was impossible so much of the time.

Chapter 22

Eva was at the ticket window once more when Beryl arrived. She looked surprised at Beryl's request to be directed to the projectionist's booth.

"Walter doesn't like to speak to anyone. Especially not strangers," she said. "He'll be very upset with me for telling you where to find him."

"What is Walter's surname?" Beryl asked.

"Bennett. Why do you ask?"

"The less you know the better. You just point the way and I'll keep the fact that you did so to myself." Eva reluctantly left the ticket booth and led Beryl to a narrow corridor off the back of the lobby.

"At the end of the hall there is a short set of stairs that leads up to the projectionist's booth. Good luck."

Beryl smiled at her then strode off in the direction of her quarry. She was quite certain nothing would make sense in the case without extracting some information from the reclusive projectionist. She moved down the corridor and then up the stairs silently. Her time spent hunting both big game and small served her well when it came to moving stealthily. The knob on the door at the top of the stairs turned smoothly in her hand and she took a steadying breath before giving it a firm shove and stepping in as though she had every right to be there. A slim man stood with his back to her. He was fitting a reel of film onto the projector. He wheeled around as her weight came down on a loose floorboard and gave off an enormous squeak.

"Dear me, I hope you don't mind the intrusion, but I simply had to find somewhere to hide from that odious man," she said to the person before her. He stood stock-still and said nothing. His expression gave nothing away either. But then it wouldn't have. The man standing in front of her was one of the many thousands of young men to have had such severe facial disfigurement as to resort to a tin mask. Beryl had seen them before often enough. In fact, the mask he wore was a popular variety. They were all hand painted and made to fit the individual, Beryl knew but she also knew many of the men who required the masks took the opportunity to have the faces painted on it portray that of handsome film stars. Walter Bennett's tin mask looked remarkably like the face of Douglas Fairbanks.

"It's the owner, you see. All I wanted to do was to watch the film in peace but he just wouldn't leave me alone. Rather quick with his hands I'm afraid. I hope you're not shocked to hear it?" she asked. He shook his head carefully, she assumed in order to not dislodge his mask. She looked around at the small room. All around the tiny space shelves were stacked to the ceiling with round tins. A waxed paper parcel with a half-eaten sandwich sat on a bench that was mounted on the back wall, along with a pair of scissors and an electric lamp.

"Of course you are. You didn't come by the need of a handsome new face by sitting in your mother's parlor sipping hot milk and reading a book of poetry, did you? A man of action by the look of you. Just the sort to help a damsel in distress. As a matter of fact, when your Mr. Mumford started getting overly familiar I remembered Polly Watkins telling me that she used to come up here and sit with the projectionist in order to avoid him while she watched the films. She said he took too many liberties in the broad daylight and that there was no way to keep him off if you made the mistake of ending up in the dark theater with him," Beryl said. Still the man said nothing.

"You are Walter Bennett, aren't you?" she said. The man nodded again slowly. "Of course you are. Who else would be working in the projectionist's booth?" Still the man said nothing until she sat down on a high stool and faced the screen. He cleared his throat rustily then addressed her.

"Polly said she came in here?"

"How else would I know about her being here with you? It was a secret, wasn't it?"

"It was. Mr. Mumford wouldn't have wanted me to let anyone in here to see the shows for free," Walter said.

"He didn't want the ladies to see them for free unless he was going to be able to get something out of it. Trying to take advantage of nice young women like Polly is just a disgrace," Beryl said. Walter Bennett stepped up to the apparatus situated in front of a small window and fed the end of the film into its slot on the projector. "Polly was lucky to have found you considering how much she loved films. It would have been a hardship to have to miss out on them rather than submit to Mr. Mumford's insisted pawing. And worse." It was difficult to gauge Walter's reaction to anything she said as his facial expression never changed. Still she was encouraged by the fact that he had not decided to flee the room and had begun to engage in conversation. She pressed on. "I understood she was here visiting you recently. Was she here to see the newest film?"

"No," he said. His voice dropped a little. "She was here to visit with me."

"The two of you were friends then?"

"We both loved film and I was surprised to find I enjoyed her company. I don't like to spend time with too many people."

"Did she say anything about being followed here? Someone told me they saw her running away from her former sweetheart, Norman Davies."

"She said something about that when I let her into the cinema." He paused. "She was upset by him following her. She thought he saw her with me and she was worried about what he would say or do. She said he had accused her of being interested in another man when she told him she was no longer interested in him."

"Did he follow her often?"

"He did. That's how I came to meet her in the first place. I heard a banging on the back door one evening and since it didn't stop I left the booth to see what it was. Polly was standing there looking small and helpless and she asked me to let her in before Norman found her. So I did. She started coming by regularly after that."

"What did she think he would do?"

"She wasn't sure. She just said he had a bit of a temper and good reason not to want to let her go."

"Did she say what the reason was?"

"No. She just said he was not an easy man to make a change once he had his mind made up about something. Polly says unfortunately she is one of the somethings."

"Was that the last time you saw her?" Beryl asked. A terrible thought had entered her mind. She realized Walter had referred to Polly in the present tense.

"It was."

"Have you spoken with anyone about her since her visit here the other night?" Beryl asked.

"I never speak with anyone besides Polly if I can help it. And I never have spoken with anyone at all about Polly. Like I said, her visits were a secret."

"Have you heard anything that has been going on here in Walmsley Parva this week?" Beryl said. "Does any gossip reach you up here in the projectionist's booth or at your lodgings perhaps?"

"I live on my own in a small cottage not far from the Wallingford Estate. I keep to myself. It's easier that way. Why are you asking me all of these questions?"

"I am so sorry to tell you this but Polly was found dead two days ago. She died sometime in the night after she left the cinema."

"Dead?" Walter dropped his hands from the film reel and faced Beryl. "How can she be dead? I don't believe you." His voice dropped to a whisper and even with what little she could see of his expression behind the tin mask she knew from his voice that Polly's death had affected him.

"I am so sorry but that is the truth. I had no idea you didn't know."

"How did she die? Was it the flu coming round again?" Beryl understood his concern. So many healthy young people had been fine at breakfast and dead by teatime during the Spanish Influenza pandemic.

"No. She was struck on the head by something hard and her body was found in a field on the Wallingford Estate."

"Someone killed her?" he asked.

"It appears that way," Beryl said. "Do you have any notion why anyone would have done such a thing?"

"Norman must have done it. No one else would have had reason to harm her as far as I know." Walter sagged against the bench as if he could no longer support his own weight.

"I'm so sorry to be the bearer of bad news. I appreciate your time, and if you think of anything else or if you just want to talk you can locate me at the Beeches." Beryl gave Walter a slight nod and left him in the projectionist's booth with his cans of film and his thoughts.

Chapter 23

Edwina couldn't help but believe that all that had occurred sprang from events surrounding the Wallingford Estate. She would liked to have said she was absolutely clear about who did what and when, that her mind was a sharp as it ever had been and her memory was completely unsullied. But that was not really the complete truth. Many little details of those days were slightly hazy in her mind. She didn't think it was her age however, as much as it was a deliberate attempt to forget. Those years held little appeal for most and she had heard others say they were unclear on much of what had happened during the war years. Fortunately she had always been an avid record keeper and note taker.

Her father had impressed upon her from her girlhood that the mind could be fickle but an accurate real time recording of events was not, so long as the parties doing the recording were truthful in their writings. He had encouraged her to keep a journal from the time she could write and she had made it a habit to do so. Many was the time she had found the act distressing. So much of the past few years were crowded with memories one wished to forget.

Edwina had taken to storing her war year diaries out of sight. She had no need to consult them and even less desire. The same could be said for the registers she kept on the Land Army girls and the notes in the margins as to the goings-on at the Wallingford Estate. When the organization had been disbanded the year before no one had come to ask for the records and Edwina had not volunteered them. In the first place, she would not have known where to offer to send them. In the second, she never did like to surrender her documentation of anything.

She left Charles Jarvis's chambers and set out for home. Anyone who happened to see her would have remarked that Edwina was certainly moving with more vigor than was her habit of late. They might also have remarked that she seemed to be lost in thought as she hurried in the direction of the Beeches.

Crumpet capered about under her feet from the moment she stepped through the front door. He had not appreciated being cooped up in the house on a fine day. Ordinarily Edwina would have felt guilty and would have accompanied him outside to throw a ball for him or to toss a stick by way of apology. But Edwina had larger matters on her mind and held the door for him to have a good romp on his own. It was light outside and she had no worry he would come to grief when the odd passing motorist could clearly see him.

Edwina made for the library on the side of the hallway opposite the sitting room without bothering to remove her coat or hat. She had taken to closing off all the rooms save the kitchen, her bedroom, and the sitting room as a matter of financial necessity. It cost a great deal to heat the whole house. Besides, she hadn't the energy to sweep and dust everywhere after Polly had left her employ. It had been the sensible thing to cover the furniture with white cloths and to pretend the room did not exist. It was a pity though she thought to herself as she entered it for the first time in several weeks.

The library had always been one of her favorite rooms at the

Beeches. She loved the long windows overlooking the gardens beyond and the floor-to-ceiling bookcases that lined the walls. The fireplace tiles had enchanted her as a child with their hand-painted images of mythological creatures. She paused for a moment and ran her finger lightly over her favourite, a phoenix rising from a bed of ashes.

Edwina crossed to a bookcase in the corner and bent down to a shelf near the bottom where she had secreted away the Land Army diaries and ledgers. She pulled out the journal labelled for the months encompassing Agnes' disappearance and also three ledgers chronicling the activities of the Land Girls on her roster. She carried the pile to the wide mahogany desk and pulled out the chair. In a matter of moments she was lost in the past remembering how she had felt to be someone contributing to the war effort in a meaningful way.

She squinted over her handwriting and the columns of times and dates and places. She recognized the names of girls she hadn't thought of in some time. It wasn't long before her gaze landed on Polly's name and Agnes'. There in black and white was what she had been trying to remember. Did those two ever work together? Did they have reason to spend time with Norman on the Wallingford Estate? What had their day-to-day responsibilities been like? How had they spent their time?

Agnes, as Edwina had remembered, was a gang leader. In fact she ended up in charge of two separate groups just before she disappeared. One of the other gang leaders had completed her year leaving the Wallingford Estate shorthanded. At the time there were few girls with leadership qualities and Hortense and Edwina had agreed to double up Agnes' responsibilities since she was so capable and the girls liked her well enough.

She had four girls who answered to her, which was at least one more than most other gang leaders. She hadn't ever complained about the added responsibility and Edwina had never heard a word against her from the other girls. Two of her charges were adept at milking and often were assigned to tasks involving the dairy. They milked in the morning and again in the evening and also turned their hand to some of the animal husbandry like caring for ailing cows or bottle-feeding orphaned calves.

The other two girls were assigned to agricultural duties. Polly had been one of them. They worked the fields, plowing and weeding, harvesting as the crops came in. The dairy girls did not have any overlapping duties with Norman Davies as far as Edwina could see. The agricultural girls, however, did. In fact they worked with him almost daily and Edwina had made a note on one of the ledger pages that Norman was becoming a very responsible part of the establishment himself despite his initial frustration with being left out of the action abroad. Edwina remembered as she read the notes that she had worried about his attitude and had discussed as much with Hortense at the time the estate opened.

Agnes had a job of her own above and beyond supervising the others. It was a cold and lonely business and it was a testament to her character that she had volunteered to drive the milk float. Early each and every morning, seven days each week, Agnes loaded cans of milk onto a wagon and hitched it to a resentful pony. At first Agnes had been scared to death of the creature who tried to kick and to bite her. But over time they seemed to have formed an understanding and Agnes could be heard talking soothingly to Joe as they headed out to make the deliveries.

Each day Agnes and Joe would amble as quickly through the village as Joe's short, arthritic legs could manage. They stopped at all the houses and businesses along her route that requested milk and left the amount that could be spared according to supply and to the ages and occupants of the premises. Edwina ran her finger along the rows of writing chronicling the names and quantities requested. The route was long and took Agnes hours to complete each day.

Much of the year she set out in darkness but she always came back with a cheerful countenance. Edwina remembered remarking on the girl's attitude one day upon her return. Agnes had said how much she preferred the great outdoors to the stifling conditions in a factory. She was glad to do her bit where she could see off into the distance and breathe fresh air.

Her comments that morning were one of the reasons Edwina had found it so difficult to credit her disappearance. The ledgers brought it all back in a flood of memories. The last few days had caused her to turn increasingly to the past in her mind and she found it was not a place she was enjoying visiting. She ran her finger along the column containing the names of the properties Agnes routinely visited for deliveries and Edwina envisioned her route. She was still hunched over the table concentrating on the path Agnes would have travelled when she heard the front door open. Dusk was beginning to fall. Beryl had arrived home in time for tea.

"I'm in here," she said, pitching her voice loudly enough to be heard down the hall. "Come see what I've found."

Edwina barely heard the footsteps behind her before she felt a blazing pain on the back of her head. She never felt the pain of her body toppling forward and her face striking the desk in front of her.

Chapter 24

Beryl had not felt so worried since her first attempt at a transcontinental aeroplane journey had ended with the need for a parachute. Dr. Nelson had arrived only moments after she telephoned and she liked to think she sounded cool and collected when his wife had answered at his home. She rather thought she had not.

"How is she?" Beryl asked as soon as Dr. Nelson closed Edwina's bedroom door quietly behind himself and stepped out into the adjacent hallway.

"Resting. I don't believe she'll suffer any lasting damage but she will have a tremendous headache," Dr. Nelson said. "She was very, very fortunate not to have been killed. What on earth are the two of you playing at?"

"We aren't playing at anything. We are investigating a murder. Clearly we've been making progress since Ed has been attacked not once but twice," Beryl said.

"There is only Miss Davenport's word for the notion that she was attacked the last time."

"Nonsense, she still has bruising along her neck."

"I saw it myself. I think it far more likely her scarf got entangled in some branches of some sort. The logical explanation for what occurred was that she panicked, and being a typical old maid assumed someone was assaulting her."

"You believe she made up being attacked in her own garden because she has never married?"

"It has been my experience that spinsters have tendencies towards hysteria. I have always found Miss Davenport to be a reasonable woman but there comes a time when even the most sensible of women begin to display signs of a nervous or fanciful disposition."

"Are you saying Edwina is losing her wits because she has never married and she is slightly older than you are?"

"I am saying there is really no crime in Walmsley Parva. At least none that you two are qualified to investigate."

"You just saw for yourself that there is someone here about attacking women. Constable Gibbs is not making an effort to get to the bottom of it."

"Like I told Miss Davenport, she has likely attracted an unstable sort of person with her advertisement in the newspapers. I doubt it is more than that. You should both stay indoors at night for the time being and make a point of locking up even when you are home."

"Are you forgetting that Polly was killed? If that isn't a crime I don't know what is."

"You've already been told by Constable Gibbs, Polly wasn't killed. She died in a tragic accident. I examined her body myself and the wounds on her head were consistent with hitting it on the rock found near her body in the field." Dr. Nelson shook his head at Beryl. "If you don't stop behaving foolishly I expect your friend will suffer another tragedy before long."

"You think this is our fault?" Beryl asked. "You think we should blame ourselves for what has happened to Edwina?"

"I should think you should blame yourself. I have it on good authority that you went into the village and started spreading the ridiculous story that two women, especially those of your age, are agents of the Crown. Not only that, you asserted that you were highly skilled operatives. Your friend has suffered a great deal of loss in the last few years. I believe your stories caused her to become delusional. I am very much afraid that if you don't desist in your meddling and fabrications she will end up entirely losing touch with reality." Dr. Nelson stared at Beryl and waggled a recriminating finger in her direction.

"You think I am driving Edwina mad?" Beryl asked.

"I am cautioning you that she is very vulnerable and that you may well be responsible for her current difficulties. I have known Miss Davenport for years upon years and she was managing her life very competently before you arrived. I would not be surprised if something about you stirs up difficulties wherever you go."

"You wouldn't be the first man to say so."

"I hope for Miss Davenport's sake that I am the last. Keep an eye on her and don't encourage her in her delusions. Rest and tranquillity are what she needs to return to her usual sensible self." Dr. Nelson headed for the stairs then stopped and turned back towards her. "If you don't follow my advice I cannot be responsible for her recovery. I'll see myself out."

The light outside had faded to sooty darkness by the time Edwina heard the doctor take his leave and Beryl quietly turn the doorknob and enter her room. She turned her face towards Beryl and her eyes squinted at the hall light streaming in through the door.

"You're awake?" Beryl asked, pulling a straight-back chair over to the side of the bed from its usual place at the dressing table.

"It would be hard not to be with the doctor here fussing over me and then the two of you having that heated conversation just outside my door."

"You heard that, did you?" Beryl asked, reaching over to straighten the coverlet.

"Every word."

"Since you were the subject of the conversation, I suppose it was only right that you overheard it. Do you think we should follow the doctor's advice and leave well enough alone?"

"You mean should we stop asking questions and investigating?" Edwina said.

"Yes. Should we take the constable's word for it and believe that Agnes' disappearance was nothing to be concerned about and that Polly's death was a tragic accident?"

"I hope that question is not because you agree with that condescending man that I am a delusional, withered-up old hag with a bad case of nerves?" Edwina used her hands to hoist herself into a half-seated position. "You don't think I was making up the attack in the garden, do you?"

"Of course not. I wish I could say I was surprised by Dr. Nelson's attitude but I can't say that I haven't encountered his sort of narrow-minded resistance to independent women before. You're lucky it isn't twenty years earlier. He might have had you shut away in a madhouse for suggesting anything had happened that he did not like to hear."

"Dr. Nelson has always been a bit of a know-it-all. I can't say that I liked the way he handled things when either of my parents began ailing." Edwina winced as she adjusted her head against the iron headboard of the bed. "I am not the least bit impressed with his diagnosis in my case."

"So you wish to continue with the investigation?" Beryl asked. Her face was uncharacteristically pinched and Edwina was surprised to see lines crinkling Beryl's forehead.

"What else are we to do? I assume there was another attack on me since I find myself unexpectedly tucked up in bed with a blazing headache and the doctor fussing about without my recollection as to how any of that came to take place."

"Don't you remember anything about what happened?"

"I was sitting at the desk in the library reading over some records when I heard you come in for tea. The next thing I knew there was a terrific thump at the back of my head."

"I should say there was. It wasn't me that came upon you sitting at the desk. I found you sometime later slumped over it, facedown, knocked out cold."

"So I was attacked?"

"Unless you managed to give yourself that great walloping, then yes, you were assaulted again. For a quiet lady such as yourself this has been quite a week."

"Did you see the ledgers? The diaries?" Edwina asked.

"All I saw was you sagging over the desk. There was nothing on it but a pen holder, an ink bottle, and a paper knife we should both be grateful the assailant did not decide to use instead of whatever he or she did find to hand."

"The ledgers were from the Wallingford Estate. They were the registers I kept for the Land Army along with all of my notes about the routes and the girls and their responsibilities on the estate." Edwina closed her eyes once more.

"Well they aren't there anymore. Whomever coshed you on the head took them with him or her." Beryl jumped to her feet and began pacing the floor. "The assailant must have thought there was something in them that could connect him or her to what happened to Agnes or Polly or maybe both."

"But what could there have been in there?" Edwina asked. "I read them over myself and didn't see anything in my notes that stuck out at me."

"Whoever took them likely didn't know exactly what was written down in there. They could have assumed it held a secret they wished to keep. Do you feel well enough to remember what you read?"

"I'll try," Edwina said. "There were mostly notes about the routines at the Wallingford Estate. Who did which sort of jobs and when they did them and with whom."

"Did you see anything of note?"

"Agnes and Polly worked together. Agnes was the supervisor of two work gangs and Polly was on the one involving agriculture."

"That makes me think of something Hortense told me this afternoon. She said she thought Agnes and Polly and Norman all knew each other on the estate and that there may have been some difficulty between Norman and Agnes. Hortense saw him grabbing her by the arm behind one of the barns."

"She never said at the time of Agnes' disappearance. I wonder why that was."

"She indicated she thought he was interested in Agnes romantically and that she did not reciprocate."

"I doubt it. As far as I knew he only ever had eyes for Polly."

"Hortense said she thought Polly was jealous. She said she got the impression that one of the reasons Polly began working at the estate was to keep an eye on Norman. Hortense thought he might throw her over for one of the more sophisticated city girls who joined the Land Army," Beryl said.

"I can see how Polly might be worried about a thing like that but I don't think that Norman was a young man with a roving eye. I would have made a note of a thing like that in the ledger and all I saw about him was how he seemed to be adjusting to the idea that his service on the farm was more valuable to the war effort than serving overseas," Edwina said.

"It would have seemed irksome for many young men to be kept at home while others were able to claim the supposed glory of battle." Beryl let out a soft sigh. "Poor Norman. He was one of the lucky ones and I'm sure it doesn't feel like that to him even now,"

"We know it doesn't. Remember yesterday he said he thought his lack of foreign service was the reason Polly wanted to cut off her relationship with him," Edwina said. "I suppose that sort of a wound to a man's pride could have made him turn violent. He always was a bit of a hothead when it came to his reputation."

"But could he have thought there was something in your ledgers that pointed to him harming Polly or Agnes? Everyone in Walmsley Parva knew he had an interest in Polly. He needn't have stolen the ledgers to keep that a secret."

"I can't think what it would have been and now I am not sure we will ever know. If the ledgers are gone I can't check them over to see what might have been of value," Edwina said. "Do you think the person who attacked me was trying to hurt me or were they trying to get the ledgers without me knowing their identity?"

"I have no idea. The assailant could have snuck back into the house later I suppose if they didn't want to hurt you. I think we'd best assume the worst and be pleasantly surprised if no one really tried to murder you," Beryl said. "Although, after what happened to Polly, I don't think we have much cause to believe someone did not wish you real harm."

"Do you think a woman could have done this?" Edwina asked. "I feel like the power of the blow was enormous."

"With the right weapon there is no reason a little girl couldn't have done it," Beryl said. "All you would need is something with a good decent heft that you could wrap your hand around and really swing."

"Something like the spanner you told me about at Blackburn's Garage?" Edwina asked.

"Something very much like that. We can't rule anyone out without more information."

"Then we'd best get back to asking questions."

"Are you certain you'll feel up to it? I can go on without you if you need to spend tomorrow in bed resting."

"If I am to maintain the reputation you've given me as a highly trained and effective agent in His Majesty's service I'd best be on my feet tomorrow morning and back on the trail.

After all, if Dr. Nelson is willing to say such disparaging things to my dear friend, what will he be saying around the village?"

"Then I suppose we had best divide up the suspects. Who's on your list?" Beryl asked.

"I'm afraid Norman is at the top of my list. He has reason to be angry with Polly if she threw him over, and the information you gathered from Hortense makes me wonder just what he might have had to do with Agnes' disappearance. He was also on the spot for each occasion."

"Do you want to interview him again directly?"

"I'm not sure. After today, I confess I am a little afraid of going out to his cottage on my own."

"You could always ask your Mr. Jarvis to accompany you. I'm sure he would be delighted to do so."

"I've already told you, he's not my Mr. Jarvis. Besides, I thought you said we needed to consider everyone a suspect until we ruled him or her out through careful enquiry. That should include Charles."

"As you like."

"Who is your chief suspect?" Edwina asked.

"I would dearly love it to be that odious Mr. Mumford but I am rather afraid it just might be Michael Blackburn."

"Because of Norah's tale about his obsession with Agnes?"

"That and a couple of other things. I am not convinced he wasn't the one driving my car when Polly would have been leaving the cinema if she stayed for the late show like Walter the projectionist said that she did," Beryl said.

"From what Norah had to say he might have been off-kilter enough to do anything. Who's to say he didn't behave the same way towards Polly that he did with Agnes?"

"You think he might be the man Polly threw over Norman for?"

"Why not? He's handsome and young and has a good job that doesn't involve either working a farm or working in domestic service. And he served overseas."

"Which makes him the sort of man Norman thought she was interested in."

"Exactly."

"I think I'll go talk to Mr. Mumford in the morning just to satisfy my curiosity. Maybe I will have luck on my side and he will confess to Polly's murder with almost no pressure," Beryl said smiling. "What do you want to do?"

"I think I shall go into town and make sure everyone sees me and knows I am still amongst the living. My presence may serve to unnerve someone enough to let something slip that they might not have done without me appearing." Edwina tried to put on a brave face. She wanted to interview other suspects but she wasn't sure she was quite ready to tackle anyone head-on anytime soon. She didn't wish to admit it to herself, let alone Beryl that she was well and truly rattled.

Just outside the doorway footsteps fell along the corridor. Edwina's head jerked in the direction of the sound. Beryl placed a steadying hand on Edwina's trembling one clutching at the coverlet as. Crumpet dashed inside and leapt onto the bed. He crawled onto Edwina's lap and lay down with his chin on her chest. Edwina slid back down under the covers and heaved a deep sigh.

"I'll let the two of you sleep and we'll be back on the case in the morning."

Chapter 25

Beryl awoke as the door behind her opened and left her unsupported. Crumpet ran over her lap and scampered down the hall, his toenails clicking on the polished wooden floorboards.

"Did you spend the night sitting here?" Edwina asked.

"I couldn't sleep in my bed wondering if someone was going to try to make another attempt on your life, Ed. I feel like no matter what you said last night that you wouldn't have become involved in all this if it weren't for me telling whoppers at the post office."

"You sound like Dr. Nelson. If I didn't want to be involved I would have said so. I am a grown woman with a mind of my own. One needn't go cavorting about the globe in men's trousers to develop opinions and the moral strength to express them." Edwina stepped over her friend and started down the hallway. She paused at the top of the stairs. "But if you really want to make it up to me you can be the one to fix the breakfast this morning for a change."

Edwina regretted her request almost immediately. Toast was beyond Beryl's ken. What she had done to the eggs was best left unmentioned. She certainly couldn't be trusted in future with the making of tea. Edwina had tried to explain there was more to the process than thrice dunking a scantly filled tea ball in tepid water but Beryl couldn't hear her over the spattering from the stove. What had become of the sausages was crueler than the fate of the pigs from whence they came. Edwina took one look at her plate and claimed her injuries had left her without an appetite.

Beryl cracked a kitchen window in an effort to clear the acrid smell of smoke by the time they returned home. Edwina accepted a lift to the center of the village. While she prided herself on following through with her commitments and putting on a brave face, the truth was her head was still pounding and the trees and buildings along the way looked a bit wobbly.

Beryl took no notice of Edwina's discomfort as she whizzed along the county lane. Edwina could just imagine what her friend would have been like seated behind the wheel of an aeroplane, the propeller beginning to spin and the sound of the engine filling the cockpit. She imagined Beryl was in her element at such times and she felt the creeping dread that the delights and intrigues of Walmsley Parva would not hold Beryl's interest for very long. Despite the whirlwind she stirred up round her, Beryl was great company and Edwina felt slightly queasy at the thought her friend might jet off once more.

"Just here will do, thank you. I should not like it getting round that I required a lift if we are to put about the story that I am uninjured and back on the case in top form," Edwina said. Beryl pulled over to the side of the road just out of sight of the village proper. "I'll meet you back at the Beeches."

"Delightful." Beryl fished into her pocket and drew out a fistful of coins and notes that she handed to Edwina. "What if you use some shopping as a cover for being in the village? You could buy yourself a new hat."

"What would I want with a new hat?" Edwina asked.

"Didn't I mention?" Beryl asked. "The hat you were wearing yesterday was rather badly done by during the attack. It was positively bashed in. I don't think it will look well on you anymore."

"I can pay for my own hats, Beryl."

'Don't be so prickly. It isn't as if I came by the money by honest hard work."

"How did you come by it then?" Edwina wasn't entirely certain she wanted to know once the question popped unbidden and ill considered from her lips.

"I bested a vulgar man who was a fellow guest at my hotel at a game of cards. He was a liar and a cheat and he deserved his losses."

"You won the money by gambling?" Edwina felt a bit light-headed. She liked to think she was broader minded than many women in her social position but gambling with unsavory men was not something she felt she could condone.

"The car, too," Beryl said. giving Edwina a wicked grin. "The poor fellow was so vexed at being beaten by a woman as well as a foreigner at that that he couldn't stop doubling the bet. In the end he was left sitting at the card table with nothing but his smalls. I don't suppose you'd like to make a gift of a very handsome newfangled wristwatch to your Mr. Jarvis by any chance? They're all the latest thing now. Inspired by pilots, you know."

There could be no doubt; Edwina felt a bit faint. She told herself it was the bump on her head, not her shocked sensibilities. If smalls meant in American what it meant in British English she was not sure she could look Beryl in the eye. The very idea of it made her feel peculiar. She took a calming breath and forced herself to respond.

"I believe he has a rather fine pocket watch already. And he's not my Mr. Jarvis," Edwina said as she opened the motorcar door.

"Just as well. We may need to pawn it before long," Beryl said. With that she peeled off, leaving Edwina standing in a swirl of dust contemplating how she would live down the shame of anyone knowing Beryl had pawned anything, let alone a nearly naked man's watch. She leaned up against a nearby walnut tree and gathered her wits.

She would miss her hat but truth be told it had become a bit of an eyesore. A new one would be a delightful luxury. And it wasn't as if she had engaged in any immoral card dealings. Besides, she told herself, if Beryl called the man a cheat then it was a certainty that he was one. Perhaps he deserved to lose his motorcar and his finery. He might have gained them by swindling someone else out of them.

With a new spring in her step and the idea of a cheekily fashionable hat filling her thoughts, she made her way into the village. Up ahead the smell of fresh bread drifted from the bakery. Horses pulling wagons filled with coal and pumpkins and sacks of grain trundled past, their hooves clopping against the cobblestone street. Her head began to throb with the noise of it all. Before she could decide where to stop she saw young Jack the newsboy standing at his usual corner calling out the headlines. She had meant to buy a newspaper when she reached the village, and her conversation with Beryl had driven the thought straight out of her mind.

"Good morning. Jack. I'll take one please," she said stopping before him. Jack always seemed to her to be the sort of boy that would rise above his circumstances given a bit of a chance. He made her think of the novels in which a poor child with no connections rises up through a series of strange fortunes to become the owner of a thriving factory empire. "Anything interesting in the news today?"

"You are, if you don't mind me saying so, miss. Everyone is talking about you." He bobbed his head and snatched off his cap when she dismissed his offer of change for the amount she'd paid for the paper. If Beryl had provided her with ill-gotten gains to spend, she was most definitely going to use the money in ways that soothed her conscience. Jack would do nicely as a first attempt.

"Whatever for?" Edwina asked.

"Folks say you took a nasty thump to the head and the doctor had to bring you back from the very brink of death. All the while a blood-thirsty murderer prowled your house waiting for the chance to finish you off." Edwina wasn't pleased with the look of glee on Jack's face as he shared the tale of her difficulties. In fact she worried a little about his moral centre. Were all boys his age so gleeful when confronted by the possibility of intrigue and violence?

"As you can see I am no worse for the wear no matter what people are saying." Edwina held out her gloved hand for the paper. "Which people were saying that I had been at death's door?"

"The butcher, Mrs. Mumford. Miss Rathbone, of course. Everyone will be by teatime, I should think." He jammed his cap back onto his head and started to turn his back before changing his mind. "If you don't mind me asking, Miss Davenport, are you working on the case with your friend, Miss Helliwell?"

"We are collaborating on an investigation. Why do you want to know?"

"It's just that I met her the other day and she said that there might be something I could do to help with the investigation. I see lots of goings-on all day here at the corner and more besides. I'm out all hours." He shifted his weight from one foot to the other excitedly.

"What would a young man who is as hardworking as you be doing out all hours instead of heading home to rest up for the next day?" Edwina asked.

"Like I told Miss Helliwell, I fetch me dad from the pub at

closing time. Mum worries he won't find his way home on his own so she sends me. He's there most every night." Edwina looked at Jack's dark eyes the color of her nightly cup of cocoa and felt a wave of sadness at the life he was leading. She was even gladder she had given him a little over the amount for the newspaper. "I see plenty of things on the way home from there. I'd like to help Miss Helliwell any way I can. And you too, of course."

"Did you happen to walk up the street past the cinema four nights ago about the time the pub closed?"

"Like I said, I fetch him every night. Four nights ago would have been the night Polly Watkins died, wasn't it?" he asked. "I saw her, you know."

"You did?"

"Sure I did. I see her all the time."

"Do you remember what was she doing?"

"The same thing she does several times each week. She was getting into that cab Michael Blackburn drives."

"She took rides from Michael Blackburn several times each week?"

"Sure. She had been taking them for a while."

"Are you sure Michael was the one driving the cab?"

"I saw him clear as day. He was parked just past the corner where the cinema is. Right under a street lamp. And he got out and opened the door for Polly like a gentleman when she came down the alley."

"Did you see where she was coming from?"

"I didn't. If she was leaving the cinema she would have been round the other side of the street, wouldn't she? I don't know what business she would have had coming round from behind the building."

"Was anyone with her besides Michael?"

"I didn't see anyone else that night. I think she was all by her lonesome but Dad and me were getting off home as quick as we could so I might have missed someone, I suppose."

"Did she have anyone with her any other night?"

"Not with her, no. But sometimes Norman Davies, the man who delivers the fruit and veg to the greengrocer, would be hanging around trying to talk to her just before she got into the cab. Only a few days ago they were arguing and he grabbed her by the arm before Michael Blackburn pulled him off of her."

"Are you quite certain about all of this, Jack? It is very important that you tell me only the exact truth. Miss Helliwell will not be impressed by lies to increase the dramatic quality of your story."

"I swear on my sister's life." Jack drew an X with his finger across his chest. "Will you tell Miss Helliwell what I said? Will you make sure she knows I'm the one who told you?"

"I will make sure she hears about it straightaway. This may be very important. I am very grateful that you told me."

"I'll keep my peepers peeled for anything else then, shall I?"

"Only if it is safe to do so. I shouldn't like to hear you too had been thumped on the head and brought to the very brink of death by a blood-thirsty madman." She gave Jack a nod and turned on her heel. The delights of a new hat would have to wait. She needed to speak with Michael Blackburn.

Chapter 26

Mr. Mumford kept late hours. Beryl knew he didn't head to the cinema until at least noontime, based on her conversation with Eva the ticket seller. It was easy enough to track him down to his small but comfortable house on a lane that ran parallel to the high street. She knocked on the door of the cottage and waited briefly for the door to open.

"Miss Helliwell, what a surprise," he said, looking up and down the lane. "Are you here without Miss Davenport?"

"Edwina was otherwise engaged this morning and I had a few questions I wanted to ask. Hope it won't be a problem that I came on my own?"

"Not so long as you aren't here to pay a call upon my wife. Minnie has gone out on her errands. She is always busy with one thing or another."

"She must have a lot to keep her busy with her business, I shouldn't wonder," Beryl said, stepping over the threshold and following Mr. Mumford through a door right off the front hallway. The same sensibility that filled the Silver Spoon Tearoom could be seen in the chintz festooning every available surface of the Mumford home.

In fact, Mr. Mumford, with his craggy face and angular appearance overall, seemed at odds with his surroundings. He offered Beryl a chair and then folded down onto a dainty wingback clearly designed for the far more diminutive Mrs. Mumford and positioned right next the window overlooking the street.

"We are both busy, busy people. She with the tearoom and I with the cinema. In addition, we have our pastimes like her Women's Institute involvement and my cinematography group." He reached out to the curtain with a knobby finger and twitched it out of the way to view the street. "So since you aren't here to visit with Minnie, what brings you to see me?"

"I wanted to ask you about your cinematographer's organization. I understand you often encourage aspiring actors and actresses to join. Is that true?" Beryl leaned back into the chair and appeared to be prepared to stay for a while. She gave herself a mental pat on the back as he squirmed slightly in his chair. She didn't want to distress Mrs. Mumford unnecessarily or cause undue marital discord but putting him ill at ease might convince him to be expeditiously forthcoming with the information she requested.

"Were you thinking about joining the group? We would be flattered to have you but I'm afraid you might find our efforts amateurish compared to your experience on camera."

"I don't know that I would say that. Yes, it's true I've been on a variety of newsreels but I've never turned my hand to any sort of acting. I simply show up and do whatever it is that I do. I simply perform as myself and it seems to work just fine for the journalist's purposes. What you do is completely different."

"How do you know so much about my organization?" he asked, peering out the window once more.

"Polly Watkins told me all about it when I first met her. She was very enthusiastic about her involvement."

"That was not my understanding of how things stood with her. In fact, she had not participated for some time."

"I'm very surprised to hear it. She made it sound like she was very active and that there were all sorts of benefits to being a member."

"Like what?" Mr. Mumford's tone grew wary and he glanced out the window again.

"She mentioned the encouragement you gave to women to keep trying to get jobs as actresses. She said you were happy to take photographs of them to use in their portfolios." Beryl noticed Mr. Mumford visibly stiffen. "I understood you even generously provided the club members with free admission to the cinema in order to stay up with the latest trends in film."

"What of it?" Beads of sweat welled up above Mr. Mumford's salt and pepper colored eyebrows.

"I wished to compliment you on this wellspring of generosity. It isn't every man who would be so giving of his time and energy to help out struggling young women in the pursuit of their dreams."

"I like to think of myself as a sort of quiet benefactor. A benevolent uncle type if you will."

"A great deal of the credit should go to Mrs. Mumford too, should it not? It isn't every wife that would be so understanding of the time you freely spend with a variety of attractive young ladies."

"What are you implying?"

"I am merely supposing that your wife is an extraordinary woman and that she must hold you in the highest regard if she has no compunction about your involvement in an organization such as yours. I should like to congratulate her on her bighearted attitude. I should very much like to know I have her approval before I could consider joining."

"I can't see any reason for you to go to the trouble to do that. Minnie is, as you say, a bighearted sort of person and you would only embarrass her by making a fuss over her generosity."

"The very least I could do would be to thank her in advance for all the money you would be saving me on cinema tickets.

Considering all the times Polly visited for free I can't imagine that wasn't a monetary sacrifice on Mrs. Mumford's part as well as your own."

"I'd really rather you didn't say a thing about it to her." Mr. Mumford shifted forward in his chair and planted both hands on his trouser-covered knees. "Now that I come to think of it, I'm not sure we have any openings at this time for new members of the cinematographer's club." He stood and gestured toward the door.

"I must say, I'm surprised at your attitude, Mr. Mumford. I should have thought you'd be eager for new members. Not to sound callous, but shouldn't there be an opening recently vacated by Polly?" Beryl crossed one long leg over the other and slouched even farther down in her chair. "This really is a comfortable room. I shall tell Mrs. Mumford when she returns and finds me sitting here how much I have enjoyed speaking with her husband in her delightfully welcoming front parlor." Mr. Mumford sat back down across from her.

"What is it that you want?"

"I want to know if you killed Polly Watkins." There was no sense beating around the gooseberry bush. Mr. Mumford was too eager to get rid of her. Beryl was certain no matter how bright her smile, Mrs. Mumford was at least a bit suspicious of her husband. If he had her complete faith he'd have no reason to be so distressed to think of his wife finding out about Beryl's visit or about the details of his cinematographer's club. His eyes bulged from his head most satisfactorily at her question and the beads of sweat that had gathered on his brow tumbled down his cheeks and ran along the sides of his nose. He was far too uncomfortable for her to think he had nothing to hide.

"You think I had something to do with Polly's death? Don't be daft. It was an accident and everyone except you and Miss Davenport know it." He pulled a handkerchief out of his trouser pocket and dabbed at his face.

"Insulting me is not likely to make me think better of you. I'd say your interest in the cinema is not as wholesome as you would like your wife to think and that you are enticing young girls into compromising positions. I think Polly got tired of you pressuring her in unseemly ways and she threatened to tell your wife what had been going on. It wouldn't surprise me if you killed her to keep her from saying something."

"I take offense to your totally spurious suggestion."

"Most people are offended by the notion of murder, Mr. Mumford."

"But you haven't any proof that I did anything to Polly."

"I know Polly was a member of your organization and so was the missing girl, Agnes Rollins. Did she threaten to tell your wife about your behavior, too?"

"Now you are being ridiculous. I don't know who you've been talking to, but if Polly was murdered, as you seem to believe she was, there is at least one person who makes a much better suspect than me."

"I find that hard to believe, Mr. Mumford. Look at you all adither looking out the window every few seconds worried your wife will come home and find you in a compromising position."

"It's the God's honest truth. Polly told me all about trying to end things with that young man Norman Davies but he wasn't having any of it."

"That's not what Mr. Davies says. He says she stopped seeing him and that he was heartbroken about it. She was the love of his life. I am disinclined to believe he would harm her."

"He wasn't heartbroken. What he was, in fact, was a bully and he couldn't begin to accept that she might wish to be with another. She was ready to move on and so tired of his persistent pursuit of her that she actually asked me for advice on how to be rid of him without making too much of a fuss."

"Are you admitting that you are someone with expertise on

how to be rid of someone without calling attention to that fact?" Beryl asked. "As far as I'm concerned that makes you a person of interest in the unexplained disappearance of Agnes Rollins." Mr. Mumford flinched.

"I don't mean to imply that I am some sort of an expert at intimidating people. It's more that Polly saw me as a man of the world, you understand, and she thought I would be able to make some useful suggestions."

"I see. So what did you advise?"

"I said she should tell him if he didn't desist in his attentions she would go to the police with what she knew."

"Did she really know something that would get him into legal difficulties?"

"I assumed she did. Everyone in the village knows that he is a shifty sort of a fellow."

"I haven't heard anyone call him shifty in the least. In which way does everyone think his character flawed?"

"I like to imagine as a man of some standing in the community I am above spreading common gossip." Mr. Mumford pursed his unattractively thin lips. Beryl thought he looked like a sweaty snapping turtle.

"I think you have to ask yourself if you are enough of a gentleman to be arrested on suspicion of a murder you believe someone else committed. Because without a real reason to suspect Norman Davies, I'm afraid I still suspect you. After all, I only have your word for it that Polly had any sort of information to hold over her former sweetheart."

"I see your point. Perhaps as Polly is no longer able to be hurt by my lack of resolve I could be less vigilant in my stance."

"I thought you might be persuaded to be forthcoming. So let's hear it." Beryl tapped her fingers against the arm of the chair. "After all, if you hurry, I might be gone before your wife comes home."

"It was back in the war days, you see. Norman Davies was

working up at the Wallingford Estate. Not to put too fine a point on things, he was abusing the trust placed in him."

"In which way?"

"He was in charge of much of the warehousing and inventorying of the produce and livestock the estate raised. It was a position easy to take advantage of, if you know what I mean."

"I don't know that I do. He miscounted, misplaced, misappropriated?"

"All three. Nelson was running a good little business for himself stealing from the estate and selling meat and milk and veg on the black market. It was quite an operation."

"And Polly knew about it?"

"Well, she would have done, wouldn't she? She joined the Land Army herself and was there to see with her own eyes what was going on."

"You believe without a doubt that she was aware of Norman's underhandedness?"

"Why wouldn't I? She didn't defend him when I suggested she threaten to take that information to the police. She knew, all right. Besides, how would a humble lad like Norman Davies come up with the money to fund a farming venture of his own? Especially with the economy being as blighted as it is at present."

Beryl thought for a moment. It made perfect sense with what Edwina had told her she discovered the day before when speaking with her Mr. Jarvis. Polly had asked him about crimes committed during the war. As much as she would have liked Mr. Mumford to be involved in what happened to Polly, it seemed as though the right thing to do would be to question Norman Davies once more. Still with nothing but Mr. Mumford's word on the matter, Mr. Davies could simply deny any involvement. Why wouldn't he? She would need a little more detail in order to put the pressure on him to tell the truth.

"Do you know to whom he sold his stolen goods?" She detected a fresh runnel of sweat appearing on Mr. Mumford's brow. The poor man would be completely dehydrated before long at the rate he was perspiring. "You weren't involved yourself, were you?"

"I had no reason to be. How would I possibly benefit from making such a purchase?"

"Perhaps not in your cinema business but Mrs. Mumford might have had many uses in the tearoom for eggs, milk, and butter, mightn't she?"

"I shan't say anything about my wife's business. What I am willing to tell you is that first choice of anything would have gone to Sidney Poole the butcher and Gareth Scott the greengrocer."

"Why them?" Beryl asked.

"Sidney is Norman Davies's uncle and Gareth Scott was his father's oldest friend. He would have wanted their businesses to thrive and they would not have turned him in if they had been caught with black market foodstuffs. Not that anyone would have been likely to complain at the time. We all were grateful to be able to buy a few extras now and again."

"You've been most helpful, Mr. Mumford." Beryl stood and gave him her hand just as the front door pushed open and Mrs. Mumford called out a cheerful greeting. "Oh dear, it looks as though you shall have some explaining to do after all. I must be going."

Chapter 27

Michael was not at the garage when Edwina arrived. Instead she found him out on the village green sitting on a bench near the duck pond. The day had warmed nicely and the sun shone down pleasantly on her head, reminding her that she still needed to shop for a new hat.

"Good day, Michael. Mind if I sit for a moment?' Edwina asked, coming up alongside him.

"I'm glad of the company. Although I have to admit, I am surprised to see you. Everyone is saying you are laid up in bed with a dent the size of a duck egg in back of your skull."

"I just heard much the same thing from Jack the newsboy." Edwina paused. Plenty of people were sure to see her on the green. She needn't be afraid of Michael while sitting in plain sight like she was. Still, her stomach fluttered ferociously as she steeled herself for her next comment. "It wasn't the only interesting thing I heard from Jack though when I bought my paper just now."

"Really? Do tell what Jack had to say this morning that was as interesting as a lovely lady like yourself being coshed in her own home." Michael turned one of his famously charming grins on her and Edwina felt sorry for what she was about to say.

"He said he is called upon by his mum to collect his father from the pub most nights of the week."

"Jack's father had a bad war. Many's the man who seeks to blot out such memories in a bottle. But I do feel for the boy. It might be better if his father hadn't made it home." Michael picked at the grain of wood in the slats of the park bench with his hand. "That isn't exactly news though. Jack's been sent on that errand ever since his father was demobbed months ago."

"It wasn't fetching his father that was the news, although I was not aware of that. It was what he saw while doing so."

"Which was?"

"You."

"What about me?"

"You were seen giving a ride in your cab to Polly on the night she died."

"Maybe I did and maybe I didn't."

"Are you saying Jack was making up stories?"

"He may have been confused about the night he saw me. It has been a few days since Polly had her accident."

"It wasn't an accident, Michael. It was murder."

"Not according to Constable Gibbs."

"I'm sure it won't surprise you to know Constable Gibbs is not the highest ranking law officer in Great Britain."

"Even so, the boy was likely mistaken. I drive lots of people around in my cab. That's what I do."

"He claims to have seen you driving her from somewhere along the high street out of town on several occasions lately. Can you tell me where you picked her up and where you let her off?"

"I haven't said I took her anywhere in my cab. The word of a tired boy steering a drunken father down the road in the night is hardly a better judge of what I was doing than I am."

"Are you refuting his statement?"

"I'm telling you to mind your own business." Michael stood abruptly and strode off in the direction of the corner where Jack could generally be found. Edwina regretted mentioning the boy immediately. She set off following Michael at a discreet distance. Her knees wobbled with relief when Michael turned off at the garage instead of making for Jack.

She considered shopping for a hat but decided her head would only begin to ache worse if she actually tried any hats on. And where would the pleasure be in not trying on hats in a milliner's shop?

She made her way into the greengrocer instead where she purchased a sack of baking potatoes, a bunch of onions, and a peck of apples. The greengrocer, Gareth Scott, looked at her with trepidation when he announced the bill. Edwina was inordinately relieved to have the money from Beryl at the ready, no matter how she came to have it.

Norman Davies had gone to market a few villages over that day. Beryl was glad of the chance to take the car for a longer run. Beryl firmly believed an automobile like hers needed to be taken out and run at full tilt once in a while, much like a large dog. She imagined it languished if left cooped up too long and trips back and forth from the Beeches to the center of Walmsley Parva were not enough to satisfy its heart's desires. Or Beryl's if it came down to it. She was surprisingly content with village life thus far, but still she had to admit she would not find a stretch of open desert to race across going amiss after so many days poking slowly along country lanes.

The sun beat down through the windscreen and Beryl felt lighter in her heart than she had in some time. Finding Ed on the floor had been a harrowing experience but it had gotten the blood pumping in a way that had been sorely lacking in recent months. To be honest, longer than she could remember. She had no cause to complain about anytime when she considered the losses and difficulties so many others had suffered. But she couldn't deny she was glad to have something fresh blowing through her life.

She turned off towards Parnham St. Mary when she saw a wooden sign nailed askew to a nearly leafless tree. She ran along at full tilt for another mile or so then fetched up in a village clotted with carts and people and all manner of beasts crossing the road at the behest of grizzled old men holding ancient-looking crooks.

Beryl found a lay-by along the road and left the car under the gaze of a striped tabby cat whom Beryl was certain would leap onto its warm hood as soon as she was out of sight. Up ahead in the village square, tables and tents and stalls with striped curtains fluttering in the breeze filled every available space. Beryl wandered up and down stopping from time to time to look at eye-catching wares or to sample a bit of something that looked tasty.

After a few discreet inquiries she managed to locate Norman Davies and his cart filled with produce. She watched as he handed a net bag laden with two tidy cabbages to a rosy-cheeked young woman. From the way he lingered over handing it to her it didn't appear that he was as filled with grief as he might have been, considering the recent loss of his former sweetheart.

"Mr. Nelson, isn't it?" she asked.

"That's right. Do I know you? You look familiar."

"We haven't actually been introduced but you may have seen me around Walmsley Parva. I've moved into the Beeches with my good friend Edwina Davenport."

"I don't believe I have. But you do look familiar."

"It may be because I stood watch over Polly Watkins's body as Edwina went for help. I believe I spotted you staring at me the whole time I was out there on my own."

"I don't remember staring at you."

"You were looking out from the steps in front of your cottage. But don't let it worry you. It was becoming dark and you were likely unable to see me clearly."

"I'll take your word for it. What brings you all the way out here? You know we have a market day tomorrow in Walmsley Parva, don't you? My fruit and veg are justifiably famous but most folks find they can wait a day for them." Mr. Davies gave her a large smile, pleased it would seem by his own joke.

"Produce that you sell is why I am here, Mr. Davies. But actually, I am more interested not in what you are legitimately selling here today, but rather what you didn't have the right to sell back in days you worked at the Wallingford Estate." Beryl watched as Mr. Davies' smile faded from his face. She was having quite an adverse effect on the local male population.

"Am I supposed to know what you are talking about?" He turned his back on her and devoted considerable attention to aligning carrots in neat rows in their scuffed wooden crate.

"I could raise my voice so that you can more easily hear me. You might rather I keep it down. People in Walmsley Parva benefitted from your little side business but I am certain the people in the surrounding market towns would not look at it as kindly if you hadn't offered them the opportunity to partake of it as well." Beryl raised her gloved hand and shielded her eyes as she appraised the crowd surrounding them. Mr. Davies whirled round and faced her once more.

"All right, keep your voice down. What do you hope to gain out of dragging up that old business?" he asked.

"Miss Davenport and I are as committed as ever to discovering exactly what happened to Polly. Unfortunately, as is the case for so many women who meet with violence, the trail leads to a man who claimed to have esteemed her."

"I already told Miss Davenport that I loved Polly and wouldn't have hurt her for the world. I was trying to win her back."

"I understand that she was not pleased by your continuing

attentions. I also have it on good account that Polly asked someone she respected for advice on how to get rid of you once and for all. That person suggested she use what she knew about your black market business to pressure you to leave her alone."

"Really? Who would be talking rubbish like that?"

"I'm not sure it would be best for village relations to share the name with you."

"Suit yourself. It doesn't matter because it isn't true."

"What isn't true? That you stole produce and livestock from the Wallingford Estate or that Polly tried to blackmail you about it to keep quiet?" Mr. Davies looked down at the bushel basket of onions in front of him.

"That Polly would tell anyone." He looked up at her. "She just wouldn't do that."

"I heard she was well and truly done with you. What makes you so sure she wouldn't say anything?"

"Because she was involved in the thefts. And even if she didn't want to have anything to do with me anymore she wouldn't have wanted to land herself in trouble, too." Mr. Davies crossed his arms over his chest and leaned back against the side of his wagon. "Polly knew all about what was going on up at the Wallingford Estate. It was why she joined the Land Army in the first place."

"There were rumors that she joined because you were paying too much attention to the other young ladies on the estate and that she was jealous. I heard she joined to keep an eye on you."

"That's all talk. She was just as eager as I was to earn a bit of extra money. She wasn't jealous. She knew I chatted up the other girls to keep them on my side if anything came out. They would turn a blind eye for a man who told them things they wanted to hear and brought them the occasional present bought with his ill-gotten gains."

Beryl took a deep breath of crisp air and considered what she had already heard. His story made sense if she could verify that

Polly knew about the thefts. If Mr. Davies would be willing to tell her to whom he sold his items she might be able to verify what he claimed.

"Unless you have someone besides yourself who is willing to tell me that he or she knew that Polly was involved in what you were up to, I think you are still the very best suspect in her death."

"My uncle, Sidney Poole the butcher, will tell you. And the greengrocer, Mr. Scott, will say the same. They'll both let you know that Polly even made deliveries for me sometimes when I was held up at the farm."

"Yes, but they have reason to be loyal to you, don't they?" Beryl said. "Is there anyone who might not be as taken with you that could support your claims?"

"Mrs. Mumford. She bought plenty of milk and eggs. And she's never liked me none. She preferred to accept deliveries from Polly instead of me. She said my boots were always too filthy to appear in her precious tearoom, even at the back."

"Why would she admit to buying black market items to help out the likes of you though? I should think it would be in her best interest to lie."

"She offered to give Polly a brooch in exchange for some inventory instead of money one day. Polly had admired it, you see, and she wanted to own some pretty things like she'd seen on women in the films. Polly worried about what I'd say when I found out that she'd accepted it, but I said if that was what she wanted I was pleased for her to have it. I said whenever she wore it she could remember what I was willing to do to build a good life for us."

"Why would Mrs. Mumford admit she gave Polly jewelery?"

"Because I have the brooch now. When Polly told me she didn't want to walk out with me anymore, she gave it back to me. She told me it wasn't right to be reminded of a future she didn't want a part of and that I should find another girl to give it to instead."

"Can the brooch be linked to Mrs. Mumford in any way?"

"I don't know. Polly told me it had belonged to Mrs. Mumford but I only had her word for it."

"If you still have it could you let me borrow it so I can take it to the tearoom to see if I get a reaction to it from Mrs. Mumford?"

"I've got it right here in my pocket. I've kept it with me ever since Polly gave it back to me, hoping I'd convince her to change her mind and I'd have it at the ready to give back to her." Mr. Davies slipped his hand into his trouser pocket and pulled out a scrap of flannel. He unfolded it gently and held out his open palm. There in the middle sat a large enameled pin shaped like a butterfly. "I'll get it back though, right? It's all I have left of Polly, except the memories."

"I hope to return it when you are in Walmsley Parva tomorrow," Beryl said, tucking the token into her own pocket. "Until then."

Beryl walked back to the car with a great deal on her mind. The striped tabby was nowhere to be seen. Beryl set off in the direction of the Beeches and as she drove back to Walmsley Parva she couldn't help but think how different the village seemed to her now than it had only days before. Beryl had thought village life would be quiet and had worried she might become disillusioned with it rather quickly. She was not so self-centered as to be glad Walmsley Parva sheltered a murderer but she was well aware that someone else's loss of life had given her a new lease on her own.

Chapter 28

Edwina struggled all the way home with her parcels but she did her best not to let it show. If the good people, and not so good people, of Walmsley Parva were to be convinced of her rude good health she would need to give them a decent show. She felt eyes peering out at her from behind row after row of fine net curtains. So, despite the heaviness in her limbs she forged on toward the Beeches, waiting to collapse until she reached the sanctuary of her own gate.

She lowered her shopping basket to the stone step at the front door. Truly, she felt most unwell. Her head throbbed and there appeared to be two of most everything in her line of sight. Before she found the energy to push open the door, she heard whistling coming from round the side of the house. Simpkins.

Her jobbing gardener came to a full stop and audaciously ran his gaze up and down her person. It was one thing to suffer appraisal by the greengrocer you had owed money to for weeks on end. It was quite another to endure the same from your own appallingly inadequate staff. She wished she had the energy to devise a scathing rebuke. As it was, she didn't have the strength to open the door.

"You don't look so good, miss," Simpkins said. He bent down and gathered up her basket then pushed open the door. With his free, albeit filthy, hand he took her by the elbow and steered her into her favorite chair in the sitting room. She wasn't sure what to make of it when she awoke sometime later, the sound of voices drifting toward her from the kitchen. She struggled to her feet, finding the world had returned to normal with each object in view appearing only once. She followed the sounds and the scents of food toward the kitchen.

"Hello, Ed," Beryl said. She sat at the kitchen table, a celebratory glass of something in her hand. Really, the woman could put it away like a common sailor. More surprisingly was the sight of Simpkins dressed in a frilly pinny, tending something upon the cooker. He lifted a fork at her when she stepped through the door by way of a greeting.

"Have a good rest, did you, miss?" Simpkins asked. "You look a powerful sight less peaky than you did when I found you all squashed up against the door like you was." Simpkins had to be the most impertinent gardener in all the empire. Edwina was almost glad her mother had not lived long enough to see the effect the war had had on the servant class.

"I am quite recovered, thank you, Simpkins." Edwina took a tentative step towards the cooker. "Why are you wearing my pinny?"

"To keep my clothes clean, of course," Simpkins said. He shook his head slowly and gave Beryl a look that said he thought Edwina was still not quite herself. Edwina considered mentioning his clothes were more likely to get the food dirty than the other way round. Not to mention her pinny would require boiling if she were ever to consider wearing it again.

"After seeing the shape you were in, Simpkins offered to fix some luncheon. I thought after the hash I had made of breakfast you would appreciate having something decent to eat."

"I could smell the remains of what she did to the eggs straight through the walls of the house and on into the garden when I arrived to get on with my duties this morning," Simpkins said. "My dearly departed wife never could get the knack of eggs either. Or any other foodstuffs for that matter."

"What did you do about meals then?" Beryl asked.

"I made them all. My Bess was a fine woman but there was nothing in our wedding vows that required me to choke down her cooking." Edwina pulled out a chair at the table. She didn't have the will to wrest her cooker from Simpkins' hands and it would have been beneath her to try to do so. Besides, she was just the tiniest bit curious about this unorthodox side of her gardener.

Beryl had the knack for drawing that sort of confidence from people. All these years in her employ and Edwina had not the slightest notion that Simpkins helped in any way around his own home. He was so indolent whilst working at hers she wouldn't have countenanced the possibility that he might be more motivated in his own. It occurred to her that Beryl might have had more luck at persuading Michael Blackburn to admit to chauffeuring Polly about the village than she herself had.

"I was bringing Al here up to speed on the case as far as we know it." Beryl pointed her tumbler of something tawny in Simpkins' general direction. If Beryl had not pointed at him Edwina would have been at a complete loss as to whom she could be referring. She barely managed to stifle the question when she remembered Albert was Simpkins' Christian name. Not that she was sure anyone who took the position he did on the double digging of asparagus beds could be said to be possessed of Christian anything. Irrefutably the man was a heathen.

"A bang-up job you did of it, too. Folks were nattering on

about how the two of you were off your gourds saying Polly had not met with an accident. But hearing the facts laid out all neat like, I've come round to your way of thinking." Simpkins reached for a trio of plates stacked on the counter next to the cooker and began to fill them with something more savory smelling than Edwina preferred to admit.

"I knew you were a sensible man from the moment I laid eyes on you," Beryl said. She turned to Edwina and dropped her voice. "Excepting, of course, when it comes to the matter of brush piles." She lifted her fork and held it aloft as she waited for Simpkins to place a plate in front of Edwina and then to settle himself in the chair next to her. As soon as all three were served she dug with abandon into the meal set before her.

Edwina wasn't sure what to make of any of it. She wondered if there were any chance she was still tucked up in bed in a swoon and all this was just a feverish dream brought on by her head injury. Otherwise there was no making sense of the fact that her jobbing gardener was sitting with his filthy hobnail boots stretched out beneath her kitchen table sharing a meal. Neither Beryl nor Simpkins seemed to find anything amiss with the entire situation.

Edwina consoled herself that neither of them had been raised to the same standards as she had been. Simpkins couldn't be held accountable for not tuning into the finer nuances of society. Men so often assumed they belonged everywhere. As for Beryl and the American habit of ignoring class structure altogether, the less said about that, the better. Still, it made one's meal undeniably less of a pleasure when one was forced to view the manner in which Simpkins shoveled it down. Nevertheless, there was no gainsaying the fact that this particular jobbing gardener was a surprisingly excellent cook. In fact, it was the best meal Edwina had eaten in longer than she could remember. This realization only made matters more vexing. As delightful as the potatoes tasted, Edwina was finding them difficult to swallow.

"You've told him everything then," Edwina asked. "About the investigation?"

"Only the notes you and I have already shared. We decided it would only be right to wait for you to join us before I mentioned what I discovered today."

"How very thoughtful of you to wait," Edwina said. Yes, she decided, the potatoes were definitely not agreeing with her. She placed her fork against her plate and gave the other two her complete attention. "Don't let me keep you any longer." Beryl squinted at her slightly and shifted in her chair.

"I'd very much like to hear how your morning went first. Did you find anything of interest?" Beryl asked. Edwina was not inclined to be forthcoming in front of Simpkins. Who was to say he wouldn't blather about all their business whilst down at the pub? "Although no one would blame you if you were unable to discover anything. After all, you were looking a little peaked when I left you."

"Peaked or not, she managed to lug home a hefty weight of veg. I take my hat off to her even if she didn't come up with anything to add to the case."

"I'll have you know I didn't spend all my time doing the shopping. I had an interesting chat with Jack the newspaper boy," Edwina said. "He seemed very eager to impress you, Beryl. He mentioned you met him already."

"Good lad that Jack," Simpkins said, winking at Beryl this time.

"I did, just the other day. What did he have to say?"

"He told me he had seen Polly getting into Michael Blackburn's cab at just about closing time when he was walking his father home from the pub."

"Really?" Beryl said.

"Yes, really. I located Michael on the village green and he refused to say one way or the other if he had given Polly a lift on the night she died."

"So there is more reason than ever to suspect Michael of being involved in something he ought not be," Beryl said.

"Being so uncooperative doesn't make him look innocent," Edwina said.

"You can't blame a young feller for getting his back up though. He might not have any reason other than simple contrariness," Simpkins said. Edwina could believe Simpkins was more than capable of speaking on that subject. "You ought to have Beryl here give it a go. She's good with the menfolk, if you know what I mean," he added. Edwina wasn't sure what she would do if he winked at either of them after that statement. Fortunately he was sufficiently distracted by a bit of leftover roast stuck between his teeth that he was too busy to bother.

"I was thinking much the same thing. You seem to have developed quite a rapport with the Blackburns. I think it really might do more good for you to try to get the truth out of him. Or his sister, if need be."

"I'll speak with him about it tomorrow I think. I find people often soften on many subjects after a good night's sleep," Beryl said. "Do you have anything else you want to mention?"

"I'm afraid that's all I have," Edwina said. "I'm sorry to say I headed for home after my conversation with Michael. How about you?"

"If you recall, I approached Mr. Mumford at his home while Mrs. Mumford was out on errands. He wasn't too keen to have her return home to find us there unchaperoned."

"A bit of a roving eye, that one," Simpkins said. "Mrs. Mumford's got cause to be jealous from what I hear." He leaned across the table and winked at Edwina. Honestly, that's what came of breaking bread with the staff.

"My thoughts exactly. I suggested he had done away with

Polly because she was going to tell his wife about what he had been up to. That's when he offered up another suspect."

"Who?" Edwina and Simpkins asked in unison.

"He said Polly had asked him for advice on how to stop her former sweetheart from pursuing her. He said he told her to apply a bit of blackmail."

"What would she be able to blackmail him with? He was a simple village boy."

"You'd think that, but Mr. Davies had hidden depths. It took a bit of doing but I managed to get Mr. Mumford to disclose that Norman Davies was selling goods stolen from the Wallingford Estate to local merchants during the war years."

"But that's entirely contrary to the war effort," Edwina said. "To the work we were all doing up at the Wallingford Estate."

"Contrary or not, Mr. Mumford assured me that he was indeed helping himself to produce and livestock from the estate and selling them on to the butcher and the greengrocer."

"How did Mr. Mumford know about this?" Simpkins asked. "Was that good-for-nothing ladies' man involved too somehow?" His voice held a combative note and he nodded at Edwina like she would share his outrage. She was surprised and somehow comforted to realize that she and Simpkins were on the same side of an issue at last.

"I asked the same question. He didn't wish to give me a clear answer, especially when I suggested to him that his wife had bought some of the milk and butter for the tearoom. He didn't confirm the accusation nor deny it."

"I always did wonder how she managed to have such delicious cakes and pastries throughout the shortages when everyone else was turning out ghastly little bricks. Every time I complimented her on them she just said she had a few secret recipes that stretched everything more than most," Edwina said.

"It sounds as though the only mystery was how she got

away with buying black market items for so long without falling under scrutiny."

"People were too downtrodden to ask those sorts of questions, Beryl. Everyone was just trying to make it through the day let alone the whole war. Pulling together as a community was one way we managed, and we weren't looking to accuse our neighbours of wrongdoing at the time." Edwina looked at Simpkins and he gave her a nod that looked a lot like approval. Such a strange few days it had been. Perhaps one had to have lived through it all to really understand. Perhaps she had more in common in many ways with the man wearing hobnail boots in her kitchen than she did with the woman who had shared her girlhood dreams.

"Well, times have certainly changed. Wrongdoing is cropping up everywhere. Mr. Davies fingered his own uncle and Gareth Scott the greengrocer as buyers of the stolen items. He also said that Polly would not have blackmailed him because she herself was involved." Beryl reached across the table and speared a piece of turnip with her fork.

"Could he prove that?" Edwina asked. Beryl reached into her pocket and pulled out a bit of flannel, which she handed to Edwina.

"He lent me this to try to extract the truth from Minnie Mumford. Not that she is likely to want to tell me anything after catching me alone with her philandering husband this morning. He claimed Mrs. Mumford gave this to Polly in exchange for some black market items and that Polly gave it to him when she broke off their understanding."

Edwina placed the small packet on the table and unwrapped it. There in front of her lay a brooch fashioned of brass and enamel. It was worked in the shape of a butterfly and it was easy to see why Polly had thought it a worthy payment for her delivery.

"How are we to prove that Minnie Mumford gave it to

Polly? He could be making up the story that Minnie gave this to Polly," Edwina said.

"I don't know about that bit. I was hoping one of you might have a suggestion." Beryl turned an expectant look towards Edwina.

"You know, now that I come to think about it I daresay I remember Agnes commenting on it one day. I was up at the Wallingford Estate and she was having a heated discussion with Polly about it. It was the only time I remember them arguing. Polly had pinned it to her Land Army uniform and Agnes said it was not regulation and that she should take it off before she got herself into trouble with Hortense."

Simpkins reached out and traced a knobby finger delicately over the brooch.

"I've seen Minnie Mumford wearing a brooch just like this years ago," Simpkins said.

"How can you be so sure?" Edwina asked. She hardly thought he seemed the sort of man to take a keen interest in ladies' finery.

"Not long after my Bess died I got into the habit of taking my tea at the tearoom whenever I had a few extra shillings. It made a nice change from sitting at home on me own." Simpkins paused. "One day I noticed Mrs. Mumford was wearing a brooch that looked just like this one. When I told her my Bess had had one just like it she got all toffee-nosed about it and I never saw it on her again. Puts on airs, she does, and I expect it jabbed her pride to have her finery worn by someone she thought wasn't her equal."

"I'm sorry to hear she was so rude to you but does your recollection prove she owned this brooch? I still think she could say that she's never seen it before," Beryl said.

"I know just how it could be done but I think it is a job for Miss Davenport," Simpkins said turning to Beryl. "You are ever so good with the menfolk but Miss Davenport here is one for the gentlewomen. She speaks their language and even though she might be a bit of a stickler she has their respect." Edwina felt a faint glow warm her cheeks at Simpkins' compliment. She listened more carefully than she might usually have done as he proceeded to tell them just how she could prove the brooch had belonged once to Minnie Mumford.

"Right you are, Al," Beryl said when he was done. "What do you say, Ed? I'll tackle Michael in the morning and you can take on Mrs. Mumford?"

All Edwina could do was to nod.

Chapter 29

The Blackburns lived in a flat above the garage. It wasn't large or even very attractively furnished but it did have the luxury of convenience. Beryl took the steps at the back of the garage. She knocked on the wooden door at the top of the steps and stood waiting for someone to answer. As she held tightly to the banister she looked out over the rolling fields nearby and the ribbon of sparkling river beyond. Walmsley Parva was a beautiful little place. If you didn't mind the odd murder.

Despite the nature of her visit to the Blackburn residence Beryl felt the same sense of well-being she had leaving Parnham St. Mary the afternoon before. It seemed the country air and Ed's companionship had renewed her zest for life. Her heart skipped a beat when she thought how it was just luck that she had seen Ed's advertisement in the newspaper. What would have happened to her if she had not? Beryl realized she was gripping the handrail as if her life depended on it. She gave herself a little shake to banish any dark thoughts to the back of her mind. There was far too much to do to entertain their like today.

Norah opened the door wearing a pair of loose trousers and a man's open-necked shirt. Beryl approved. She had long enjoyed wearing such practical garments herself and was delighted to see other women doing likewise. Not that she didn't love a dramatic ball gown, but the lure of the sensible combined with the forbidden made trousers irresistible.

"Good morning, Norah. I wonder if Michael is home?" Beryl asked.

"Is there something wrong with your motorcar?" Norah asked, stepping back to allow Beryl entry.

"I just need to talk to him about something, that's all," Beryl said, following Norah in through the open doorway. "Did he tell you about the talk he had with Edwina yesterday?"

"No, he didn't. He didn't say much of anything all day when it comes to that. I asked you two not to say anything about Agnes to upset him. Why can't you just leave well enough alone?"

"This isn't just about Agnes anymore, Norah. Did you know he drove off somewhere with Polly on the night she died?"

"Who said that he did?" Norah asked.

"Young Jack, the newspaper boy."

"Did Michael tell you he had Polly in the cab?"

"He doesn't deny it. I'm not saying he admitted it either but they were seen together driving out of town at the time the last film of the night at the Palais let out."

Norah crossed the small sitting room to the sofa and slumped down on a sunken cushion at the end of it.

"I don't know what to do anymore," she said. Beryl sat down beside her.

"You're worried about what he has been doing because of what happened to Agnes?"

"No. That's not it. I know he didn't have anything to do with what happened to Agnes. I'm worried that he is having some sort of return to his precarious state of mind. I can't stand the thought of him slipping back into being the sort of person who can't even recognize when he is being spoken to."

"Has he shown any signs of a breakdown?' Beryl asked.

"He hasn't been himself in days. He doesn't eat. He's jumpy and every time I mention Polly he gets defensive."

"Don't you think it might be because he has something to hide?" Beryl asked. "You have to admit, Agnes disappeared after he showed an interest in her, and then after a witness saw him driving Polly away she turns up dead. One would be insane themselves not to wonder if the two circumstances are linked."

"For the last time, I know he had nothing to do with Agnes' disappearance." Norah raised her voice and banged her fist down on the arm of the sofa. "Agnes is alive and well and living in London." Her eyes grew large in her face and she covered her mouth with both hands. "Oh dear. I wasn't supposed to say."

"That's all right, Norah. I think it will be for the best if you tell me exactly what happened."

Norah sat in silence gnawing on a thumbnail for a moment and then began to speak in a low voice.

"Agnes and I were friends. We met when I first went up to the Wallingford Estate to fix some broken machinery. A good mechanic can work on all sorts of engines and I liked to do my bit for the war effort so I was up there quite a lot."

"Is that why she paid special attention to Michael?"

"Yes, it was. She chose Tarzan because I told her he had loved those books when he was a youth. She sat right next to his bed and touched his hand now and again as she read because she knew how distressed I was by his illness."

"But then she disappeared."

"About three months after Agnes had started reading to the soldiers she came to me out of the blue and said she was leaving the Land Army and would be heading to London."

"Wasn't that unusual? I thought the Land Army workers committed to a one-year term," Beryl said.

"They did, which is why I was so surprised when she said she was leaving. She hadn't fulfilled her obligation. When I asked why she was going she said she was expecting a child and that she was going to change her name and go to London where she would introduce herself as a war widow."

"The poor girl. She must have been so distressed," Beryl said.

"I believe she was at the time. She really seemed to enjoy her work at the Wallingford Estate and I don't think she was looking forward to leaving it for a job in a factory in London. But she couldn't stay here."

"Was the baby Michael's?"

"Heaven help me, that was my first thought, too. I actually asked her if Michael had forced himself on her in any way and she said that he hadn't. I wasn't entirely sure that I believed her after the way that he had behaved but I wanted to do so more than anything."

"So she vanished without a trace and you never told anyone that she was alive and well? You just let everyone worry that she had come to harm?" Beryl asked.

"It seemed like the right thing to do at the time. Now it seems unkind. I didn't realize how much it had plagued Miss Davenport all this time."

"You realize, don't you, that this secret may have contributed to Polly Watkins' death?" Beryl asked. "As soon as we started asking question about Agnes, Polly was killed. Michael may yet have something to hide."

"He didn't know about the baby. She made me swear not to tell anyone. Until now I haven't." Norah looked at Beryl with tears in her large blue eyes and Beryl wished to believe her. It was, however, a murder enquiry.

"You don't know her new name or her address in London, do you?" Beryl asked.

"Why do you want to know?"

"Because I am going to need to verify for myself that what you are telling me is true. I will need to go up to London with Edwina and see Agnes Rollins in the flesh for myself."

"But then she'll know I didn't keep her secret," Norah said.

"Which is worse? Two sympathetic women making discreet enquiries way off in London or the two of us continuing to ask questions about Michael right here in Walmsley Parva?" Beryl asked.

"She calls herself Agnes Martin now. I have the address written in a cookery book in the kitchen. Michael would never look for it there." Norah moved off the sofa and into the kitchen. She returned holding a piece of paper in her hand and she stretched it out to Beryl. "Here it is. When you see Agnes will you tell her that I miss her and I hope that she is doing well?"

"I'll be sure to let her know that you were asking after her. I can't help but ask, why would she tell you about the baby instead of just slipping away?"

"Because she was going to London and she was planning to get a job in a munitions factory. She was worried about what would happen to the baby if she were hurt or even killed in one of the accidents that were so common in those places. She didn't have any family at all and she didn't have any other friends she would trust with her baby. She said after the way I did my best for Michael she knew she would trust me with the care of her baby if it came down to it."

"Did you ever meet the baby?"

"No, I never did. I didn't want to try to explain to Michael why I was going up to London. Besides, he gets quite anxious if he has to stay at home overnight alone. The trains are reliable but you never know what could happen to delay a journey. I never wanted to risk it."

"Thanks for trusting me with your secret."

"Please just don't let Michael know that Agnes is able to be found. I don't think it would be good for him. I especially don't think he needs to know she bore another man's child."

"Do you think he could have found out another way? Did anyone else have that information about Agnes?" Beryl asked.

"I doubt it. Agnes was friendly enough with Polly but I think she knew Polly couldn't be trusted to keep such an important secret. If she were as smart as I believed she was, she would have known better. I don't think there is anyone else she would have told about a thing like that," Norah said. "I really don't believe there could be any way that Michael knew."

"You realize you still haven't told me if Michael drove Polly somewhere on the night that she died."

"I was rather hoping you had forgotten with the excitement of discovering that Agnes was alive and well."

"I'm afraid I am not quite so old as all that. I haven't lost all my marbles yet and left them to roll round the nursing ward floor." Beryl shook her head at the younger woman. "So tell me, did he drive her somewhere on the night she died?"

"Michael has a strong sense of honor for his fellow soldiers. He doesn't like to put them in harm's way either in their bodies or in their minds either."

"I understand the instinct. There is something between compatriots that the rest of the world cannot ever quite understand. Polly wasn't a fellow soldier though unless you are including the Land Army in the military to the same extent as the army or the navy."

"No, of course not. I only meant he had a great respect for his fellow soldiers and would have considered requests for secrecy from one of them of the highest order."

"So someone else asked Michael to keep the secret of Polly being in his cab?"

"Yes. And Michael did. He hated to lie to Edwina. He was

brought up better than that but his code with the fellow soldiers goes deeper than common courtesy."

"Yours doesn't though, does it?" Beryl asked. "Your loyalty isn't to the armed serves that broke Michael's spirit but rather to Michael himself."

Norah looked at Beryl then slowly nodded. "Michael had a standing engagement to drive Polly home from the cinema three times each week." Beryl's heart beat faster and her nose twitched at the thought that the trail was heating up.

"That seems a bit expensive for a daily maid, doesn't it?" Beryl asked.

"Polly didn't pay for it. Walter Bennett, the projectionist at the cinema, contacted Michael a couple of weeks ago and made the arrangements. He hired Michael to drive Polly home."

"In the cab?" Beryl asked. "To her house?"

"That's right."

"Why would he do that? Isn't it a bit strange to go to the expense of hiring a cab for someone you barely knew?"

"It wouldn't have been much money. Michael always gave other soldiers a deeply discounted rate. It barely covered the petrol. I assumed Walter and Polly knew each other better than anyone else realized. Michael never said. In the cab business it doesn't pay to ask too many questions."

"You must end up picking people up at places they ought not be and dropping others off at locations at least as damning."

"Something like that. Discretion is a large part of developing repeat business."

"Did Michael ever drive Walter Bennett anywhere?"

"Not that I know of. If he did he never said. Walter only hired him to drive Polly and only back to her house, as far as I knew."

"This still doesn't get him off the hook for her murder, you know. He was seen with her and then she was found dead."

"I know he didn't hurt her. He wouldn't have hurt anyone. That's just not who he is."

"Then convince him to talk to me or to Edwina. If anyone else saw her get out of his cab the night she died and then saw him drive away it would be a great help in convincing us to look elsewhere for her killer," Beryl said.

"I'll do my best but he's been very tight-lipped about the entire business. I think Polly's death bothered him more than he wants to admit. We were just starting to have the expectation that young people would have chance of living a normally long life again. What with the war and then the Spanish Flu it has taken a long time and some deliberate forgetting to let in a little bit of hope." Norah looked down at her hands fidgeting in her lap. "He's been so distracted he's even started making errors with his work."

"Then you had best get him to talk to me. Even if he didn't kill Polly he may well kill an unsuspecting customer through negligence," Beryl stood and made her way to the door. "I'll be sure to tell Agnes hello from you."

Chapter 30

The Silver Spoon Tearoom was warm and smelled faintly of nutmeg. Edwina looked around with admiration at the tins of tea and the sparkling porcelain pots and cups. Minnie was an inspiration. One felt quite sanitary about her operation. Edwina wished she were there to swap recipes instead of to interrogate her about black market involvement. There was simply no good way to broach such a subject.

At least there was no one else present. At least for the moment. Which was only to be expected as the tearoom was still closed. Minnie had looked surprised to see her when Edwina knocked on the door so far ahead of opening time. She was in the midst of polishing the cutlery from the looks of things. Silver teaspoons and butter knives lay on a thick layer of toweling on one of the tables near the center of the room along with a pot of some sort of paste.

"What brings you by, Edwina?" Minnie asked, seating herself once more at the table and taking up her polishing cloth.

"I felt a little cooped up in the house and wanted a bit of a walk so I came on into the village. I was passing the shop and when I glanced through the window I saw you sitting here all by yourself with this great mound of silver. So I thought I'd ask if you needed any help with it. I've always quite enjoyed doing the silver."

"That's very kind of you. The job has to be done from time to time but it can be a bit daunting." Minnie waved her rag at the pile. "It's much easier of course when you use the right sort of polish. I've tried all sorts of recipes, you know and my own recipe seems to work the very best. Sometimes I think I ought to sell it right along with the tea considering the way customers always ask me how I keep things so bright and shiny."

"I should think that quite a good idea. You know," Edwina said, reaching for the pot and holding it to her nose, "it smells quite pleasant really."

"Rose geranium oil. Nothing so lovely as that as far as I'm concerned. I add a few drops at the end just before I bottle it. The scent fades over time but it's nice for a few days," Minnie said. "I'd be happy to give you a jar if you'd like. I often do when someone I know admires it."

"I'd love one. And a very great help it must be to have an effective preparation to use. You certainly can't count on finding staff to keep things spic and span," Edwina said.

"You just can't get the help these days, can you? Not for love or money."

"Not like when we were girls, is it?" Edwina asked. She removed her coat and draped it over the back of a chair and sat in the seat next to Minnie. She took up a soft cloth from a pile on the table and dipped it in the paste pot. She applied it to a spoon blackened around the ornate scrollwork of the handle. She began to rub in earnest and was gratified almost at once to see a rich lustre emerging from beneath the tarnish.

"Not in the least. I sometimes despair. You know I do. I've often felt as if the war and all that came with it just upended the entire natural order of things. It used to be there were standards. Pride in one's work. A sense of duty. But now it's all about glamour and adventure and trying to look like cinema stars." Minnie savagely rubbed at the handle of a cake knife. Edwina couldn't help but wonder if they were really talking about the state of world affairs or perhaps something a bit closer to home.

"It can feel worrisome at times, can't it? Running this place on your own is a remarkable achievement. I've heard Mr. Mumford speaking about you very proudly when you aren't around to be embarrassed by the praise." Edwina realized she was behaving just as she had when she had told fibs as a schoolgirl for the greater good. Mr. Mumford had never praised his wife in or out of her earshot to Edwina's knowledge. But in this case, there was no reason the truth was a better choice than a little white lie. Especially if it helped Minnie to admit to her part in the black market purchases.

"That's very kind of you to say, I'm sure," Minnie said, her eyes widening in surprise and her zeal for energetic buffing slowing down a bit. "It hasn't always been easy, I'll say that much."

"I've always admired your business sense. I don't know how you did it. Especially the way you turned out such delicious morsels all through the shortages. People came for miles around to partake of your cakes and buns. Well, they still do, don't they?"

"They do indeed. You know the increasing ownership of the motorcar is making places like this one more popular all the time. People are making a practice of stopping in for a bit of refreshment on their way along the road to the seaside or on their way to a weekend at a cottage in the countryside."

"You know, I think you'd be doing home cooks with small budgets a real service if you were to publish a cookery book sharing the recipes that kept this business flourishing through the war years. There are so many families that are in dire circumstances and would benefit greatly from your wisdom." Edwina glanced over at Minnie who all at once seemed more interested in the bowl of a serving spoon that was justified.

"I don't think that I am any more qualified to speak on such things than the average cook. I am quite sure I would have no special expertise to write such a book."

"Nonsense. Everyone in Walmsley Parva is consumed with curiosity about how you pulled off such confectionary and culinary feats. You are a legend both far and wide as the best place for miles around to find a proper cup of tea and a delicious slice of cake. I am quite certain that the ongoing success of your business has to do with that reputation."

"It's very kind of you to say so. Although tearooms are very popular no matter who runs them, I'm sure."

"You may be right about that. Beryl told me that she passed several tearooms on her way down here from London." Edwina glanced at Minnie's face as she dipped her buffing rag into the polish jar once more. "I do hope the competition won't create downturn in your own business."

"I can't see why other tearooms would. After all, as you say, my reputation is enough to attract people from a distance. And motorcars easily traverse that distance. I trust I shall continue to do well."

"Still, it seems it would be important for your reputation as a baker of almost mythic ability to remain intact if your business is to continue to be profitable."

"Yes, that's likely true enough. But why shouldn't it?" Minnie asked.

"Because of this," Edwina said, laying aside a small pair of silver sugar tongs. She unclasped the latch on her handbag and pulled Polly's brooch from inside it. Minnie gave a small start then looked Edwina brazenly in the eye.

"Edwina, I believe you were hit on the head a good deal

harder than you realized. We were discussing tearooms, not cheap little bits of jewelry."

"Don't you recognize it?" Edwina asked.

"Should I?"

"I think that you should. It belonged to you not so very long ago."

"I don't recall owning such an item. And even if I did, I can't say that my reputation would be tarnished by possessing a cheap bauble."

"I'm told you gave it to Polly in exchange for some black market baking ingredients from the Wallingford Estate when it was up and running." Edwina fixed her gaze on Minnie's face. Fear, then obstinacy, flitted across it in quick succession. "I don't mean to put you in a bad position, Minnie, and I don't want to expose your secret. But I do need the truth."

"You are accusing me and insulting me in my own shop. I think you should go."

"If I leave, I will have to ask other people the same question I would rather ask you."

"You have no proof. Only baseless accusations."

"It was your brooch. I can easily prove it." Edwina rose and crossed to the section of wall centered between the front door and the coat rack. She lifted a framed newspaper clipping down from the wall and carried it back to the table. She placed it down in front of Minnie. "That's you on the day the tea shop opened. And that's this same brooch pinned right to your blouse for all the world to see." Edwina gently tapped the glass.

"What do you want to know?" Minnie's voice was barely above a whisper.

"I just need you to confirm that Polly was involved in selling the stolen items from the Wallingford Estate. It has bearing on why she died."

"Do you think I had something to do with her death?" Minnie's voice rose again and took on a hysterical note. "Buying a bit of black market butter is one thing but murder is quite another."

"No. I never said that. I am asking in pursuit of the truth of someone else's involvement. You are just supporting or refuting the assertions of another." Edwina laid her hand on Minnie's trembling one. "I really do just want to know about Polly. I won't say a word about your purchases."

"Not to anyone?"

"I will be discussing it with Beryl of course but neither she nor I have any intention of carrying tales anywhere at all."

"You promise not to tell Prudence?"

"Minnie, I know she is your friend but I wouldn't tell Prudence the day of the week if she asked," Edwina said. Minnie gave the faintest of smiles.

"She is rather a gossip, is Prudence. All right. Since you know everything already I'll tell you. Polly admired my brooch every time she saw it. The girl liked a bit of frippery and who could blame her? You know what girls like her are like, always attracted to things with some shine to them."

"I know just what you mean," Edwina said.

"One time when she came in money was a bit tight. Many of the folks around here had contracted the Spanish Flu and so fewer patrons were coming in. When Polly admired the brooch during a delivery I offered it to her as payment instead of money."

"I remember those weeks. It seemed almost everyone was ill. Prudence had to close her shop. The reading room was closed. Simpkins didn't come to work in my garden. I think even the doctor's family was ill at that time. It is no wonder you had little extra to spend." Edwina nodded.

"Polly was glad to have it and when I asked her later if Norman had minded she said he was pleased for her to have a piece of jewellery instead of having the money. Everyone was happy with the arrangement and I never thought of it again."

"Thank you for telling me."

"Do you think less of me, Edwina?"

"I think everyone has enough grief to bear these days without making more for our neighbours. Let's never think on it again."

"Really?" Minnie asked.

"Why don't you hand me that cake server. It looks like it could use a good going over."

Chapter 31

Beryl had promised she would meet Edwina in the village before luncheon. She could hardly contain her excitement. She headed for the Silver Spoon Tearoom but hauled up short when she looked through the window and even from a distance could tell that Edwina and Minnie were deep in conversation. Taking a seat across the street, she turned her thoughts to the case at hand.

Michael was still the strongest suspect. That was, as long as Minnie confirmed Norman's story about how Polly ended up with the brooch. She was distressed to think that Michael had killed Polly, but there were so many young men who had come away from soldiering changed men, and not for the better. Even though she had not said so outright, Beryl was certain Norah was terribly concerned about her brother's state of mind.

She still wished Mr. Mumford would be found to be the one who had done it. He may have moved them closer to a solution to the case but she truly disliked the way he took advantage of young women, and she thought his treatment of his wife was reprehensible. As far as Beryl could see, Minnie would be better off without him. By the time Edwina pulled open the tea-room door and spotted her, Beryl had come up with a whole speech to deliver to Minnie on the joys of divorce.

"So what did she say?" Beryl asked, pushing her women's rights battle cry into the back of her mind.

"She confirmed Norman's story. He was telling the truth about Polly being involved in the illegal sales."

"That is good news. I promised to return the brooch to Norman today at the market. Let's walk over and I'll tell you what I discovered. I am quite certain you will never guess."

"Agnes is alive? She's a mother?" Edwina said. She blanched, then wobbled, and finally grabbed Beryl's arm. "Why didn't Norah tell us before? She knew how worried I was about Agnes when she disappeared."

"She was protecting her friend. Not everyone is charitable about momentary indiscretions."

"A child is hardly momentary."

"Nevertheless, she wished to avoid ridicule. I, for one, don't blame her. I likely would have done the same thing had I unfortunately found myself in her shoes."

Edwina, she noticed, was very quiet on the subject of what one should do if a baby arrived on scene without a father. It wasn't like her to be so reticent concerning her opinions.

"We shall have to speak to her to confirm she is alive and well," Edwina finally said.

"I agree wholeheartedly. I propose we motor up tomorrow and camp out at her address until we find her."

"Can't you go without me? I hate to leave Crumpet on his own for long."

"You hate to leave your precious Walmsley Parva for long. Crumpet can keep watch over your brush pile and ensure that Simpkins doesn't do away with it again," Beryl said. "Besides, you are the one who will recognize this Agnes. She's using a new name now, remember, and has no reason to own up to her previous name just because I tax her with it."

"Oh, all right. But promise me we will come back by nightfall."

"I promise nothing, Ed. It is an adventure and any promise to stick to a schedule will be broken as a matter of course. I'll tell you what; while we are in London I will take you to the best milliner in the city to replace the hat you lost in the tussle with your intruder. If that doesn't sweeten the deal, I don't know what will."

"Let's wait and see what our adventure brings before you decide to turn it into a shopping expedition. Is that Norman up ahead?"

They crossed the green and stopped in front of Norman's cart. Beryl had a sneaking suspicion she was looking at much of the same produce she had viewed the day before. It seemed trade was not swift in the neighboring town.

"Have you come to return my property?" Norman asked as he looked up and noticed them there.

"We have," Edwina said, handing the brooch back to him with care. "Safe and sound."

"It seems Miss Davenport was able to persuade Mrs. Mumford to give credence to your story," Beryl said.

"Does this mean you no longer are accusing me of murdering Polly?" Norman asked.

"It means there is one less reason to believe that you would have done so. But no, you are not entirely off our list of suspects."

"Why not?"

"One reason is that we've had it on good authority that you were seen grabbing Agnes Rollins by the arm. It makes you seem like a man who would behave violently. Would you care to explain why that was?" Edwina asked.

"Agnes said she knew about the thefts. She threatened to tell

Hortense Merriweather what was going on. I panicked and grabbed her. When she pulled away I told her she was crazy and that she would look a fool if she went to the matron with no proof."

"Did she go tell Hortense?" Edwina asked.

"She must not have done since the matron never asked me about it. And you know her." Norman turned to Edwina. "If there was anything the slightest bit off she wanted it corrected. And quick."

"How long was this before Agnes went missing?"

"No more than a few days, I think. I was worried about it but Agnes seemed to have other things on her mind. I tried to keep out of her way but even though I bumped into her a few times after that she never mentioned it again," Norman said.

Beryl gave Edwina a long look. Likely worries about her own situation had driven all other thoughts from her mind. The theft of a few cabbages and some butter would have seemed small compared with deciding what to do about a baby. Edwina nodded slowly at her.

"Thank you for your honesty, Mr. Davies. We'll let you get back to your customers," Beryl said. She and Edwina stepped aside and allowed a stout woman with a large basket to shoulder past them.

"All the more reason to go to London to speak with Agnes, wouldn't you agree?" Beryl said as they walked away.

Chapter 32

The next morning, at just past daybreak, Beryl descended the stairs to find a pile of blankets, coats, and a large valise heaped up near the door. She heard noises coming from the kitchen and followed them to find Edwina in a state of frenzied preparation.

"Ed, what are you doing?" she asked, staring in awe at the production spread out before her.

"You never can be sure what you will encounter whilst away from home. I prefer to be prepared," Edwina said. From her tone it was clear her friend did not wish to be jollied along. Beryl stood watching as Edwina wound several feet of bandage material into a neat wad. She held her tongue as Edwina packed a picnic hamper with a loaf of bread, a dozen boiled eggs, and a small wheel of cheese. Her curiosity got the better of her when her friend reached for a glass bottle adorned with a chemist's label.

"What in the world is that?" she asked.

"Quinine." Edwina said.

"We are going to London, Ed," Beryl said. "Not to the Amazon."

"That's what you say now, Beryl, but with you, one never knows."

"There shan't be room for all this if you keep it up. Besides, we need to get on the road if we are to have enough time to get to town and back again by your bedtime," Beryl said. That did it. Edwina snapped the lid of the hamper shut and hurriedly donned her coat. Both women carried an armload to the motorcar and Beryl pulled open one of the back doors.

Edwina set the picnic hamper on the bench seat and bent to tuck a spare pair of boots on the floor.

"Are these yours?" she asked, holding a pair of work gloves up for Beryl to see.

"No, they aren't mine. I've never seen them before," Beryl said.

"How did they get in here?" Edwina asked. "Do you think Michael or Norah left them by accident when they were conducting the repairs?"

"I hope that is when it happened."

"How else would you explain it?"

"Maybe they were left by whomever was using this car the night Polly died," Beryl said.

"You don't think they belonged to Polly, do you?"

"No, but I do think they might have belonged to whomever killed her," Beryl said. Edwina looked down at the gloves. For a moment Beryl thought she might hurl them from her.

"Then I'd best tuck them away somewhere for safekeeping just in case we need them as evidence at some point," Edwina said. "I shall be ready to go momentarily."

Edwina reluctantly left Crumpet and her beloved garden in the unsupervised hands of Simpkins. He promised both would be none the worse for his stewardship but her doubts remained firmly fixed. While she was eager to see Agnes Rollins with her own two eyes, she was not looking forward to the journey. She would have tried to persuade Beryl that the train service to London was the more practical choice but she hadn't the money to pay the fare. She was most reluctant to accept any more funds than absolutely necessary from her friend.

By the time they'd been on the road for half an hour Edwina's nerves were completely jangled. There were far worse things to say concerning the condition of her digestive system. First there was the cat that darted across the road in front of them. Then there were the tight turns and little hills that Beryl took at enough speed to lift and then immediately to drop one's stomach. Weaving in and out of London's traffic only made things worse.

Beryl however seemed to relish the entire ride. She nattered on almost constantly about the pep of the motor and the beauty of the scenery and the pleasure of being able to pull over anytime one wished to do so. Not that there was any sign of Beryl slowing down whatsoever.

Carriages with horses, buses, and pedestrians flooded the streets. Everywhere Edwina looked there were signs of activity. She had been to the city before, of course, but it had been many years. Her mother had been ill and there was the worry about leaving her for long. The war years did not make one inclined to stray the least bit from what little comfort could be found, and in truth Edwina had found London to be more overwhelming than comfortable.

Beryl seemed to know her way around though and steered confidently, if somewhat recklessly, through the maze of streets and people. She pulled up in front of a brick building with little to recommend it and to Edwina's relief, came to a complete stop.

"This is the address Agnes gave to Norah," Beryl said. They sat in silence for a moment evaluating the situation. The neighbourhood did not inspire enthusiasm. Laundry flapped out of an upper-floor window and Edwina was dismayed to see that sheets and garments, which should have been white, were marred by soot. Litter skittered in the stiff breeze that moved between the buildings and the smell of unnamed dank things reached her nostrils. "Shall we see if she's home?"

They stepped out onto the street and Beryl opened the door to the building with far more confidence than Edwina felt. No sooner had they stopped to inspect the names on the mailboxes than a red-cheeked woman yanked open a door right next to them.

"Who are you looking for then?" she asked, crossing her sizable arms over her even more outsized bust.

"We are here to see Mrs. Agnes Martin," Beryl said.

"Don't I know you?" the woman asked. "You look familiar."

"You'd be surprised how often I hear that. I must just have one of those faces."

"It says A. Martin has a flat on the fourth floor," Edwina said. "Shall we see if she's in?"

"She won't be in until the evening. She works at some sort of office in the city."

"Do you know where?" Beryl asked.

"No. I just know that she works all day during normal business hours and she comes back by six every evening. I let my tenants keep to themselves so long as they pay their rent on time."

"I suppose we shall just have to find a way to entertain ourselves until she returns," Beryl said, giving Edwina a bright smile.

"The milliner's I think first, don't you?" Beryl asked. She couldn't help but notice that her friend had been terribly quiet throughout the journey. Ed was not much of a city person and Beryl was determined that the visit to London in the company of one who knew it as well as she did would change her mind. "I am eager to hear what you think of their selection. Hop in."

Edwina blanched. "Is it very far from here, this millinery shop?"

"No, I suppose not," Beryl said. "Why do you ask?"

"I thought it might be a pleasure to walk there. I find I can see more when I travel by foot."

"Why in the world would that be?" Beryl asked with astonishment. She had seen so much of the world by using most every form of transport there was. Feet were in no way her preference.

"Because when I am on foot I find that I don't close my eyes in terror," Edwina replied.

"Ah, that would explain it." Beryl tucked her arm through Edwina's and the two set off at a leisurely pace. "I'll try to drive home a bit more sedately then. Are you sure that is all that has been on your mind? You've been unusually quiet ever since I told you that Agnes was still amongst the living. Honestly, I expected you to be more pleased."

"I think you're imagining things, Beryl. Let's look for hats."

Beryl gave Edwina a whirlwind tour of the city. It was strange, she noted to herself, that she was the foreigner but in London, Edwina was the one who seemed like a stranger. Beryl found she delighted in showing her friend the sights of the city and she also immensely enjoyed indulging Edwina at the shops they visited. It took some convincing but in the end she managed to purchase two hats, a dress, and a pair of gloves for her friend. She had done her best to persuade her to also take home a fine wool cardigan that brought out a rosy glow in her cheeks but Edwina had refused, claiming she could easily knit one herself. She had suggested purchasing a small gift for Agnes' child and Beryl had readily agreed.

Over luncheon at the Georgian Restaurant in Harrods department store Edwina confessed she had not had so much fun in years. Her eyes sparkled and her voice grew uncharacteristically loud.

"I hadn't realized how much good a change of scenery could do," she said as she poured a cup of tea for each of them. "Being here has been like a breath of fresh air."

"I'm so glad you've enjoyed the day. I haven't had so much fun in ages myself."

"You're just saying that to make me feel better about being such a poor little country mouse," Edwina said.

"No, it's the truth. I have been here there and everywhere but I haven't really had companionship on my journeys."

"That can't be true. You always have an entourage of sorts. Journalists, porters, even bandits if the newspaper articles are to be believed. Surely there has been plenty of people to keep you company." Edwina cocked her head sideways and looked at Beryl out from under the brim of one of her new hats. She looked so much like the inquisitive girl she had been that Beryl felt the room fall away and had the strange impression that they were in the dining hall of Miss DuPont's Finishing School for Young Ladies once more.

"There is a great deal of difference between company and companionship, Ed. I am more pleased than I can say that you placed that ad for a lodger in the newspaper and even more pleased that I saw it. This has been the best adventure I've been on in many years."

Edwina glanced over at the clock on the wall. "I think it's late enough that the next step in adventure can go ahead. If we hurry I think we can arrive at Agnes' flat about the same time she does."

Darkness had fallen and they made their way back to Agnes' address by dint of the streetlights. Edwina was dazzled by the way the city continued to thrum with life even after the sun had set. They were accosted once more by the woman guarding the front of Agnes' building who informed them she had arrived home a few moments before and had not gone back out again.

They took the stairs as there was no lift. Edwina was a bit disappointed by that although she did not mention it. She had felt quite childlike enough throughout the course of the day without revealing such a juvenile sentiment as that. As they reached the top of the final flight of stairs Edwina was surprised to find herself nervous about what would happen when Agnes opened the door. She had no desire to invade Agnes' privacy and was loath to cause her embarrassment of any sort. Beryl was oblivious to any qualms Edwina had and made swift work of thumping with a heavy hand upon the door.

Agnes opened it and stood on the threshold looking much as she had the last time Edwina had seen her. Her clothing was different, of course, as there was no call for a Land Army uniform at this late date. She did not look entirely happy to see them. A slight gasp escaped her lips and she took a step back not to invite them in, Edwina thought, but rather to put distance between them.

"Hello, Agnes," Edwina said. She felt an overwhelming sense of protectiveness for the younger woman. If she had felt discomforted by the idea of encountering Agnes even though she was aware the meeting would take place she could only imagine how much more rattled Agnes must be feeling. "I'm so sorry to have startled you. We should have written or sent a telegram. But we simply didn't have time to wait for a letter to reach you and so many people now have adverse reactions to telegrams that I didn't wish to risk distressing you by sending one."

"May we come in?" Beryl asked. Agnes nodded, still speechless. They stepped into the tiny bed-sit and looked around. Nothing was new but neither was it untidy. Sitting on the floor in the corner sucking on his thumb was a boy, aged somewhere around a year and a half.

"Allow me to introduce my friend Beryl Helliwell. You have

most likely read about her in the newspapers from time to time. And this is your little boy then, is it?" Edwina asked. Without waiting for an answer she walked over to the child and knelt next to him on the well-worn carpet. "Hello, young man. Would you like to see what I have in this bag?" She pointed at the paper sack she held. The boy nodded slowly then reached out his hands. Edwina lifted a toy rabbit with long silky ears from the bag and handed it to him.

Agnes found her voice and remembered her manners. "What do you say, Benjy?" she asked her son.

"Thank you," he said as he reached for the toy. Edwina stroked his smooth curls then got to her feet.

"May I offer you some tea?" Agnes asked. "I was just starting to prepare a meal."

"We have simply stuffed ourselves already and couldn't eat another bite. But please don't let us keep you from getting on with your preparations. I'm sure Benjy needs his meals on time," Beryl said.

"I suppose Norah must have told you where to find me," Agnes said. "She's the only one who knew."

"She did but it wasn't easy to convince her to do so," Edwina said. "We wouldn't have disturbed you if it wasn't important."

"What is so important?" Agnes asked.

"It's Polly Watkins," Beryl said.

"Really it's more about Michael Blackburn. Norah wouldn't have shared your secret if she weren't justifiably concerned about her brother," Edwina said.

"Michael? He hasn't had a relapse, has he?" Agnes' face clouded with concern. She darted a quick glance at her son and Edwina wondered if she had reason to fear for his safety where Michael was concerned.

"No, nothing like that. There's no nice way to say this so I'll just come out with it." Edwina glanced at Benjy and lowered her voice. "Polly is dead and it looks very much like Michael might have killed her."

"Polly Watkins was murdered?" Agnes gripped the edge of the chair close at hand. "You say Michael may have done it?"

"He was the last one known to have seen her alive. She was seen getting into his cab the night she died and no one has come forward to say they've seen her alive again," Beryl said. "He won't even confirm that he had her in the cab, let alone where he took her. Norah says he had been hired to drive her home from the cinema but his uncooperative attitude makes him look guilty."

"I am so sorry to hear about Polly. I always liked her. When will her family hold the funeral?" Agnes asked.

"Tomorrow afternoon at the church in Walmsley Parva. Will you come?" Edwina asked.

"I'll have to think it over. It could be very awkward." Agnes looked over at her boy. "Why does anyone think Michael might be involved?"

"He was the last one seen with her before she died. It's especially worrisome because of how Michael acted while he was in the hospital. We know that he became unusually possessive of you during the time you spent reading to him in the hospital. We wanted to verify that you were in fact alive and well. Honestly, I feared from the time you disappeared that you had been killed and your body had been hidden away somewhere," Edwina said. "It simply was not like you in the least to shirk your duties and to leave without a word to anyone."

"I never meant to worry anyone. I suppose I was just so caught up in my own concerns that I acted selfishly. I am so sorry to have caused any grief."

"I understand why you left without a forwarding address and I don't even think you did the wrong thing. It's just that it looked like a pattern of behavior on Michael's part and we needed to be sure you truly were alive and well."

"Norah had good reason to make something like that up, you see," Beryl said. "She is very protective of her brother even now that he seems to be mostly mended."

"I'm glad to hear that he is fine and I don't think he was the sort of man to do violence to others. Did anyone question the man Polly was walking out with? Norman Davies, I think he was called. If anyone in Walmsley Parva was a criminal type, it was him," Agnes said.

"You're talking about the stolen produce and livestock from the Wallingford Estate?" Beryl asked. Agnes nodded. "Will you tell us about it?"

"I had been concerned for some time about discrepancies in our inventory. Whenever I asked Norman about it he gave me an excuse. First they were plausible like an accounting error or an unexpected illness in one of the lambs. But then he became defensive and started saying I was imagining things. I said we had either the worst stock-keeping system and unhealthiest animals in the county or something dishonest was going on. He dismissed my concerns and said I thought I knew more than I did about the way the farm worked. He acted confident but I could tell he was worried despite all his bluster."

"Did you prove that he was stealing?"

"I did. I decided to get to the bottom of it for once and for all so I hid in the storeroom where the butter was kept. I had noticed a couple of pounds would go missing every few days during the night. It took a couple of nights of keeping watch but before long Norman let himself in and left with not only some butter but some cream as well."

"Did you tell him you had proof?" Beryl asked.

"I did. He laughed in my face until I told him I was planning to go to the matron, Hortense Merriweather, with the accusation. He grabbed my arm and started shaking me. I pulled away and I wished I hadn't told him what I had decided to do."

"Did you end up telling her?" Edwina asked.

"Of course I did. He was stealing from us all, from the boys on the front even, by taking the products from the Wallingford Estate. I wasn't working my fingers to the bone so that Norman Davies could simply help himself to whatever he took a mind to grab."

"What did Hortense say about it? Did she seem surprised?" Beryl asked.

"Naturally she was very upset. I only wish I had been there to see what happened when she reported him to the authorities. Unfortunately things took longer than she had expected and I left before it all got sorted," Agnes said. Edwina cocked an eyebrow at Beryl who gave a tiny shake of the head. Agnes did not need to know that Norman was never prosecuted for his crimes.

"So you left for London very soon after discovering what he was up to then?" Edwina asked.

"Only a couple of days later, in fact. It is rather difficult to think about."

"I'm sure it is but could you bring yourself to explain how you came to leave? Polly's body was found at the Wallingford Estate and it seems that every part of our investigation keeps bringing us back to things that happened on it at the same time you were stationed there," Beryl said.

"Why are the two of you asking these questions instead of the police?" Agnes asked.

"Constable Gibbs remains the enforcer of the law in Walmsley Parva," Edwina said.

"I see. I can't imagine she's raised her esteem of women who were in the Land Army in the time that has elapsed since I was enlisted."

"It doesn't appear that she has. The search for you was conducted halfheartedly and only at my insistence. She decided Polly had met with an accident as soon as she arrived at the crime scene," Edwina said.

"Not only that, but Edwina was attacked while she was

looking over the ledgers from the estate. The person who assaulted her took them away. Is there any reason you can think of that someone would want them?" Beryl asked.

"What did they contain? Not the inventory records?" Agnes said.

"No. Hortense had the inventory ledgers. Mine were about the skills and availability for each Land Army worker and where they were sent to work. I had the milk, produce, and livestock delivery routes marked out. I had the list of the girls that had already left the Land Army and those that were still on the roster."

"None of that sounds like something worth stealing, does it? Or hurting you over, does it?" Agnes asked.

"No, it doesn't, but nevertheless someone did steal them after knocking me unconscious," Edwina said. "I just can't give up the idea there was something important inside them."

"Which is one more reason we have been looking into Polly's murder. We'd like to know who assaulted Edwina," Beryl said. "Any little bit of information you remember could be a great help."

"Was there anything unusual that occurred that week? Anything at all?" Edwina asked.

"You mean besides the fact that I abandoned my post and ran off to London under a new name?" Agnes said.

"Yes, besides that. How did you decide to leave for London? Was it your idea?" Edwina asked.

"I'm not sure. It all happened quite quickly."

"Perhaps if you tell us what you do remember for sure that would be a good start," Beryl said. "Just try to remember what you did. Was it an ordinary day, the last day you were at the Wallingford Estate?"

"Well, it wouldn't have been a few weeks earlier. Unfortunately it had become quite common. I was out with the milk float doing the early delivery and I was ill. Sick in the morning, you understand." Agnes looked over at Benjy. "I had to keep stopping the float and being sick at the side of the road."

"That must have been a difficult morning," Beryl said.

"I had gotten quite good really at pushing through but for some reason that last day I was sicker than usual. I worried maybe that I had fallen ill with something even more serious than having fallen pregnant. Flu or something like it," Agnes said. "I had to pull the cart to the side of the road so many times I was late delivering the milk. In fact, I was so late that Hortense came out looking for me."

"Hortense went looking for you?" Edwina asked.

"She met me on the route," Agnes said. "I was just straightening up once more when she came round the side of a small cottage. I remember thinking it was such a sweet-looking little place with its cheerful blue door just before I lost some more of my breakfast. Hortense said Prudence Rathbone had called to complain that I was late with the milk and that she'd seen me being ill and she assumed I was feeling the effects of a night of drinking."

"Prudence said that about you?" Beryl asked.

"She did. Hortense was very angry and she told me she would drive us back to the estate. When we finally got back to the barn she said it served me right to be ill and that she expected me to stable the pony. Dreadful, stubborn creature that animal was," Agnes said. "I remember I was so light-headed and weak that I could barely manage to unhitch the pony. Matron said she had resisted listening to the gossip from Constable Gibbs that all the girls in the Land Army were no better than they ought to be but it was clear to her that morning that the constable had been right all along. She'd seen the proof with her own eyes."

"Hortense must not have liked that."

"No, she didn't. She said I had disgraced my uniform and should be ashamed of myself. She wanted to know what sort of example I set for the other girls sneaking out and drinking. She wanted to know where I had gone and how I had managed to get out and back in again without anyone seeing me. She said she couldn't let this sort of thing spread to the other girls. She kept badgering me until I finally told her the truth."

"You told her about the baby?" Edwina asked.

"I just blurted it out. Before I knew what I'd done I told her everything. It was a relief really. I had felt so alone." Agnes crossed the room and picked up Benjy. She sat on the edge of the slim iron bed and held her son close.

"What did Hortense say when you told her?"

"She surprised me. She said it was a terrible thing for a young woman to go through all alone. She felt it was her responsibility to try and make things right. She said if she had done her job better I wouldn't have found myself in the position I was in. She also said she didn't want my condition to become known and to reflect poorly on the work the Land Army was doing. She said it had been difficult enough to appease the locals without one of the girls falling pregnant."

"How did she propose to keep anyone from finding out? Did she tell you to leave Walmsley Parva?"

"She said she wouldn't report me to the people above her in the Land Army administration and she suggested I leave Walmsley Parva and head to London where it would be easy to find a factory job, especially if I said I was a war widow. She even gave me some money for travel and helped me to leave early the next morning before anyone else was up."

"That was very generous of her. How did you leave the village?"

"She used the farm truck to drive me to the station in Parnham St. Mary and I boarded the train there. She said it would make it harder for anyone to find me should they go looking if I didn't leave from the station in Walmsley Parva."

"Have you ever seen Hortense again?" Beryl asked.

"I haven't seen anyone. The only one I've had any contact with since I left Walmsley Parva was Norah."

"You haven't contacted the baby's father at all?" Edwina asked.

"No. I thought it best not to make things more complicated than they need to be. I thought about doing so at first but at this point I've been telling everyone that I meet that I'm a war widow that I've almost convinced myself that I am." Agnes stroked Benjy's head. "It's better for everyone this way."

Chapter 33

The back garden of Heronwood House still showed a bit of color in its long herbaceous borders. Rose hips clung to bare branches and some pansies bloomed valiantly at the edges. Hortense stood with her back to Edwina snipping some rosemary branches with a pair of garden shears.

"I don't know how you manage to keep it all looking so nice with no help at all," Edwina called out across the lawn. Hortense turned and raised the bunch of rosemary in greeting. "Even with Simpkins pitching in a couple of times each week my garden doesn't look half this tidy."

"It keeps me occupied between volunteer obligations. You know how it is when you don't have enough to keep busy." Hortense headed to a wooden bench in front of a grove of azaleas and sat down. Edwina joined her.

"Beryl and I ran into an old acquaintance yesterday on our trip to London."

"You went up to London?" Hortense said. She made a snorting noise. "You never go up to London."

"I needed a new hat," Edwina said.

"You went all the way to London to purchase a hat? Whatever has gotten into you?" Hortense said. "We have a perfectly serviceable millinery here in Walmsley Parva."

Edwina had been surprised at herself and the pleasure she had found shopping in London. There was something freeing about going to shops where no one knew you and no one had a notion of the sort of person you were supposed to be. Not one of the shop assistants had realized they were helping an impoverished spinster from an insignificant village. They simply saw her as another woman who wanted a hat. Some of them had seen her as Beryl Helliwell's friend. It had all been rather marvelous. Hortense's comments made it feel all the more special. Edwina sat up a bit straighter.

"I felt in need of something a bit more than just serviceable. I had a notion to buy something rather more glamorous than that."

"Glamorous? At your age? It sounds to me like that friend of yours is putting notions in your head that ought not be there. Either that or you were rather more badly injured by that knock on your head than anyone realized," Hortense said.

"I didn't really come by to discuss hats, Hortense. I thought you would be interested to know that the person I ran into when I wasn't making a fool of myself in the shops was Agnes Rollins. Or Agnes Martin as she calls herself these days."

"Well, that's a surprise. You must have been relieved to finally know where she got off to."

"I was quite relieved. Especially after what has happened to Polly. It was good to finally know Agnes was safe and sound. I only wish I had known sooner what had become of her," Edwina said. "I was disappointed to discover you could have put my mind at ease long ago."

"I did what I felt was in Agnes' best interest. I'm sorry if you felt I could have done better by you." Hortense gazed off into the distance.

"You certainly could have. You know how distressed I was about Agnes at the time. Constable Gibbs has still not forgiven me for pestering her for weeks on end."

"I did what I thought was in the best interest of a young girl with a life-destroying problem," Hortense said. "Surely you wouldn't have wanted me to betray Agnes' confidence in me?"

"Do you think I would not have kept her secret?" Edwina asked.

"It wasn't about you. I promised Agnes I wouldn't share her whereabouts or her reasons for leaving so abruptly with anyone."

"Why did she leave so abruptly? It wasn't as if she was showing. She could have stayed on the Wallingford Estate, earning her wages and having a free roof over her head. Why did she leave so quickly?"

"I received a call from Prudence complaining about a late delivery. Agnes had been ill right at her front door and she had a great deal to say about it. I was convinced that with Prudence's poisonous mind it would take very little for her to decide that Agnes was not ill from too much drink. Lives are ruined that way. It felt as though enough lives were being ruined every day with the war and the influenza."

"So you decided to go out looking for her?" Edwina asked.

"It seemed the only thing to do at the time. I was trying to limit the damage that had already been done. I didn't want anyone else to see her being ill at the side of the road."

"I likely would have done the same. But there is something else that I don't understand."

"Which is?" Hortense asked.

"Agnes says she reported to you that Norman Davies was stealing produce and livestock from the Wallingford Estate and that she told you all about it. It doesn't seem like the sort of thing you would let go?"

"It isn't usually. I did what I thought was best in that situation, too."

"You thought it best to allow thieving from the estate? Stealing from the soldiers and the villagers?" Edwina said.

"It was on account of his help. I simply would have missed his expertise and his muscle far more than I missed a few pounds of butter or the odd pint of cream."

"You had plenty of help, didn't you?"

"I had a willing group of inexperienced girls. What I needed was someone with the least idea of how to be a farmer. Norman was too vital to the success of the entire estate to turn in to the authorities for stealing."

"You allowed a thief to stay in a position of responsibility because you needed his skills too much to lose him?" Edwina asked.

"It seemed worth it at the time. The stakes were so high. You know what it was like, the worrying about food production. About starvation. A little skimming off the top seemed a small price to pay for Norman's expertise."

The two women sat in silence for some moments. A bird warbled in the tree above their heads and the breeze lifted the ends of Edwina's scarf. She wondered what else she could ask of Hortense that might push the investigation forward. Even with the success of finding Agnes alive it felt little had actually been accomplished. She took a stab in the dark.

"I wonder, do you remember the route that Agnes drove the milk float? Where she made her deliveries every morning?"

"I ought to. I had to take over her duties on top of my own after she headed off to London."

"How did you manage it all?"

"Thankfully I had the farm truck to use. It made things much faster than hitching up Joe the pony the way Agnes had to do."

"You didn't use Joe to make the deliveries, too?"

"Of course not. I had to get finished as quickly as possible and I never liked that beast. Agnes only used him because she didn't know how to drive," Hortense said. "I made the deliveries and still got back in time to see to the business of the estate without a glitch."

"Do you happen to remember the properties on the route? Where you stopped and made the deliveries?" Edwina asked.

"If I put my mind to it I suppose that I could but I thought you had all that written down in your records, didn't you?"

"I did, but the person who assaulted me not only bashed me over the head, he or she took all my ledgers from the Wallingford Estate, too."

"You think that a woman could have hit you hard enough to have knocked you out?" Hortense asked.

"Of course. Shouldn't we be the last people to question what women are capable of after seeing all the hard work on the Wallingford Estate? You and I both know that with enough determination women can do anything they put their minds to."

"I suppose you could be right."

"So do you remember the route?"

"Let me think. I headed out from the estate and took the east road into town. The houses all along the way between the estate and into the village needed deliveries. I went along the high street. I stopped at Prudence's since she was on the route and then up the lane running towards the reading room and the church. I stopped at all those houses along the way that had asked for deliveries." Hortense looked up at a woodpecker knocking away on a tree at the edge of the wood. "I stopped at the doctor's place before I headed back out to the west side of town and back to the estate. It made a fairly tidy loop."

"That doesn't sound like anything that should have caused someone to take the ledgers. It just doesn't make any sense. None of it does," Edwina said. "You don't know who the father of Agnes' baby is, do you? I keep thinking there has to be something from her days at the Wallingford Estate that explains what happened to Polly."

"Didn't you ask Agnes who he was then while you were in London?"

"I didn't feel right about asking her," Edwina said. "And she didn't offer the information either."

"What makes you think she ever offered it to me?"

"I just thought since you were such a help to her that she might have confided that to you as well."

"Well, she didn't. And frankly I'm glad. I shouldn't have liked to have known and tried to keep myself behaving civil to a man that would leave a nice girl like Agnes in such a bad way."

"You think he was a local lad then?" Edwina asked.

"I can't see how he could have been otherwise. Agnes was either working on the estate or reading to the soldiers in the hospital wing. She wasn't like Polly going out dancing and the like at every weekend. She didn't wander far afield and I doubt she would have had the opportunity to meet someone from far off."

"You have no one you suspect of being the man responsible?"

"There are a number of possibilities, of course, but I would be very uncomfortable naming names. Unlike you, I don't fancy myself a detective."

The two sat in companionable silence for some moments watching the clouds scud across the sky and the shadows flit across the garden beds. Edwina ran her hand along a stand of lavender planted next to the bench and released its heady scent.

"If you think of anything you think I should know you'll get in touch, won't you?" Edwina asked as she stood to go. She turned her face towards the long border opposite once more and gazed at it with admiration.

"I will if I think of anything but I shall be surprised if there is any more for me to tell."

"Are you sure you also can't tell me how you manage all this?" Edwina gestured towards the plantings. "I wonder if you would be willing to give Simpkins some tips."

"My only tip about Simpkins is that he'd be more use fertilizing the garden from beneath it rather than above it. I'd cut my losses with him as soon as possible. I don't know why you keep him around."

"I suppose because my mother thought so much of him. They were always of a mind about the garden, those two. Besides, having him is better than having no help at all." Edwina hoped she sounded more confident than she felt. Defending Simpkins was alien territory and would take a great deal of getting used to.

"I thought that was exactly what he was, no help at all."

"He watched Crumpet while Beryl and I were in London. That has to count for something," Edwina said. "He is also a surprisingly decent cook."

"How on earth would you know a thing like that?" Hortense asked. Edwina wished she had not opened her mouth so wide.

"You'd be surprised the things you uncover in the course of an investigation."

"I've noticed your investigation hasn't left you much time to help out with the jumble sale. When can I expect you to be back at the village hall volunteering?" Hortense asked. "What's more, are you ever going to wring a commitment to help with a celebrity fund-raising scheme from that lodger of yours? After all, what good is it to have someone famous living amongst us if it can't be made to profit somehow?"

"Beryl hasn't seemed terribly eager to step into the spotlight since she's been here. I don't feel comfortable asking her to do anything she'd rather not do."

"No one is ever eager to help with things like the jumble sale, Edwina. That's why God put women like us in every community. Someone has to remind people of their duty to King and country."

"Not everyone can be as good a citizen as you, Hortense. At least not all the time." Edwina stood and brushed a dried leaf off her long skirt. "I'll be along to the village hall to help just as soon as I can."

Chapter 34

Edwina stepped into the hallway and heard voices coming from the sitting room. Finding Simpkins in the kitchen had been enough to get used to. Discovering that Beryl had taken the notion to entertain him in the sitting room was another thing altogether. She carefully unwound her scarf and removed her new hat. She cocked her head towards the sound of the voices and steeled herself to face the fresh effrontery of the outside staff inside the house. Any finer feelings she had shown towards him at Hortense's house immediately fled as she considered his boots upon her hearth rug.

She stepped into the sitting room prepared for battle but not for the sight of Agnes and Benjy sitting on the sofa.

"Look who decided to take the train down to see us," Beryl said.

"Agnes, what are you doing here?" Edwina asked.

"I thought it over and I couldn't sleep thinking about both Polly and Michael. Even if everyone in Walmsley Parva finds out the truth about Benjy I couldn't refuse to attend the funeral once I knew it was happening." Agnes paused. "I also thought maybe if I saw Michael I could convince him to tell you what he knows. He always did have a soft spot for me."

"Do you really think that is wise? Norah didn't want to tell Michael where you went for fear he would suffer a setback," Edwina said.

"He'll suffer a worse one for sure if he ends up arrested for Polly's murder," Beryl said. "I think we should risk it."

"The funeral is this afternoon. What about Benjy? Surely you don't want him to attend?" Edwina looked down at the small boy and thought how such an event would be trying for all concerned.

"I don't have much choice. Where I go, he goes, except to work."

"Beryl could keep him here with her," Edwina said. "She didn't really know Polly, and if Benjy stays here, gossips like Prudence Rathbone will keep their attention on Polly where it ought to be, not on speculating about your son."

"Would you really?" Agnes asked, turning to Beryl. "I was rather dreading trying to keep him quiet at the service. I wasn't looking forward to facing all the inevitable whispering either, if I tell the truth."

Edwina was surprised to see her intrepid friend turn ever so slightly green. Beryl's eyes widened, and if Edwina didn't know better she would have said her friend was terrified of the baby. In fact, she seemed temporarily robbed of the power of speech. Finally she nodded as slowly as if she were encased in aspic.

"That's settled then," Edwina said. "Are you able to stay the night in the village and return by tomorrow's train?"

"I haven't any place to stay," Agnes said.

"Nonsense. You can stay here at the Beeches. We'd love the company, wouldn't we, Beryl?" Edwina said. Beryl didn't answer. She simply kept staring at Benjy as if he were some sort of alien creature that couldn't be trusted not to lash out. Edwina was stunned by Beryl's behavior and couldn't help but feel a bit like she was getting her own back after the way Beryl had foisted altogether too much of Simpkins' company on her of late. In fact, from the look of her, it might even balance the scales concerning the terrifying trip to London at Beryl's hands the day before.

"I'll show you up to one of the guest rooms. I believe we even still have some toys from my brother's childhood in the attics that I could bring down. Beryl will surely want something with which to entertain our young friend," Edwina said. "I'm sure she'll be happy to get to know him better while I show you around." She took Agnes by the arm and left Beryl standing next to the mantlepiece with an anguished look on her face.

Polly's service filled the small church to capacity. The whole village, it seemed, had turned out. Polly's parents sat in the front row, their heads bowed and their shoulders slumped. Edwina dressed in the dull black ensemble she had worn for her own mother's funeral several months earlier and had managed to avoid ever since.

Heads turned when she and Agnes entered the church. Whispers made the rounds and Agnes gripped Edwina's arm with ferocity. Edwina was glad she had suggested that Benjy remain out of sight. Not that Edwina thought Agnes should be ashamed of him. Still, it made matters easier not to add to the excitement her unexpected appearance seemed to cause.

Edwina noticed the Mumfords sitting a few rows ahead on the right. Norman, she noticed, had a place in the front row sitting right next to Polly's parents. Michael and Norah were there as were Hortense and Prudence. Dr. Nelson and his wife sat in a pew with Charles Jarvis. Edwina even spotted Walter Bennett, the projectionist, standing at the very back of the church despite his apparent reluctance to ever appear in public.

Sidney Poole the butcher and Constable Gibbs sat near the door.

At the end of the service Edwina and Agnes stopped to pay their respects to Polly's parents before strolling on out of the churchyard. Edwina did not want to appear as though they were hurrying but neither did she want to expose Agnes to unnecessary questioning. Norah stood at the far end of the churchyard holding on to Michael's arm and leaning towards his ear. Edwina would have given a lot to hear what she was saying to him. He shrugged her hand off and closed the distance between them in a few quick strides.

"Agnes, it is so good to see you," he said, catching her hand in his own. "Where did you take yourself off to? And why did you leave without saying good-bye?"

"I had obligations in London and I couldn't get out of them, Michael. I'm very sorry if I hurt you by leaving without warning," Agnes said.

"I'm just so glad to see you safe and sound. Miss Davenport here had the countryside turned on its ear looking for you in the days after you left."

"She did indeed." Constable Gibbs stopped next to Edwina and looked Agnes up and down. "I told you at the time there was no reason to get so heated about Miss Rollins leaving town. Just as there is no reason to think anything criminal happened to Polly. I hope you've learned your lesson about meddling in things amateurs ought to leave to the authorities." Constable Gibbs scowled at them both and turned on her heel.

"Even though I wasn't missing, I'm more touched than I can say that you put such effort into looking for me. Most people would not have bothered."

Michael reached out and touched Agnes' sleeve. "Will you take a walk with me?" he asked. "I have so much I'd like to say to you."

Agnes looked at Edwina and then back at him. Norah stood hovering just a few feet away. Edwina could feel desperation coming off of Michael in waves but wasn't sure that it meant he posed a threat to Agnes. Agnes gave Edwina a small smile of reassurance.

"I would be delighted to visit with you but only if Norah agrees to accompany us. After all, I'm not the sort of girl to ignore one friend in favor of another," Agnes said. Edwina couldn't be sure because of the distance but she thought she heard Norah exhaling a long-held breath.

Norah stepped up and linked her arm in Agnes'. "Come along to the garage and see what we've done to the place while you've been away."

"Sounds delightful. Miss Davenport, I'll be back to the Beeches in time for tea if that suits you and Miss Helliwell," Agnes said.

"If you aren't back by then I will put out a call to Constable Gibbs to come find you. Maybe she will do a better job a second time around if the need arises." Edwina watched as the three younger people walked off in the direction of the garage. Michael waved his good arm about exuberantly while Norah held on to Agnes' waist like they were long-lost sisters. Edwina was startled when Charles Jarvis' voice filled her ear.

"You must be quite pleased to finally have that mystery solved." He nodded towards the retreating trio.

"I am, actually," Edwina said.

"I wonder if everyone in Walmsley Parva shares your view," Charles said. "There may be those who were just as happy for her to stay missing." They stood silently watching the funeral-goers file past. Edwina felt the sudden desire to rush home to the safety of her own four walls.

"Miss Davenport, you look as though you've taken a turn. Please allow me to accompany you home." Edwina looked at

Charles, a man she had known for years, and wondered how much she really knew about him. Or any of her neighbors for that matter. It seemed to her that the person responsible for Polly's death had likely attended her funeral. Edwina could not say with any degree of truth that any one of them acted in a way that implied guilt. A cold shiver ran up her spine. She didn't relish the idea of walking home on her own but the idea of trusting Charles was suddenly not appealing either.

Just then she heard the honking of an insistent horn. She turned to see Beryl's motorcar approaching with, to her eyes, what constituted reckless speed.

"Thank you so much but as you can see Miss Helliwell has come to collect me." Edwina gave him a bright smile and then made a mad dash for the cherry red car. She was so glad to see it that she forgot how much Beryl's driving terrified her.

"What have you done with the baby?" Edwina asked, looking around the motorcar and seeing only Beryl.

"I just couldn't manage a moment longer. He was so very small and fragile looking," Beryl said. Her hands gripped the wheel tightly and Edwina thought her voice sounded unnaturally high.

"What have you done with him, Beryl?" Edwina asked, her heart starting to hammer in her chest.

"No need to worry, Ed. He's in good hands. I've left Simpkins in charge of him."

"Simpkins?" Edwina could not believe her ears. What was it with Beryl and her gardener? "You left a helpless baby with a man who can't be trusted on the matter of limestone and azaleas?"

"I don't know anything about limestone or azaleas. I know even less about babies. I think it is very narrow-minded of you, Ed, to assume I was a better candidate for the job of child minder than Simpkins just because I am a woman. He did well with Crumpet while we were in London."

"A dog is not the same as a human baby. As you ought to know."

"I've never even successfully cared for a fish in a bowl. Simpkins seemed a better choice." They rode the rest of the way back to the Beeches in silence.

Chapter 35

Simpkins sat at the kitchen table with Benjy balanced on his knee, crooning a tune Edwina was horrified to realize was something more suited to a pirate ship than a nursery. Crumpet sat disloyally under the table with his chin on the toe of Simpkins' grubby boot. Beryl also recognized the tune and began to sing along. It appeared she had recovered her good humor just as soon as the responsibility for the baby was assuredly no longer hers.

"Good as gold he was. Such a fine little fellow," Simpkins said once he concluded his song. Edwina started to reprimand him for his choice of music when Benjy began to cry. Immediately Simpkins took up his song once more and the baby quieted.

"See," Beryl whispered in Edwina's ear. "Simpkins is far more suited to child care than I shall ever be." Edwina could think of nothing whatsoever to say. She turned to the cooker and set about preparing something for tea. Edwina trusted Agnes would be along soon. Surely Norah wouldn't let any harm befall her.

She pulled out some eggs and put them on to boil then began to slice a loaf of bread for toast soldiers when a knock sounded upon the front door. Beryl hurried to answer it and in a moment Agnes appeared with Michael a step behind her.

"I hope you don't mind but I've invited Michael round to join us. He has something he wants to tell you about the night Polly died," Agnes said. She turned to Michael. "Isn't that right?" Edwina realized she was holding her breath. Michael nodded and she slowly released it.

"Would you and the baby like to take a turn round the garden with me while they talk?" Simpkins asked. "I shouldn't be at all surprised to find a few late quinces to pick if we're lucky." Agnes gave Michael's arm a reassuring squeeze then followed Simpkins out the back door. Crumpet looked from his mistress to the garden. She nodded at him and he followed Simpkins and Agnes. Edwina hoped Crumpet was feeling a sudden attachment to the baby. She wasn't sure what she would do if her dog developed an appreciation for the gardener's company.

Beryl and Michael sat at the table and Edwina wiped her hands on her apron and joined them.

"Agnes convinced me to tell you what I know about Polly. She said it wasn't right to let my instincts as a soldier cloud my judgment back home in Walmsley Parva."

"Very sensible of her to suggest," Edwina said.

"It's very big of you to do so," Beryl said. "It isn't an easy thing to stop soldiering." Michael nodded and cleared his throat.

"I just can't believe he had anything to do with what happened to Polly, no matter how it may seem," he said. "Walter Bennett hired me to drive Polly home from the cinema on the nights she attended the late show. He was worried about her getting all the way back to her mum's place in the cold now that the weather has turned."

Edwina and Beryl exchanged a look. It would not do any good to tell Michael that his sister had already told them about

Walter hiring him. It was far better to let him tell them all he could.

"That's very thoughtful of him. So you took her home at his request the night she died?" Beryl asked.

"I picked her up like I usually did. She would come out the back of the building since she didn't want Mr. Mumford to see her. He wouldn't have liked her getting in to see the film for free if she didn't feel she owed him directly for the privilege."

"Not a very savory character that Mr. Mumford, is he?" Beryl said. "But you spirited her away and got her safely home?"

"No. That's just it. I didn't take her home." Michael exhaled deeply. "She asked me to take her to Walter's house instead. She said she had a surprise for him and that she wanted me to keep it a secret."

"Did you see her go into Walter's house?" Edwina asked.

"I walked her to the door and made sure she got inside. She smiled and waved at me through the window when I left her."

"And that's the last you saw of her?" Edwina asked.

"The very last. I didn't want to say anything because I didn't want to bring down any trouble on Walter's head. God knows the man's suffered enough," Michael said. "And I didn't want to damage Polly's reputation. It would only hurt her mum to hear that her daughter was out visiting a man's house so late at night like that. People have nasty minds, don't they, and no one would likely believe she wasn't there for some scandalous purpose."

"I'm sorry to say that I'm sure you're right," Edwina said. "Gossips would have made quite a meal of that bit of news."

"Have you spoken with Walter since he asked you to take Polly home on the night she died?" Beryl asked.

"No. I was going to try when I caught sight of him at the funeral this afternoon but he slipped away before I could reach him. When I saw Agnes all other thoughts disappeared," Michael said. "I didn't hurt her. Polly I mean. And I've apologized to Agnes for frightening her. I wasn't at all well when she was in the village. I know that now." Michael stood to go.

"I'm sure she appreciated that. Are you going to say good-bye?"

"I think I'll head out before she knows I've gone. I'm not much of one for good-byes." Michael shrugged and headed down the hall and out the front door without another word.

"As much as I'd like to think it would, I'm not sure that his explanation gets Michael off the hook," Edwina said. "He can't prove that he left her safely at Walter Bennett's cottage. We only have his word for it."

"There's also the matter of how she ended up in the field on the Wallingford Estate. Where does Walter Bennett live?" Beryl asked.

"He lives in a small laborer's cottage at the edge of the Wallingford Estate."

"This whole situation keeps circling back to the same place. Is Walter Bennett's cottage near Norman's? Is it near where her body was found?"

"No. It is like Norman's but is on the other side of the estate. It's closer to the centre of the village."

"I think the next thing we should do is to speak with Walter Bennett. We need to know what he has to say about Polly being at his cottage."

"We should go in the morning I think. This isn't a matter to discuss at the cinema and he is sure to be at work by now."

"I agree. I think we should take a look round the cottage to see if there is any evidence that Polly was ever there. If she was, that may prove Michael is telling the truth."

"And it may also prove that Walter Bennett is a guilty man."

Chapter 36

"Are you ready?" Beryl looked over at Edwina.

"We have to see it through," Edwina said. She opened the motorcar door and stepped out into the cool air. Walter Bennett's cottage stood alone at the edge of a field. A low stone wall separated it from the lane in front of it. A wooden gate shaded by an arched trellis weighted down by the bare branches of a gnarled wisteria creaked loudly when Beryl pushed it open.

They walked up the stone path to the cheerful blue door and Edwina knocked upon it with a gloved hand. When no one responded Beryl stepped forward and gave it a louder rap. From behind the door came the sound of feet and then Walter Bennett stood before them. His hand held the side of his tin mask as if he were checking to be sure it was properly in place. Beryl found herself wondering if he seldom wore it when alone in his home. She imagined that it must be uncomfortable and it would be a relief to leave it off from time to time.

"Sorry to come by so early, Mr. Bennett, but we needed to speak with you rather urgently. Some new information about Polly Watkins' death has come to light and we wanted to ask you about it," Beryl said. "May we come in?"

"The place is a tip. It isn't fit for the likes of you two," Walter said.

"I've traveled in tramp steamers across the Pacific down amongst the bilge pumps and the water rats. Edwina suffers almost constantly from the untidiness of her jobbing gardener. I expect your home holds no terrors for us." Beryl gave him a bright smile and took a determined step forward. Walter stepped backwards and gestured for them to go on through to the sitting room.

They entered a dusty, shadowy low-ceilinged room at the front of the house. Beryl sat down in an upholstered chair next to the small brick fireplace. Edwina took a place on a stiff sofa facing the windows onto the street. Beryl thought there was something pleasant about the arrangement to the room despite the surface layer of dust. A silver candlestick graced the center of the small wooden table Beryl imagined served as a pleasant place for a meal. Two needlepoint pillows brightened up the sofa. Framed watercolor prints of landscapes hung on the walls and floral curtains suspended at the sides of the windows.

"May I offer you some tea?" Walter asked.

"That would be very kind. I don't know about Miss Davenport but I never refuse the offer of a cup of tea," Beryl said. She tipped her head significantly at Edwina hoping she would be understood.

"Thank you, Mr. Bennett. I would be delighted to have some," Edwina said. As soon as he left the room both women got to their feet and began searching the room for signs of Polly. Beryl headed straight for the bookcases.

"I doubt very much you'll find evidence of Polly there. She wasn't much of a reader," Edwina said.

"Mr. Bennett is though, isn't he?" Beryl said.

"So it would seem. If you were Polly, what would you do if you wanted to surprise Mr. Bennett? Would you wander around the room? Would you perch quietly on that chair there?" Edwina asked.

"I think she would want to be on the lookout for him coming up the walkway. If I were her I would have sat on the sofa and faced the windows. If there was as much moonlight beaming down as there was on the night we found her she would have been able to see him coming up the walk." Beryl sat on the edge of the sofa and squinted. "I think she would have been here. Although I must say this isn't the most comfortable spot." She reached into the crack between cushions and pulled out a length of fabric.

"That's Polly's wrap," Edwina said. "I remember seeing her wearing it when we saw her near the cinema." She turned to the door at the sound of Walter Bennett's footsteps. Beryl stuffed it under the needlepoint pillow sitting next to her on the sofa. Walter Bennett carried two heavy ceramic mugs, which he handed to each woman in turn. Edwina carried hers to the sofa and sat beside Beryl. She suddenly felt a great need to have a friend at hand.

"I don't want to seem unfriendly but what is this information about Polly that's brought you out so early in the day?"

"We are sorry, Mr. Bennett. I'm sure it doesn't seem as early to us as it does to you. We should have considered the late hours you keep. However, we would not have bothered you if it weren't urgent," Edwina said.

"We've been told that you hired Michael Blackburn to drive Polly to her house after she spent the evening at the cinema with you. We understand that this was a common occurrence and not at all the situation you led me to believe when I asked you before how well you knew her."

"Is there any crime in being a gentleman?" Mr. Bennett asked.

"Certainly not," Edwina said. "But considering Polly was murdered, and we know she was much more well-known to you than you have admitted, it would be wise of you to be a bit more forthcoming about your relationship with her."

Truly it was disconcerting to interview Mr. Bennett. His facial expression never changed because of the mask. Beryl wondered if Edwina was finding it as difficult to gauge his reaction to questions as she did.

"Michael and his sister, Norah, claim you paid to have Polly driven home from the cinema at least three evenings each week. People might make a lot of that information if it were to get out and I can't imagine any of it will do her character credit. Somehow I don't think that is what you want for her memory," Beryl said.

Mr. Bennett lowered himself carefully into the side chair near the fireplace. "No, of course it isn't."

"We have something else to ask you about. Michael told us that he didn't drive Polly to her house the night that she died," Beryl said.

"Where the devil did he take her then?" Mr. Bennett gripped his knees with both hands.

"He says he dropped her off here. He says she asked him to do so because she wanted to surprise you. Can you think of any reason for her to do that?" Edwina asked.

Walter sank against the back of the chair. His posture telegraphed abject misery. Beryl watched as Walter pulled a handkerchief out of his pocket. He dabbed at his chin with it as his shoulders shook with silent sobs. "We are so sorry for the loss of your friend," Beryl said.

"She was more than my friend. The night she died she had agreed to be my wife," he said. "If you can imagine that. Me, a man reduced to hiding away in a dark room and avoiding all contact with the outside world, managed to get a sweet, lovely girl like Polly to accept me as her husband."

Beryl wondered about his story. She only had his word for it that Polly had agreed to marry him. The entire thing could be the crazed imaginings of a damaged man. His grief seemed genuine but it might have been guilt as much as love and longing that made him weep. Beryl also had only his word about when Polly left the cinema and in what condition. As far as she knew, he could have killed her in the projectionist's booth, carried her body to the garage just down the street, and taken Beryl's own car to transport it to the field.

"How did you come to be romantically entangled?" Beryl asked, hoping his response would either lend credence to his claim or help to disprove it. "Many couples find that their common interests spark their interest in each other. Perhaps your shared love of film brought you together?"

"That was mostly what we talked about. I said she was pretty enough to be a star in one of the films herself and she said I already looked like one. We joked about starring in a film together one day."

"She must have loved that idea considering how much she seems to have adored films. She must have had high hopes for your future together to agree to marry you," Edwina said.

"And there must have been something special between you if she put you at your ease," Beryl said.

"We talked all the time. It was like I was bursting to communicate with someone after spending so much time alone. Polly had a way of making me feel like I was interesting. Smart, too. She said I could be anything I put my mind to," he said. "She was so curious about everything. She loved to hear me tell her about other parts of the world, places beyond the village."

"Do you think she wanted to see you that night because of the engagement? Maybe to discuss the wedding?" Edwina asked.

"I suppose that is possible," Mr. Bennett said. "But she wasn't here when I arrived home."

"She wasn't here?"

"No. There was no sign of her," Walter said. "Not that I

would have had a reason to look for her. I thought she was home safe and sound. After all, why would I think she would be otherwise?"

"You didn't see this then?" Beryl asked, pulling the wrap from beneath the pillow. Walter let out another sob and he reached for the gauzy, cheap bit of cloth.

"She was wearing that the last time I saw her," he said.

"That's what we thought. Miss Davenport and I saw her heading for the cinema that evening. She was still wearing the clothing she had on when she visited you that night. So it sounds as though Michael did bring her straight here," Beryl said.

"We wondered how she came to be missing it when we came across her lying in the field. It didn't make any sense that she would walk home without it," Edwina said.

"How long did it take you to leave the cinema after Polly did?" Beryl asked.

"About an hour or so."

"Why were you so long in leaving?" Beryl asked

"I needed to splice together some broken film. I like to have everything ready for the next day before I leave at night. Besides, if I wait until it is late enough I never encounter anyone else on my way home." He held Polly's wrap up to his neck and let out another shuddering sob. "She must have gotten too impatient to wait any longer and decided to walk back on her own. If I had gotten here sooner she might still be alive. I should have gone for the constable when I arrived home that night."

"If you didn't know she was missing why would you have gone for Constable Gibbs?"

"Because I was quite sure someone had been here. This room seemed a bit disarranged and a few items were missing. At least, I couldn't find them. They didn't seem valuable enough to report them. When I found out about Polly it drove the incident from my mind."

263

"What went missing?" Beryl asked.

"An old bedsheet, the mate to that candlestick, and a pair of work gloves."

"Are you quite sure about those items?" Edwina asked.

"The cottage is tiny. I don't tend to lose things as there's nowhere for them to go," he said.

"You mustn't blame yourself. You couldn't have known anything would happen to her."

"I should have known there was no possibility of a happy ending for a man like me. How can it be that I survived driving a tank right into the shelling that did this to me"—he tapped his mask with a heavy hand—"and was nursed back from the Spanish Flu by Dr. Nelson but someone like Polly dies violently right in the tiny village where she had every reason to feel safe?"

"It doesn't seem at all fair. Life seldom does of late," Beryl said.

"We are terribly, terribly sorry for your loss. Isn't there anyone we could call to come to be with you?" Edwina asked.

"I don't want you to call anyone. I'm all on my own. If you don't mind I'd like to be alone now," Walter said, tucking his handkerchief back in his pocket. Edwina nodded and handed him her card.

"If you change your mind and decide you need to speak to someone you can ring me at the Beeches. I would be happy to come keep you company should you feel the need of companionship." She patted him gently on the shoulder and the two of them left him in peace.

Chapter 37

They were back in the car before they spoke again.

"You don't really think she tried to walk all the way home from here, do you?" Edwina said.

"From the condition of her shoes I would say most definitely that she did not."

"Why was she really at his cottage, do you think?" Edwina asked.

"You aren't really that naïve, are you, Ed?" Beryl asked. She had the satisfaction of seeing her old friend's cheeks color up like two maraschino cherries.

"Surely you don't mean that she was there to stay the night?" Edwina said.

"Well, if she was, we had best figure out what could have possibly convinced her to up and leave. And more importantly, how she managed to go." Beryl drummed the steering wheel with her fingertips. "Even though we don't have those answers we do know a couple things we didn't know before now."

"Well, we know that Polly's wrap was at Mr. Bennett's cottage and it makes it likely Polly was there herself," Edwina said.

"We also know that Mr. Bennett knows how to drive. He said that driving a tank led to his disfigurement."

"You think he was lying about finding her there?" Edwina said. "I found his grief very convincing."

"He did seem like a man who had lost his last hope. But he may be a very accomplished liar. Neither of us knows a thing about him other than that he is the projectionist at the cinema and has lost his face."

"We also know he was engaged to be married to Polly," Edwina said.

"And that he was nursed back from the influenza by Dr. Nelson," Beryl said. "When did the last wave of influenza pass through this village?"

"Just about the same time Agnes left. It was one of the reasons the search for her was less thorough than I would have liked. There were simply too few people available to conduct the search. So many villagers were confined to their beds and those that weren't were mostly home tending loved ones that were sick."

"I feel quite sorry to leave him on his own like that. To be so solitary in a time of grief is a heavy burden," Beryl said. Edwina was very quiet and Beryl thought perhaps she had brought to mind difficult memories. She was about to apologize when Edwina turned to her and spoke.

"Mr. Bennett has no one to condole with him in his time of grief. How did he call for the doctor?"

"What do you mean? Wouldn't he just telephone?" Beryl asked.

"This isn't London, Beryl, and money has been very tight everywhere. Most people in Walmsley Parva don't have telephones."

"I think after luncheon with Agnes and Charlie we should pay a call to Dr. Nelson. Perhaps he will remember who the Good Samaritan was that made the call on Mr. Bennett's behalf," Beryl said. "But I have one other question I want answered. If you can spare me for the luncheon preparations I think I'll run into the village."

"If there is one question that never needs to be asked again, Beryl, it is if I need your assistance in the kitchen."

Beryl pulled the car to the curb on the high street just outside of Prudence's shop. Excitement always left her with a hankering for sweets. She pushed open the door of the shop and stepped inside. Prudence was handing a parcel across the gleaming counter to a small woman with red hair. She shut the drawer of the till with a slam and turned her toothy smile on Beryl.

"Miss Helliwell, what a pleasure to see you in my shop once more. What can I help you with today?"

"Miss Davenport and I are having a guest for luncheon and I wanted to pick up a confection to share. I always think it's nice to have something sweet at the end of a meal, don't you?"

"Agnes Rollins is it that you'll be wanting them for?" Prudence asked. She leaned predatorily over the counter. Beryl was certain she actually saw Prudence's ears wiggle at the notion of such gossip. "I saw her with Edwina at the funeral."

"How well informed you are about the goings-on in Walmsley Parva. How long has it been since you last saw Agnes?" Beryl asked, stepping over to view the glass case filled with chocolates and nougats.

"I'm sure I can't say. A nice girl she always was. Polite, not like so many young people these days."

"I understood that when the Land Army girls first came to Walmsley Parva the people around here weren't so very eager to have them. Thought they might not be the sort of girls that were a good influence on a community."

"There were people who were opposed to them being here in the early days but after a time they came to appreciate the hard work the girls did. Mind you, everyone still agreed it was work hardly suited to young ladies."

"There must have been times when the girls did something that caused the odd raised eyebrow. At least from time to time," Beryl said with a shake of the head she hoped looked like disapproval.

"Well, not to speak ill of the dead but Polly was said to have been spending enough time at the cinema to attract attention. She had a young man she was seeing but that didn't stop her from being no better than she ought to have been." Prudence opened the case and pulled out a tray of sugared almonds. "At least that's what people say. Not that I pay much mind to that sort of thing."

"Polly wasn't the only one of the Land Army women that caused tongues to wag though, was she?" Beryl looked around conspiratorially as if to assure herself that they were alone in the shop. "Agnes wasn't always blameless from what I heard." Prudence's nostrils quivered as if she could smell scandal.

"Agnes only made herself the talk of Walmsley Parva when she disappeared and it would be fair to say when she came back into town for Polly's funeral."

"Are you quite sure there was nothing else?" Beryl asked. "No complaints about her deliveries with the milk float."

"Not that I had ever heard of. She always left my pint at the door before I came down for it in the morning."

"May I have two pounds of the chocolates?" Beryl asked. Prudence nodded and pulled out a tray of gleaming sweets. "So, you never had cause to complain to Hortense Merriweather about Agnes' tardiness with a morning delivery right before she left the village?"

"I would certainly remember a thing like that." Prudence gently placed chocolate after chocolate into a white paper box. "Agnes was a conscientious girl and I never had cause for complaint in regards to her. Why would you think that I had?"

"Just something Agnes said the other day. I must have misunderstood her," Beryl said. "These are just lovely. Shall I tell Agnes you send your regards?"

Beryl paid for the sweets and tucked the box under her arm. She walked back to the car wondering just where the confusion lay.

"And you are quite sure Hortense said she had a complaint from Prudence Rathbone about your tardiness?" Beryl asked, looking across the long dining room table. Edwina passed their young guest a platter of stuffed eggs. Beryl had been antsy from the moment she had arrived. Edwina had not given any thought to her friend's secret errand while she was hurrying to prepare the meal but now that they were seated around the table she remembered.

"I think it was Prudence. I suppose it could have been someone else and I just remember it as the sort of thing she would have said."

"But she didn't. I stopped into her shop just now and asked her about the complaint and about your reputation in town. She had nothing but glowing things to say about you."

"Prudence Rathbone had glowing things to say about someone other than the King?" Edwina could not quite believe her ears. First Simpkins was proving a useful person to have round the house and now Prudence Rathbone had complimented a commoner? The Earth must be slouching on its axis. Or maybe there was something demonic overtaking the citizenry of Walmsley Parva. One read about these things in the sorts of sensational novels she often borrowed from the reading room.

"She did indeed," Beryl said, seizing an egg and stuffing into her mouth. Edwina was pleased to see Beryl took the time, despite her obvious excitement, to swallow it before speaking. She would hate to think Simpkins was a bad influence on her friend. "Are you still certain about what you said about Hortense being angry about a telephone call?"

"Yes, of that I am certain. She met me on the route and gave me a right dressing-down. I don't think I shall ever forget it." Agnes held a cup of beef broth to Benjy's plump lips then wiped his mouth after he sipped his fill.

"Would you be willing to show me the route you took that morning?" Beryl asked.

"It wasn't just that morning. It was the same every morning. But certainly I'd be happy to do so. You don't suppose it would be a good idea to take Benjy out with us, do you? He's getting quite restless cooped up in the house."

"That is up to you. We'll take the car to make things easier. Do you think he'll like that?" Beryl asked. Edwina fervently hoped Agnes would object. In her opinion motorcars, at least not those driven by Beryl, were not suitable for children.

"I'm sure he would love it. He's never been in one before," Agnes said.

"That's settled then. As soon as luncheon is over we shall set off. Will you come too, Ed?" Beryl asked. Edwina dearly wished to give an excuse to stay home but she couldn't swallow her own bite of egg fast enough to object before Beryl had decided she had agreed. Besides, she too was curious about the route. The missing ledgers still bothered her a great deal. Each time she thought of them, the back of her head ached ever so slightly.

"Absolutely."

They were packed tightly into the motorcar in less than an hour. Beryl headed off at something she called full throttle for the Wallingford Estate and squealed to a stop just in front of the dairy barn as Agnes had instructed. Edwina clung to the notebook and pencil she had brought along to make a record of the route as Agnes remembered it.

"I started out just there with old Joe and followed the cart track at the back of the barn to the north side of the estate. It's just up along there." Agnes pointed to a hard-packed dirt lane. Edwina did her best to keep her notes legible as the motorcar jounced and bounced along the rutted path. They followed along for a moment or two before Agnes pointed out the first stop. "It certainly is faster in this than it was with old Joe and the milk float. I would have been done in half the time with a contraption like this one," Agnes said. She indicated a few more stops before Benjy started to fuss and reach towards the outside.

"Perhaps we should pull over for a moment. There's plenty of time and Benjy might like to stretch his legs for a bit," Edwina suggested. In fact, she quite agreed with Benjy and if she had been his age thought to herself that she would have been crying, too. "Look, there's a nice grassy spot for the baby to run around for a bit."

Beryl acquiesced immediately and Edwina had a sneaking suspicion the baby being in the car unnerved her. From the way she hurried out of the motorcar herself Edwina suspected that she had become quite frazzled by the presence of the small boy. Color returned to Beryl's cheeks the moment she took a step away. Edwina found it extraordinary that after all her outrageous exploits, the one thing in the world her friend seemed terrified of was a child.

"You know," Agnes said, "I believe this is quite near one of the spots I had to pull over the last time I was on this road. You were the cause of that stop too, Benjy." Agnes lifted the child above her head and spun him around in the air. In the distance Michael Blackburn's cab was drawing closer. Within a moment it overtook them. Edwina noticed Dr. Nelson in the back. She waved at him as he passed but he didn't wave back. Rather, he stared at the group of them with a stony face. Edwina wondered if he was on his way to deliver some bad news to a patient. Or had come back from doing so. Really, he did not look like himself in the least.

Benjy was content to be returned to the motorcar not long after and within a few minutes more Agnes had directed them to turn onto the lane that ran to the east of the Wallingford Estate. Edwina tried to remember what she had recorded in the ledger about the delivery routes but everything seemed a bit fuzzy. It was the head injury she hoped that did it, rather than advancing age.

"That's where I was when the matron appeared." Agnes pointed at a cottage with a thicket of bare wisteria vines clinging to a trellis at its gate.

"Hortense came upon you at Walter Bennett's cottage?"

"I don't know any Walter Bennett but I do remember the cottage with the cheerful blue door. That's the very one." Beryl pulled the motorcar to the verge again and stopped.

"Where was she coming from when she came upon you?" Beryl asked.

"I don't know really. I didn't see her approaching since I was too wrapped up in my own misery at the time. She just appeared and started scolding me."

Beryl and Edwina looked at each other then up and down the narrow road. There was nothing particularly interesting to see. Edwina did not think the missing ledgers could very well be explained by anything in their line of sight.

"Shall we go along?" Agnes asked. "I think Benjy will need his nap before it gets much later." Beryl pulled back onto the lane and faithfully followed Agnes' instructions for the remainder of the journey, winding back up once more at the Wallingford Estate.

"So that's it?" Beryl asked. "That's everywhere you went on deliveries?"

"Yes. There were no additions or subtractions while I drove the milk float. I've shown you everything. At least as I remember it."

The three of them drove back to the Beeches lost in thought.

From the lack of speed to her driving Edwina thought Beryl seemed dispirited by their outing. She was disappointed too as it happened. The case seemed to have dangling threads but none of them unraveled a thing once they were tugged upon. Beryl stopped the motorcar in its accustomed place in front of the house and sat there simply staring ahead. Agnes and Benjy clambered out noisily but Beryl slid out from behind the wheel, lost in thought.

Edwina considered asking her what was on her mind but held her tongue and hurried into the house after their guests. She was surprised to realize she was quite looking forward to preparing yet another meal for more than just herself. It certainly had been an extraordinary week. If anyone had asked her only a few days before what she thought the chances of having three more people staying under her roof as well as having developed a reputation as an intrepid sleuth she would have thought they had gone completely round the bend.

So caught up was she in the pleasures of the little domestic tasks hostessing involved that she had completely failed to notice how quiet Beryl had become. In fact, her usually exuberant friend had not said more than a few words since they returned from the Wallingford Estate. Beryl's change in demeanor finally occurred to her when she sought her out to call her to tea and came upon her sitting in the library just staring at the desk where Edwina had been attacked.

"What is it, Beryl? Is something wrong?" Edwina asked

"I've been mulling."

"Thinking over stray threads in the case?"

"Exactly. It has been quite a day for information and I can't help but feel we should be further along by now with our investigation."

"I know it isn't really your way but some things take patience, you know. I shouldn't wonder if investigating crimes was one of them."

"I don't feel impatient. I feel frustrated and as if all the bits were almost there but then nothing is there at all. I feel completely muddled and I have no idea what's next."

"Well, despite the reputation you so ingeniously developed for us, we aren't in fact experienced at all in the field of detecting. I think we've done quite well."

"You do?" Beryl turned towards her, a bit of brightening in her manner.

"Indeed I do. Just think of all the people we've pestered and the questions we've asked."

"But we're at a standstill. I have no idea what to do next. Walter Bennett may or may not have killed Polly. We only have his word for it that they were engaged to be married. Norman says he was trying to win her back but there is no proof of that either. Michael was seen with her in his cab and she was never seen again. And we haven't any way to really know if any of them can be absolutely ruled in or absolutely ruled out as suspects."

"We just need to keep asking the right questions. You'll see. We'll get back at it tomorrow first thing."

"But where would we start? We don't have any more lines of enquiry suggesting themselves."

"Nonsense. I know exactly what we shall do next."

"What's that?" Beryl asked.

"Even though I'd prefer never to see him again after his comments about my mental state, I am afraid I'll need to see the doctor. Why don't you ring his office tomorrow morning and do your utmost to convince the doctor to pay a call on us as soon as he can in order to take a look at my head."

"What shall I say?" Beryl asked. "You've spent the past couple of days running all about the village convincing everyone that you are in fine fettle."

"You can tell Nurse Crenshaw my appetite is poor and you

are concerned by the way I keep asking about my dead mother. That ought to do the trick I think," Edwina said.

"And why should we want to do that?" Beryl asked. 'You aren't actually feeling unwell, are you?"

"Never been better. At least, not in ages. While he is here we will find a way to ask him about treating Walter Bennett. Who knows where that will lead us and how quickly."

"That's what has been bothering me since we were at Mr. Bennett's cottage," Beryl said. She jumped from her seat and began pacing the room. "How did Hortense get there so quickly?"

"How did she get where? The spot where she intercepted Agnes?"

"Yes. How did she arrive so quickly? If Agnes was driving the horse and cart, how could Hortense have overtaken her so quickly?" Beryl asked. "Agnes mentioned how much longer it took to get between delivery points with old Joe than it did today using the car."

"What if Hortense drove out in the farm truck?" Edwina asked. "She must have known how to drive it. She told me herself she used it for the milk deliveries after Agnes left."

"But surely Agnes would have heard her arriving in a vehicle. She wouldn't have been surprised by that."

"No, I suppose you're right about that." Edwina thought for a moment. "I know, she cut through fields like we did the night we found Polly. You only need to stick to the roads if you are using a vehicle or pulling a cart like Agnes was doing."

"Would that shave off much time, do you think?" Beryl asked.

"It would cut it down by half, at least. She could easily have managed to get there much more quickly on foot than by the road."

"I suppose that explains it."

"You don't seem satisfied, Beryl. What is it?"

"I don't like coincidences. We know Polly was at Walter Bennett's cottage the night she died. Now Agnes brings us back to that very spot. I don't like it at all."

"Coincidences do happen though. You wouldn't be here at all if it weren't for the simple coincidence that you happened to need a place to stay at the very same time I was looking for a lodger. I know you are eager to make some sort of progress but it's no good making something nefarious out of something so easily explained."

"I suppose you make a good point. Maybe I am getting worked up over nothing," Beryl said. She gave a deep sign and then shrugged. "Shall we go in and join the others for tea?" Beryl asked.

"Do let's. I'll have the tea. We'll find you a large tot of gin instead."

Chapter 38

Dr. Nelson was even more obliging than Beryl hoped he would be. After her last encounter with him she had wondered if he would dismiss her concerns as the ravings of a withered-up old spinster. Despite her misgivings, no sooner had Nurse Crenshaw alerted the doctor to the nature of her call than he agreed to attend Edwina as quickly as he was able. That very morning, in fact. Beryl had been quite surprised at how quickly he had arrived. She wondered if he might in fact require medical attention himself as his face was pale and it was clear from the circles under his eyes that sleep had eluded him the night before.

Beryl couldn't be sure but she very much suspected the poor fellow was suffering from an evening of excess drink. She considered recommending a remedy a pilot she knew during the war had sworn was infallible, but she found she had forgotten the secret ingredient. Beryl never suffered from overimbibing. She prided herself that her constitution was uniquely suited for indulging in vices of all sorts. As she led him up the front stairs she noticed his attention seemed to be elsewhere and that he kept looking around as if searching for someone.

Edwina really did look quite convincing tucked up beneath the counterpane dressed in a gently frayed bed jacket and a lace-trimmed nightcap. Crumpet sat at attention in his basket at the corner of the bed. Edwina's hands clutched loosely at the coverlet and her eyes remained determinedly shut even after Beryl and the doctor entered her bedroom. Beryl solemnly approached the bedside and took Edwina's small hand in her large one.

"Dr. Nelson is here, Ed. He'd like to examine you." Edwina barely creaked one eye open and nodded at the doctor with the smallest of motions.

"I understand you are still feeling poorly in your head," Dr. Nelson said, lifting her wrist and feeling for her pulse. Beryl noticed Edwina's second eye open ever so slightly. She was definitely giving the doctor an unpleasant look. The poor man didn't even seem to realize it. Questioning him wasn't likely to go very well if Edwina decided to take the lead.

"I believe I overheard you mentioning that same opinion to Miss Helliwell the last time you were here." Edwina had gotten up on her high horse and kicked it into a canter. Beryl hoped her attitude wouldn't derail their investigatory efforts. "I do wish you'd think of a better diagnosis than that my mind had been unbalanced because I have never married." Beryl noticed Edwina's ire had brought a bit of color to Dr. Nelson's pale complexion. Perhaps she was more what he needed than the other way round.

"What I meant was that Miss Helliwell told my nurse when she rang was that you were experiencing headaches and double vision. I believe that is due to the injury you sustained. I'll just take a look at the wound, shall I?"

Just as he bent over her, Benjy toddled in through the open door and made straight for Crumpet's basket. The dog bounded out and ran about the room, stopping every foot or so to coax the child to give chase. The boy lurched after him squealing. He pulled Crumpet's tail and the little dog dove under the high bed. Dr. Nelson looked down and lifted the boy into his arms. Beryl watched as the doctor's eyes filled with unshed tears.

"Are you in here, Benjy?" Agnes said from the doorway. She stopped and a startled gasp left her lips as she saw her son in the doctor's arms. Beryl felt a sadness envelop her as she realized one small part of the mystery was solved. Agnes recovered herself and she hurried across the room with her arms outstretched. She lifted her chin and looked straight at Dr. Nelson. "Come to Mummy, you silly little boy." Benjy squirmed away from the doctor who seemed reluctant to release him. Without a backwards glance Agnes strode out of the room.

Beryl and Edwina exchanged a glance. Edwina inclined her head towards the door and Beryl hurried over and pressed it firmly into place. Beryl slid a chair from near the window next to the bed and patted the back of it. "Here, Doctor. You'd best sit down before you keel over." She waited until he had sunk safely into the chair then sat on the edge of Edwina's bed.

"Does Mrs. Nelson know about the boy?" Edwina asked, all irritation with the doctor evaporated in the face of his obvious distress.

"Was it that obvious?" Dr. Nelson asked, passing a hand over his forehead.

"Only to anyone with at least one good eye," Beryl said. "Between your reaction to the baby and Agnes' attitude towards you, there wasn't any doubt."

"Mrs. Nelson doesn't know about any of it. And I have no intention that she ever shall. Although, even if I told her, I'm not sure how much of it she would take in. She's not been herself since our Alan passed from the influenza."

"That flu outbreak touched so many in the village. We were speaking with Walter Bennett about it just yesterday. He said you treated him, too," Edwina said. Something about the doctor's demeanor shifted as soon as he heard Mr. Bennett's name, a sort of rigid set came over his shoulders, and a guardedness crept onto his face. Gone was the man with his heart on his sleeve. Beryl watched him closely for a signal as to why that should be. Doctors treat patients every day. Certainly Mr. Bennett had an extraordinary medical history considering his facial injuries but those occurred before he arrived in Walmsley Parva surely.

"Did he? There were so many at the time one patient sort of blurs together with the rest."

"He said you were the reason he survived the illness. Not that he appreciates it much now. The man is entirely engulfed in his grief over Polly and he told us he wished he had died before he met her."

"The ungrateful bastard." Dr. Nelson shifted to the edge of the chair. "He has no idea what we sacrificed when I agreed to treat him. He was the first case of influenza we had seen in Walmsley Parva in that second, far more virulent wave. As far as I could discover, he's the one who brought it to the village."

Beryl looked at Edwina. She felt quite certain they were closing in on something that had eluded them. Dr. Nelson was thoroughly distressed. She held her tongue and with an encouraging waggle of her perfectly plucked eyebrows, indicated that Edwina should take the lead. After all, Edwina knew far more than she did about the history of the village.

"What a terrible burden for you to carry, knowing the point of origin of the illness. How very noble of you never to have pointed the finger of blame at the unfortunate Mr. Bennett," Edwina said. Dr. Nelson cast his eyes towards his lap and Beryl wondered if he was already regretting having done just that. After all, wasn't it a doctor's responsibility to guard the secrets of his patients? Edwina spoke again, even more gently. "When you said you had sacrificed so much did you mean that your exposure to the influenza by treating Mr. Bennett brought the contagion into your own home? To your Alan?" Dr. Nelson nodded wordlessly.

"I don't even think any of my efforts on his behalf saved

him. From all we now know it seemed to just be a matter of chance who lived and who died once a person fell ill," Dr. Bennett said.

"How old was your son when he became ill?" Beryl asked.

"Just about the age Benjy is now." Dr. Nelson slumped even farther. "I shall never forgive myself for what happened to him. If I hadn't been so cowardly maybe Alan would still be alive."

"You don't seem like a cowardly man, Doctor. I think it very brave to tend to someone with influenza," Beryl said.

"I was a coward and an adulterer. If God had not thought me so he might not have punished me by taking Alan from us. If only I had the courage to confess my infidelity to my wife I would have left that wretched woman to tend him on her own."

"Which woman was that, Doctor?" Edwina asked. "It wasn't Polly, was it?"

"No. He hadn't met Polly then. Like I said, he had just come to town. He arrived already ill. I believe he caught it on a train or maybe even in the hospital where he had been recovering from being shelled." Dr. Nelson looked from Edwina to Beryl. The sound of Benjy's high-pitched chattering floated down the hall and into the room. The doctor glanced towards the door and a look of decision crossed his face. Beryl felt the tremor in her heart she always did just before taking off in a plane or jumping from a cliff and plunging into the sea. They were all toeing up to a line between before and after. "Hortense tracked me down at the hospital wing of the Wallingford Estate. She said I was urgently needed for a patient in the village with a high fever and that she would take me to him immediately. I refused, saying he could be seen by Nurse Crenshaw or someone else. I said my workload was entirely filled with the soldiers. She pulled me aside and proceeded to convince me."

"Nothing unbecoming of a lady, I hope?" Beryl asked.

"If blackmail isn't unbecoming, I don't know what is. She told me Agnes was with child and that she knew I was the father. She said if I refused to treat him she would go to my wife and tell her everything."

"So you went?"

"I told you I was a coward. I went without giving it another thought."

"Did it not seem strange to you that Hortense would strong-arm you on behalf of Walter Bennett?" Beryl asked.

"My mind was not on Hortense or on Walter Bennett. It was on Agnes and a baby and the worry that my family would be ruined by a terrible indiscretion," Dr. Nelson said. "It was only after I arrived and began to examine the patient that I realized the reason she would be so desperate to call me."

Edwina had pulled herself more and more upright throughout the course of the interview. By now she was practically leaning off the edge of the bed, hanging on the doctor's every word. Beryl stuck out a restraining hand and asked the logical question.

"Which was what exactly?"

"Walter Bennett was actually Roland Tinsdale," he said. Edwina gasped. Beryl felt decidedly left out.

"I'm sorry but you say that as if you had just named a film star or a character from Shakespeare. Who is Roland Tinsdale?" she asked.

"Hortense's brother. His entire unit was reported dead. Heavy shelling if I remember correctly. Hortense received the news just before she joined the Land Army. Why do you think it's him?" Edwina asked.

"His mask was off when I arrived. While he had terrible damage to much of his face, there was still enough of it to show the young man he had been. I might not have pieced it together if Hortense had not been the one to ask for me. But she was and I did."

"Why is he using a false name? Is there some reason he is not welcomed in Walmsley Parva?" Beryl said.

"It wasn't that. He was always a smart young man but he was a sensitive one, too. Not that you needed to be particularly that way to feel the effects of the trenches. When I asked Hortense about it later she said that everyone in his unit except him had been killed. He managed to crawl out from under all the bodies and somehow had the fortune of being hauled off on a stretcher. When he came to in hospital someone had misidentified him as Walter Bennett. When he was sufficiently recovered he managed to sneak off and has been a deserter using another man's name ever since."

"Did he really believe he would be sent back to the front?" Edwina asked.

"Apparently so. The trauma men suffered there made many of them desperate and irrational," he said.

"The entire war was irrational," Beryl said. "That poor, poor man. So he headed here to his sister but because he wasn't really Walter Bennett no one would think to look for him here?"

"That's right. I promised Hortense I would keep his secret and I have until now."

"What made you tell us this now?" Edwina asked.

"I've seen my son, haven't I? There is no going back from that. It's like a second chance. I am going to try to tell my wife about Benjy. If she can hear me I will ask her forgiveness. I want to see my only living child and I want to help to provide for him. If Agnes will let me." He looked towards the hall again.

"Agnes intends to leave later today to go back to London. I suggest you go talk to them while you still have the chance," Edwina said.

"You have been remarkably kind and open-minded about all this," Dr. Nelson said. "I would have expected you to be far more ruffled."

"I daresay because you see me as a dried-up old spinster?" Edwina asked. Beryl noticed she said it much more kindly than she might have done earlier.

"I would say the same to anyone at all. I truly regret if my remarks the other day hurt you."

"Perhaps you haven't heard the gossip going round the village. I happen to be employed as an investigatory agent for His Majesty. I should hope very little at all would ruffle my sensibilities."

"What about your head?" he asked. "I still need to have a look at it."

"I feel better than I have in ages. I just needed a lie-in, I expect." Edwina threw back the chenille coverlet and swung her feet down and slid them into her trusty carpet slippers. "Go try to speak to her before the chance slips away." Dr. Nelson straightened his tie and strode out the door. Beryl noted his shoulders were squared and he looked like an entirely different man than the one who had entered the house.

"It seems confession really is good for the soul," Beryl said. "Not that I want to test the theory out myself, mind you."

"If it worked so well for Dr. Nelson in the case of adultery, imagine how much good it will do our murderer."

"You believe you know who did it then?" Beryl asked.

"Yes, I'm rather afraid that I do."

Chapter 39

Beryl stopped the motorcar a few doors up from the village hall. The sign hanging above the door declared the jumble sale would be taking place the next day. "Are you quite sure about this? From what I've seen of Walmsley Parva, if you are wrong it won't be forgotten."

"The thing is, Beryl, I won't be able to live with myself if I don't ask. We've already set people to whispering and wondering about their neighbours by investigating at all. It isn't fair to leave so many people open to unkind speculation. In a village like this, lives are ruined that way." Edwina stepped out of the motorcar and climbed the steps to the door of the village hall. Beryl followed close on her heels.

Hortense stood at the back of the hall. "I hope you are here to tell me you've finally convinced your famous friend to appear tomorrow in support of the jumble sale?" she asked, coming towards them. "This is her then, isn't it?" Hortense met them in the middle of the room and looked Beryl up and down.

"This is my friend Beryl Helliwell. But we aren't here to discuss her supporting the fund-raiser."

"I suppose you're here to say she'll be dashing off on another round-the-world caper of some sort or other and can't be bothered with the likes of us," Hortense said, letting out an unladylike snort.

Edwina stepped over to the table filled with bric-a-brac and looked carefully at the rows of vases, cigarette boxes, and candlesticks she had placed there earlier in the week. Even in the low light one item gleamed brightly compared to the rest. It certainly hadn't been in with the others when she had organized the lot of them. Edwina reached over and held it up to Hortense.

"No, Hortense, nothing of the sort. We are here for this item. It's just what we have been looking for." Edwina held the stick to her nose and inhaled deeply. There was still the faintest scent of rose geranium oil.

"I'm afraid the jumble doesn't start until tomorrow. I have a strict policy of not allowing early sales. Even for those who help out. It's matter of principal, you see." Hortense took a step closer and held out her hand.

"I don't intend to purchase it. I am sorry to tell you it is evidence in the murder of Polly Watkins and for all we know the attempted murder of myself," Edwina said. Hortense put her hands on her hips and shook her head.

"Really, Edwina, you have become as eccentric as everyone is saying that you are. What possible reason would you have to believe that bibelot could have been used to attack anyone?"

"It's a perfect match for the one we saw on the table at Walter Bennett's cottage," Beryl said. "Walter's the cinema projectionist."

"There's no reason to think this candlestick was part of a pair that he owned. There must be any number of candlesticks that look alike. And I doubt very much there is anything on that piece to show it had been used in a crime."

"Walter told us that when he came home the night of Polly's

murder that someone had been there. Someone who burgled his cottage. They took a bedsheet, a pair of work gloves, and a candlestick that was one of a pair that exactly matches this one," Edwina said. "Why would it be cleaned and polished so carefully if it hadn't gotten dirty in some sort of unsavory way? And why polish just one of a pair?"

"What does any of this have to do with me or Polly's death? It sounds like this Walter fellow might have reason to summon the constable but it hardly means the jumble sale is harboring a murder weapon. I cannot see how this Walter has any connection to Polly at all."

"Walter claims he was engaged to Polly Watkins. We are quite sure the police will believe he killed her during some sort of lover's quarrel."

"You've no proof Polly was ever at his cottage, let alone on the night she died."

"We do actually. Her scarf was tucked down between the cushions of his sofa. Beryl and I both saw her wearing it on the night she died. It proves she was there," Edwina said.

"Michael Blackburn also swears he drove her to Walter's cottage instead of driving her home that night. He claims that Walter had hired him to drive Polly home several times each week after she had been visiting him in the projection booth," Beryl said.

"He knew how to drive and we are certain someone borrowed Beryl's motorcar from outside the Blackburn garage in order to transport Polly's body to the field at the Wallingford Estate in order to try to lay the blame on Norman Davies," Edwina said.

"This is sounding more and more like the ramblings of a certifiable lunatic. You really should see Dr. Nelson about your head injury again." Hortense shook her own head as though she were very sorry for Edwina.

"We've seen Dr. Nelson already. He had quite a lot to say about treating patients. Walter Bennett in particular." Edwina's heart thrashed like a fish on a line as she took a step closer to Hortense.

"That sounds like a breach of ethics to mention another's health history to a lay person," Hortense said. "Someone should have him up before an oversight board."

"Surely you wouldn't want that sort of scrutiny on the village now any more than you wanted officials poking around when you learned Norman was stealing from the Wallingford Estate."

"Are you implying that I have done something wrong?" Hortense asked.

"We aren't implying anything. We are flat-out saying it," Beryl said. "Either you, or your brother, Roland Tinsdale, will be charged with killing Polly. Which of you is it to be?"

Hortense's face went slack and she looked as though she were about to collapse. Edwina stepped forward and took her by the arm. She guided Hortense to a wooden chair well away from the door and pressed her into it. The doctor was likely still busy with Agnes and it wouldn't do for him to be needed to look after another head injury should Hortense topple to the floor.

"The doctor must have told you," Hortense said. "It was seeing Agnes back in the village that broke his silence, wasn't it?" Hortense asked.

"I think it was seeing his son that made him confess everything. He couldn't bear to keep a secret that forced him to be separated from the boy any longer."

"I understand," said Hortense. "I know just how he feels." Hortense lifted her eyes from her lap and looked at Edwina. "If I tell you the truth of what happened, will you promise not to tell the authorities about Roland?"

"I'll do my best not to. He's already suffered a great deal," Edwina said. Hortense nodded and cleared her throat.

"Roland arrived at the Wallingford Estate the day before I called the doctor. He was almost delirious with fever and couldn't stop coughing. I barely recognized him. Once I realized who he was I took him to one of the empty cottages at the edge of the estate. I kept running back and forth between the estate and the cottage to check on him all day. Come nightfall he was worse and as soon as the girls were all securely back at the estate for the night I hurried back to the cottage. I stayed the night there with him and was on my way out the next morning trying to get back before my absence was noticed when I saw Agnes right in front of the cottage door."

"You pretended you came for her because she was so late?"

"I did, poor thing. She was doubled over retching and didn't see me slip out of the cottage." Hortense took a deep breath. "When she told me that she was with child and by whom, I knew I had leverage with which to force the doctor to tend to Roland."

"Why did you help Agnes to leave?" Beryl asked.

"If she stayed in the village something might have occurred to make the doctor confess to his wife. Either the sight of her, or of the child. If Mrs. Nelson found out I'd have no hold over the doctor to keep my secret."

"But what about what happened to Polly?"

"I arrived at Walter's cottage on the night that she died. I often visited him late at night. No one was about then and it suited us both. I stepped inside the cottage and she was there sitting on the sofa as if she belonged there."

"You must have been startled," Edwina said.

"I was shocked. I asked what she was doing there and she said she didn't have to answer to me anymore. I told her not to be impertinent and she said she had every right to be there. She was going to be Roland's wife. A skivvy telling me Roland was going to marry her. It was bad enough thinking I had lost him because of the Germans. But to have him back only to discover he has decided to throw away his life on a charwoman? I was in a total state of disbelief. Then she walked over to me, pulled off one of her cheap gloves, and waggled her finger at me. Do you know what was on it?" Hortense asked, her voice growing more and more shrill. "My mother's engagement ring."

"What did you do?" Edwina asked.

"I accused her of lying and of having stolen the ring, like I told you before when I mentioned why I let her go. She said he had given it to her because it was his mother's and wasn't I thrilled to be having her for a sister-in-law. I couldn't believe he had told her who he really was. I didn't even think. I reached for a candlestick that was on the table and hit her on the side of the head with it. She just collapsed."

"How did she come to be in the field?"

"I wrapped her body in a bedsheet. I knew Roland would be home soon so I dragged her out the back door and left her body behind the woodpile. I ran to Blackburn's Garage and I took Miss Helliwell's motorcar and drove it back to the lane near Roland's cottage."

"We found Walter's missing gloves in the back of Beryl's motorcar. After he told us they went missing the night she died we were certain then that whomever killed Polly had used it to transport her body to the field," Edwina said.

"I'm not proud of that bit, I assure you. I tried to make it look like an accident but in case someone thought she had met with foul play I wanted the finger pointing away from Roland and towards a more likely suspect."

"Norman Davies. Why him?" Beryl asked.

"Why not him? Rather than rising to the occasion on the home front while other men were risking their lives to protect

King and country, Norman took the opportunity to profit from the situation. I didn't turn him in for his wartime crimes in order to protect Roland. I convinced myself that if the authorities realized Polly had been murdered Norman deserved to be the one to pay." Hortense let out a deep sigh. Beryl took a few steps closer and Edwina was surprised to see a look of anger upon her face.

"Are you the one who tried to strangle Edwina? Did you hit her over the head and take the ledgers?"

"Yes. I thought if I frightened you enough straightaway you might stop investigating, so I attacked her in the garden," Hortense said. She turned back to Edwina. "I was so worried that you were searching for Roland that I panicked. Later when you said you were looking at the Wallingford Estate I thought it might just be a cover. I thought the ledgers might contain information about your investigation and I wanted to take a look at them for myself."

"You let a rumor spread by Prudence Rathbone drive you to attempt murder?" Edwina asked. "Why would you do such a thing?"

"Because you are just the sort of person I believe to be capable of just the sort of investigations Prudence was crowing about," Hortense said. "After all, you were the one who was so certain that Polly hadn't met with an accident, weren't you? What was it that convinced you she had been murdered?"

"It was her shoes. A girl of Polly's class would never consider walking across a manured field in her dancing shoes to shave a little time off her walk home. She simply never would even consider it."

"Shoes. I am going to hang for a pair of daily maid's shoes?" Hortense asked.

"Perhaps the court will show more leniency to you than you did to Polly," Edwina said. She nodded at Beryl who moved towards the door. "Beryl is going to fetch Constable Gibbs now. I shall simply sit here with you until they return."

"I don't intend to tell anyone else what I've told the two of you. I shall say that she enraged me by quitting my employ. No persons of consequence will fail to realize how such a thing would unbalance my mind sufficiently to lash out. No one need ever know that Walter is Roland. My brother will be safe and that is enough for me."

"Roland isn't your brother though, is he?" Edwina asked. "He means even more to you than that."

"Have you always known?" Hortense asked.

"I have always suspected. Being away at finishing school did not keep the rumor mill from reaching my ears. All the ladies in town were quite aghast to think your parents were still giving in to carnal impulses so late in life," Edwina said. "I'm rather afraid the men in town had rather a different view of the matter."

"You're right. Roland is not my brother. He is my son. I formed an ill-considered attachment as a young girl and paid dearly for it. The under gardener if you can believe it. When my condition became impossible to ignore my mother took me on what we said was a trip to the Highlands of Scotland and she returned with Roland a few months later claiming him as her own. I went off to a finishing school not unlike the one you and Miss Helliwell attended for a year before I was allowed to return. Father never treated Roland well in the least despite always wanting a son."

"I remember my own father speaking of it. Nasty business," Edwina said. She reached out and clasped Hortense's hand. "You truly don't want your son to know the truth of his parentage. His mother at least?"

"I most certainly do not. In his mind his parents were upright members of the community. All I want for him is to find someone new and to create a life he loves. It will be hard enough with a sister convicted of murder. He needn't know something even worse than that. I know you don't owe me anything, Edwina, but will you keep my confidence to yourself?" Hortense looked at her with pleading eyes. It made no difference in the end, Edwina thought. And who didn't have things they wished to keep to themselves? Compassion cost so little in the grand scheme of things.

"I promise, Hortense, your secret is safe with me."

Chapter 40

"You've been quiet all evening, Ed," Beryl said from the depths of the wingback chair on the far side of the crackling fireplace. "After what she did, I hope you aren't fretting over what will become of Hortense."

"No, I have something else on my mind," Edwina said.

"What is it then? You haven't said more than a few words since we returned to the Beeches. You hardly touched your dinner and you've been staring into the fire like you were expecting it to deliver a message from the great beyond." Beryl swirled her glass of whiskey then took a small sip.

"I can't help but wonder if all of this is our fault. If we hadn't perpetuated the rumor that we were crack investigators Hortense never would have been so concerned about Roland's safety. I'm not sure she would have killed Polly if she didn't believe we were looking into Roland."

"I'm inclined to believe Hortense would have killed Polly no matter what. Walter's engagement to Polly had nothing to do with us. Hortense was clearly set against the match and I don't think it had to do with his safety. It had to do with her prejudice."

"I still feel like we set something terrible in motion with just one lie."

"What lie? As it turns out, we are investigators. If it hadn't been for us, Hortense would have gotten away with killing someone," Beryl said. "You should have seen the look on Constable Gibbs' face when I tracked her down at the post office and told her Hortense had confessed. I don't know when I've ever had such fun."

"I hardly think murder should be considered an amusement, Beryl," Edwina said. "But I must admit, I know just what you mean. I suppose life here will be quite dull now that Agnes has been found and Polly's murderer has been revealed. I expect you shall be wanting to head off for far more thrilling vistas before long."

So that was it. Edwina did not wish her to go but she wasn't the sort to come out and say such a thing. Beryl felt a warm glow wash over her that had nothing whatsoever to do with the fire. She realized in a flash that leaving Walmsley Parva, or Ed, was the very last thing on her mind.

"We may have gotten to the bottom of an old mystery and a new one." Beryl flashed her friend a sparkling smile. "but that doesn't mean there is nothing else that needs investigating."

"You think there is something else nefarious going on in Walmsley Parva?" Edwina leaned forward in her chair, a flicker of hope passing over her small features.

"I'm certainly going to stick around to find out," Beryl said. "That is, if you can put up with me for a bit longer."

"I can't think of anything I'd like more."